Praise for *Filth Eater*

"This sure and exciting melodrama with archaeological thrills rivals Indiana Jones in entertainment and Dr. Leakey in information. Highest kudos for the entire family to read the *Filth Eater*."
—Dr. Lew Hunter, UCLA Screenwriting Chair

"A skillful blend of anthropology and intrigue, *Filth Eater* is a real page-turner!"
—Dr. Harriet Ottenheimer, Kansas State University

"In an intriguing blend of archaeology, sexual titillation, and high-level political chicanery in Mexico in the 1980's, Stanley Struble presents a fast-paced scenario that will engage a spectrum of readers whose interest in Mexican culture may range from intense to non-existent."
—Jim Tuck, *Guadalajara Reporter*

"A tale of brutality and murder for the sake of securing priceless artifacts, *Filth Eater* exposes sins of greed and gluttony aimed at procuring vast riches at any cost...sic...possess a vivid insight into the pitfalls of modern social structure."
—Cheryl Golden, *Omaha Reader*

"An intriguing look at the Mexico of just a few years ago as well as a glimpse of the Spanish conquest and the problems it brought."
—Sally Fellows, *The Whole Truth Review*

Praise for *Sins of the Jaguar*

"Stan Struble takes you on a roller coaster ride of action, love and mayhem that puts you on edge wherever you sit, then causes you to stand and cheer his fabulous, *Sins of the Jaguar* adventure on a breathtaking final drop to the end. Forget Magic Mountains and Disney. *Sins of the Jaguar* smokes them all!!"
—Lew Hunter, Chairman, UCLA Screenwriting School

"A fast-paced anthropological thriller with fascinating surprises at every turn. Combining archaeology and detective work, Professor David Wolf and Special Agent Luis Alvarado search for a kidnapped diplomat in remote Tarahumara territory. What they find threatens to change the archaeological history of the area, and have far reaching environmental implications. A great page-turner, as well as fun reading for anyone interested in Mexico, Native Americans, and anthropology."
—Harriet Joseph Ottenheimer, Professor of Anthropology and American Ethnic Studies, Kansas State University

"The sense of place and historical/archaeological information kept me involved in the first part of the book, and the suspense of how the unlikely group would survive and whether all would pull through kept me reading until the very end."
—Sally Fellows, *The Whole Truth Review*

George & Grace;

Family & friends with literate souls. Thanks for your support.

Sins of the Jaguar

Stan Struble

Stan Struble

PublishAmerica

Baltimore

First printing

ISBN: 1-59286-845-2
PUBLISHED BY PUBLISHAMERICA, LLLP
www.publishamerica.com
Baltimore

Printed in the United States of America

Dedication

For Valerie,
grammar tyrant and scaly creature lover,

and to Lucas, Tim and Grace—four good reasons to keep writing.

And to
Rose Marie Roberts, Butch and Ted Neuburger
and Father Flanagan's Boys' Home, Boys Town, Nebraska.

Acknowledgments

Many, Many Thanks

Jim Bunstock, Ellen Kodis-Salmon, Lew Hunter, Harriet Ottenheimer, and Sally Fellows; literary lions, colleagues and friends. Thank you for your help, support and patience.

Special Acknowledgment

Without the patience, charity and friendship of the Gonzalez-Corso family of Guadalajara, Jalisco and San Cristobal de Las Casas, Chiapas this book would never have been written. *Tengo un debo lo que nunca pagaria.*

Prologue

The midwife hurriedly moved about the dark candlelit room, her growing disquiet evident in the flickering shadows as she stuffed bloody linens into a plastic trash bag. The scent of blood and death overpowered the acrid witch's brew of air that leaked into the room through dirty, cracked windowpanes. She glanced at the dead woman on the bed, crossed herself, and looked at the young man from the corner of her eye. He seemed ghostly, almost frightening, his expression tortured as he stood over the petite, lifeless body. A bulbous tear, leaving a clean trail down his grimy cheek, slid untouched to his chin where it dangled briefly before falling onto the newborn baby in his arms. The child, a moonfaced Down's Syndrome baby, appeared horribly deformed; its stomach and intestines lay glistening and exposed. A sucking noise from a moist hole in the baby's chest accompanied each breath.

Fear and sorrow, the twins of despair, were again visiting the weak and helpless in this desperately poor Mexican village near the U.S. border. Accustomed to tragedy in the midst of poverty, the villagers slept unaware, tired from the endless struggle of scratching out an existence in the desert of Nuevo Leon.

"*Voy para el Sacerdote,*" the midwife insisted, her Spanish heavily accented with Indian dialect.

"No. No priests," said the child's father, turning to look at the midwife, as if just noticing her presence.

"*Señor....*"

"No," he repeated, quietly but firmly, his eyes blazing with the fire of a zealot. "Leave me. You've done all that you can do. I need time to think."

"You need help, *señor.*"

"Get out...now." The voice floated softly, but his eyes betrayed a fervor. The midwife crossed herself without thinking, started to protest, and then thought better of it. "*Sí, señor*," she mumbled, crossing herself yet again, "I will pray for the Virgin to intercede for your wife."

The brooding man ignored her, staring at the dying child cradled in his large, callused hands. He began to shift his weight in rhythm, slowly swaying and rocking the infant. A sad smile tugged at the corners of the man's mouth, then he began to hum. With a slow melodious chant, he sang in a language the midwife didn't understand. She crossed herself one final time, shivered with dread, then abruptly headed for the door. With a fearful backward glance, she hurried outside, preferring the blackness of night and poisoned air to the strange young man.

The song continued uninterrupted as the child whimpered and issued pitiful, wet sucking noises from its chest. The song completed, the father sang another, then another, and finally, when the baby lay silent and still, his lifeless body limp and his spirit departed, the man lovingly kissed him and placed him next to his mother.

The father walked outside into the cold, stinking night and breathed deeply of the soiled desert air, tasting the everpresent acrid residue of progress from TexMex Chemical and other factories lining the northern horizon. Millions of white lights blinked cheerfully, lighting small industrial towns while the factories belched mushroom clouds of black smoke into the sky. The toxic, particleladen spew spread far and wide before falling to earth, poisoning and defiling the land and water. He looked around at the flimsy, filthy shacks that comprised the town and housed the work force for the factories. No electricity, no sewage treatment, and the only drinking water polluted with mercury, arsenic and lead.

The factories had killed his wife and baby, he reasoned, just as they killed the land and the sky. Everywhere he looked, he saw creeping death and smelled the odor of insane progress. The factories dumped, spat, and excreted heavy metals and carcinogens, unhampered and unregulated, the legacy of numerous free trade agreements.

He paced the dirt road outside his home, his mind in turmoil, his body oblivious to the desert cold. Anger simmered, unfocused and fluid; his loss like a burning coal, then a furnace. Finally, seized with a white-hot anger, he strode to his pickup truck, retrieved a gas can from the bed and carried it to his one-room home. He splashed the contents throughout the hovel, slowing only to drench the bed thoroughly. Bending low, he kissed the gold amulet with jaguar-haped jewels around his wife's neck. He straightened, touched her cheek, took one final look around, and left, closing the door behind him.

Standing resolutely, his face to the sky, he spread his arms and began to sing the Gift of Death Song. Finished, he lit two matches and threw them at the house. He walked south into the desert while a red flower blazed behind him. He would return after purifying his spirit and seeking a vision from his totem animal, the jaguar. He would return to visit death upon the factories and politicians.

Kidnapped

(One Year Later)

Ruth Johnson, Assistant Honorary Consul of the United States and presently stationed in the city and state of Chihuahua, in Northern Mexico, slipped off the headphones to her Sony Walkman. She carefully twisted the cord so as not to snag a curl, then turned to stare out the window into the dark night. Spectacular scenery, now ghostly shadows fleeing the dawn, flew past the windows of the Chihuahua to Los Mochis Vista Train.

The most incredible train ride in the world, 405 miles of nearly impassable mountains, tunnels, trestles, and colorful landscapes, sped by unnoticed and unappreciated as she watched with numb indifference. The clack of steel rails and the shifting, swaying car hypnotized her and dulled her interest, creating a lull in her attention. A muted Jimmy Buffet song percolated from the headphones, distracting her emptiness. She turned it off and returned to the window, ignoring a gray-clad, mustachioed conductor who traversed the aisle with practiced patience, moving in rhythm to the sway of the train, intent on crossing to the next car.

A miserable ending to a bad relationship, but at least it's over now, she consoled herself. Her blue eyes dipped to look at her ring finger, now void of Doug's engagement ring. The finger felt naked and elicited a pang of guilt. But guilt for what? she asked herself. For ending a troubled and doomed relationship? Both parties agreed that the relationship had not developed to the point of commitment, leaving an uncomfortable awareness that their love had failed, but with neither willing to be the first to say, "This isn't going to work."

A working vacation in Mazatlan was a bad idea. She should have stayed in Chihuahua and never allowed Doug to talk her into going, she berated herself.

But that wasn't entirely true, she realized. Chihuahua and her job at the Consulate weren't going well either. She had gladly accepted a position as Assistant Honorary Consul of the United States after two dull, numbing years in Colombia as an attaché who specialized in meeting nobodies at the Bogota airport. She had been elated at the prospect of rubbing elbows with the most powerful movers and shakers in the Northern Hemisphere. Chihuahua was no longer a jumping-off spot in the northern desert. Even the Europeans came with startling regularity. They went first to Mexico City, but always stopped in Chihuahua, Mexico's largest and richest state, to talk and bargain for its natural resources.

The dissatisfaction she felt prior to entering the diplomatic corps grew stronger daily. The failed marriage and death of her daughter had left Ruth with a gnawing suspicion that life might not turn out as she hoped. She had learned that bringing excitement and dedication to every endeavor did not ensure success. Some things were beyond her control, and others couldn't be negotiated away—hers or those of the U.S. Government. Many were simply intractable and didn't lend themselves to resolution. She realized that life had no easy formulas. In order to negotiate, you must offer something desirable in exchange for what you want, and she felt she had nothing of value, only an overriding sense of guilt because of her dead child, a marriage on the rocks, and a series of unsatisfactory jobs.

How do you barter with God? How do you negotiate a relationship with a man? These defeats, she realized, lay at the root of her unhappiness. She had become a stand-in for the real players, a prop to be manipulated for someone else's purposes; a former mother and exwife, and now an Assistant Honorary Consul.

A flunky. Just a damn flunky, and not even any good at it, she chastised herself, balling a fist in helpless anger.

Choked with emotion, she felt warmth bathe her face. She dug in her purse for a handkerchief to stem the flow of salty tears.

"*Señora*, are you okay?" asked the grizzled conductor, seeing her tears and stopping in alarm. "*Señora....*"

"No...please. I'm fine." She waved him off with a handkerchief-clasped hand.

"But, *señora....*"

"No...I'm sure. Thank you." She smiled in spite of herself, dabbing her eyes, then rose to go to the restroom, directing a smile at the conductor as she passed.

She rinsed her face in cold water and lightly toweled it with coarse, brown paper towels from a wall dispenser. The train shifted and swayed, occasionally jerking, making it difficult to stand unsupported. She took a step backward and appraised herself in the mirror; a brownhaired, doe-eyed, middle-aged woman with narrow eyebrows stared back. The mirror image moved synchronously, mimicking each movement.

She looked sick, she decided, like a damn cadaver. She needed a major life change. Sighing, she stepped toward the mirror to repair the tears' damage to her makeup and adjust her hair.

Unexpectedly the train lurched violently, hurling her into the wall and smashing her face into the mirror and shattering it! Stunned, her legs collapsed and she sank to the floor, overcome with pain and nausea. The car jerked again, then began to squeal as four diesel locomotives locked their brakes in an attempt to forestall a derailment.

Tears mingled with blood as she groped to pull herself erect. Panic seized her and she gasped for breath. A wet, warm ooze flowed from cuts above her eye as she battled a rising hysteria. *Not my face! No!*

Finally, the train screeched to a stop. With a cold fear wrenching her gut, she rose to her knees, stood and staggered toward the sink basin. Her face! "Oh God!" she cried piteously. She opened a faucet, wetted her handkerchief and wiped and rinsed blood from a deep cut on her forehead.

The bathroom door banged open, and there stood a gray uniformed conductor. But it wasn't the one that she knew, the one that had earlier offered help. This man had a scraggly beard on a square face set above broad shoulders. Tall and longarmed, his eyes burned with a fervor. He looked too big for his uniform.

"*Señora?*"

"Help me, please," she begged. "I need a doctor." She reached for him.

"Certainly, *señora*." And he accepted her arm, pulling her toward him with strength and sureness.

She smelled a piercing chemical odor. Had the wreck caused the awful stink? It smelled familiar. She looked into his eyes—the last thing she remembered—the gleam of his dark eyes before a reeking, ether-drenched cloth covered her mouth and nose. A sinking, leaden feeling made her swoon, then she panicked and struggled and tried to scream, but he held her firmly and applied the anesthetic until she grew limp.

He picked her up and carried her from the bathroom, exiting the train on the side leading to the canyons and gorges south of the railroad line. He toted her a short distance, then stepped behind a line of sheltering boulders and down into a ravine where an accomplice stood impatiently with a burro.

"Is this the one? What happened to her face?" queried the accomplice.

The abductor ignored the question and laid the captive over the burro. They quickly secured her with ropes, loosely tying her to keep her from falling until she awoke and could ride.

They turned to go. Suddenly the ground seemed to shudder, swell, subside, and then shudder again.

"What was that?"

"Small quake...you know. Happens several times a year."

"Yes, but it's been happening a lot lately."

The bearded abductor, Fr. Martin of the Batopilas parish, remained intent on his task and ignored his younger brother's comment. A full moon illuminated the trail and cast eerie shadows as they began the slow, tortuous descent into the deep canyon. A large, feral jaguar watched from a distance, and then began to follow. The priest, sensing its presence, turned and searched for the cat. He could feel its glowing, yellow eyes watching his every move. Finding it, he shivered with revulsion, then turned his attention to the trail again. He would try his best to ignore its presence and control a growing fear that the jaguar stalked him. They moved slowly along a narrow path used only by the Tarahumara Indians that linked the lowland villages with the foreign economy of the railroad and its tourists.

Ruth Johnson, Assistant Honorary Consul, was traveling on the back of a donkey to her new home—a remote cave in the Copper Canyon in the Sierra Madres.

"I hate having that damn beast around."

"She's a friend, nothing more," replied Mike, younger brother of Fr. Martin.

The priest snorted, disbelieving, then turned and warily searched the hillside to ensure the large cat kept its distance. He pulled on the halter rope, urging the donkey forward.

"Her face is cut, and you didn't bring her luggage," argued Mike.

"She doesn't need any."

"But she's a woman and...."

"She won't need any where she's going. It's just an extra burden. Do you want to carry it for her?"

The younger brother looked ahead at the twisted trail, and then up the sheer walls of the mountain. He shivered. "No...I guess you're right. It's just that she's a woman and we've never involved ourselves with a woman before. Women have different needs than men."

The priest stopped the burro and eyed his accomplice. "Women? You've only known one woman. What do you know about women? Don't start wringing your hands and whining now. This was your idea, too. Remember? What about your convictions? What about our purpose? What about the needs of the Raramuri? Don't try hiding behind any convoluted reasoning processes. You're not as smart as you think. This is all for the cause, brother. Understand? You can't have a war without getting dirty." He jerked the halter tether and continued down the narrow mountain path, his keen eyes sorting shadows from rocky debris and hidden dangers.

Mike paused and looked one last time up the mountain path to the string of lights illuminating the derailed train cars. He caught sight of his friend, the jaguar, and gave it a hand sign, then hurried to fall in behind the donkey that resolutely negotiated the rocky trail down into the moonlit valley.

Kidnapping, sabotage, and murder were dirty businesses, he told himself; but then again, so was death from pollution, poverty, and despair. Why weren't there any easier answers? It was an old story, just as Martin had said: "The end justifies the means."

He settled into the rhythm of the walk, slowly descending into the valley. In a couple of hours, they would begin walking uphill into the sierras to a place so remote that, besides himself, only his strange brother and their father knew its location. He would stay with the woman to ensure her proper care, but his priest-brother, Fr. Martin, must return to Satevo. Fr. Martin would telephone authorities in Chihuahua to announce the kidnapping of the diplomat, and why. There was no backing out. The war had turned ugly.

Mike looked over his shoulder to see that his cat followed. The jaguar, a brooding black shape with fierce yellow eyes, stood in silhouette in the moonlight. He made a motion of recognition to the beast, then turned to follow the donkey. Mike drew comfort from the fact that his friend, the jaguar, accompanied him, but a nagging guilt remained. He looked at the limp shape of the unconscious woman strapped to the donkey, and a persistent feeling of shame assailed him.

What had he done? he asked himself, already feeling remorseful. He never should have come. He looked once more to see that the jaguar followed, then turned his attention to the trail.

Snakes

(One Week Later)

Professor David Wolf sat on the patio of his rented cabin high in the Sierra Madres of Chihuahua, drinking a cup of nearly tepid tea and enjoying Mexico's version of the Grand Canyon—Las Barrancas de Cobre (The Copper Canyon)—when the phone rang. When his wife called, he put aside a potsherd and hurried inside. Initially irritated at the intrusion, he smiled—pleasantly surprised to hear from an old friend, Luis Alvarado, formerly a captain on the Mexico City Police force and now a special agent for the Federal Policia in the Northern states of Mexico. David's new wife of six months, Alexandra, returned to the patio and threw the last of her sweetbread crumbs to her new friends, a flock of brown finches.

"Luis?"

"Who else, *gringo*? What are you doing in the most remote place in Mexico? You've already found Moctezuma's gold. Have you changed professions to prospecting?"

The professor grinned, appreciating Luis' friendly banter. It recalled a sense of loss at his friend having left Mexico City one year previous for a new job as a *federale*. Loss is always accompanied by regret, even if your loss benefits a friend.

"Hey…I have a telephone in my cabin and two trail bikes sitting outside the door to get us around. I can see the Vista Train and its passengers if I want to hike a little."

"Tell me, David, how many times have you ridden the bicycle?"

Caught in a lie, thought the professor. He and Alexandra had once attempted to ride a short distance downward into the canyon, when they encountered five or six rattlesnakes sunning themselves on the path. This

15

quickly ended the excursion, and the uphill return trip reminded him that although he felt fit and vigorous, he had fifty-two years under his belt. They had slowly puffed their way up the mountain, pushing the bikes and stopping intermittently for rest. Aging is a humbling experience.

"Hey, you know me," lied David. "Can't stay off it. It's all those years in the field, backbreaking work, long hours, climbing up and down pyramids twenty or thirty times a day, and all those years wheelbarrowing dirt. I feel like I'm nineteen."

"He acts like it sometimes, too," shouted Alexandra from behind, cozening up to slip a hand inside his plaid shirt. He leaned into her embrace and received a few nibbles on his neck.

"Sounds like I need to get lost somewhere if it'll do that for you. How about some company, David?"

"Company? Who do you have in mind? The last time we spent time together it became a little too exciting: lots of people dying, my students beaten up and, if I remember correctly, you received a couple of bullet holes for your efforts."

"A small thing, professor," boasted the *federale*. "You know how resilient the Mexican male is." (The professor could visualize Luis standing straighter as he spoke, and see his chest swell). "I've completely recovered and on the job again. Angela wants to visit with Alexandra. Besides, I've got something important to talk to you about. You know...an anthropology thing."

"Oh, yeah?" said the professor, his interest perking. "Like what?"

"Jaguars."

"Jaguars?"

"And murder."

"Murder? Jaguars don't murder. They hunt and kill to feed themselves and their young. Only primates murder," David philosophized, immediately recalling several examples, "especially humans, as we all know. Chimpanzees and other nonhuman primates have been known to murder." He slipped into academic recall mode, oblivious to nuance or inference.

"David...please. That's all very interesting," interrupted Luis. "I'd love to discuss...er...primates with you later. However, the jaguar I have in mind is most definitely a human murderer. Care to hear about it?"

Ah, a mystery, thought the professor. He loved a good anthropological mystery. "Tell me, Luis, are you going to ask me questions about Indian tribes and jaguar motifs?"

"You're a smart man for a *gringo*, professor."

"How long will it take for you to get here?"

"Actually, Angela and I are calling from up the mountain. We're here, in Creel, to see you. We just got off the train."

"What!" exclaimed David.

"What is it?" asked Alexandra, concerned at his outburst.

He waved her off. "Think you can find our cabin?"

"I'm a detective, David. What do you think?"

"We'll be waiting. And Luis...."

"Yeah?"

"Watch for the rattlesnakes at about the third curve. There's a den somewhere along that line of boulders."

"Rattlesnakes, David?"

"And boots. You did remember to wear boots, didn't you?"

"Rattlesnakes? Boots? Just a minute, *gringo*." Luis' voice became muffled, as if he'd covered the phone mouthpiece.

The professor grinned and waited, listening to the one-sided, urgent conversation. Standing in the doorway to eavesdrop, Alexandra smiled, shook her head and gave him the shame-shame signal with her index fingers.

"Listen, David, if you're not doing anything right now, maybe you could give Angela and me the scenic tour down to your place. I mean...you know...we might miss something important...a view or something."

"I'll be right up, buddy," David turned and grinned at Alexandra, "and Luis...."

"Yeah?"

"Did you bring your gun?"

"Certainly, David, I...."

"Good. Because they've sighted pumas roaming the cliffs west of here two days ago."

"Pumas!" Luis exclaimed.

"I'll be there shortly. Just relax and breathe the mountain air."

"David...."

He hung up, turned to face his wife, and both burst out laughing!

"You're shameless," she admonished. "How could you do that to our friends?"

"I'm sure they'll return the favor. Besides...his macho nonsense needs toning down. He'll be a little more humble this way."

The professor reached for his walking stick. "Want to come along?"

"No. The maid saw some snakes up the hill this morning and I don't want to take any chances."

"Snakes?" The professor tried to remain expressionless. "Up the hill?"

"Yes," she replied, her face unreadable, "she couldn't recognize them in the early morning light."

"That right? Well, guess I'll just have to be careful," he said, trying not to betray his fear. The professor hated snakes. Thirty years of archaeological fieldwork had left him a reservoir of memories, some of them frightening, and a healthy dread of crawling reptiles.

He leaned forward for Ali's kiss, listened for the inevitable instructions all females give their husbands when they leave home, then closed the cabin's cedar plank door behind him. A brilliant white orb showered light over the spacious canyon and mountains beyond as he carefully scanned the ground for snakes. He heard the door open again.

"I was just kidding about the snakes, *querido*," she smirked. "Thought you deserved a taste of your own humor!"

He made a half-hearted lunge for her, but she slammed and locked the door, chortling as she did. He smiled fondly, appreciating the joke, and reminded himself of how lucky he was to have found such a wonderfully compatible companion so late in life.

Blocking the sun's glare with his hand, he glanced quickly up the boulder-studded trail leading to the lodge then began the slow, uphill trek, looking left and right as he walked. At 52, he knew he was lucky to be so healthy. No sense in getting snakebit after living this long. He planted his stick firmly on the rocky path, following the well-worn trail up the summit, the stick extending in rhythm as he began to pace himself for the thirty-minute walk. His anticipation at seeing Luis and Angela grew with each step. Soon they would be talking of jaguar murderers, and so he began to daydream as he stepped off the distance to the lodge.

A Meeting of Old Friends

Bald eagles with outstretched wings glided thousands of feet above the Copper Canyon, cutting circles in a cloudless blue sky, lazily riding unseen wind currents as they searched for a rodent to bring to the nest and their young. The professor grew dizzy watching their tireless slow promenades, and so he leaned and looked over the patio wall, his arms supporting his weight, neck outstretched. Below, one of four major rivers in the Copper Canyon area boiled away into a series of un-navigable cataracts. Torrents of white water roared through a boulder-strewn riverbed and launched itself into thin tresses of white mist, crashing into a cauldron of spinning whirlpools.

He never tired of looking into the canyon and imagining the geologic processes and millions of years it took to create this masterpiece. A pamphlet at the lodge had informed him that the canyon country comprised 10,000 square miles of the northern Sierra Madres, all of it bedeviled with amazing gorges, ravines, and at least four canyons deeper than the Grand Canyon in Arizona. Much of it was covered with dense forests of oak, hemlock, and austere pine; all of it was populated with more than 50,000 Tarahumara Indians. A veritable paradise, and as yet undiscovered by the Americans across the border.

"...Anyway," continued Luis, "when your office told me you were on sabbatical in Creel, Angela and I decided to surprise you." He clunked a scuffed black boot onto a stool, then tilted a bottle of Corona to his puckered lips, hesitated a moment, and finished with, "I've heard of this place—been meaning to visit for years—but we can't stay long. Maybe a couple of days." He took a long pull from the bottle, then wiped his mouth with a sleeve.

The view had riveted the professor and he still searched the canyon walls and bottom. Only reluctantly did he turn away to answer Luis. "Hope so. It's a long way to travel for a two-day visit. If I had a choice...I'd stay forever.

Mexico City runs an easy last to just about anywhere I've been lately."

"I hear that," agreed the mustachioed *federale*, taking another drink from his beer, then exhaling loudly. "Angela and I haven't missed it a lick. Chihuahua…now there's a good city. Cleanest place I've ever lived. Now the kids are talking of moving north."

"Hey," said David, remembering, then slapping the bottom of Luis' boot. "What were you hallucinating about on the phone? Jaguars? A jaguar murderer? If I didn't know better, I'd say you were working too hard. But that can't be the case, can it?"

"No respect," grumbled Luis, "no respect for a master sleuth who's solved countless mysteries and saved thousands of innocents from the crimeinfested barrios of Mexico City." He lowered his boot to the floor, leaned back into his chair, and reached into his right pant pocket. He extracted three translucent green stones, several blue-green rocks, and a delicate gold pendant with a blue-green stone at its center.

"Ever seen anything like this before?"

"Could be anything," offered the professor, giving the stones a quick perusal, "but this is probably gold and the stone turquoise." The clear green stones gleamed and sparkled, though a few had been scorched by fire. The blue-green stones were smoke-blackened, irregularly shaped and pitted. Something black and brittle edged them—probably metal melted from the fire. "What do these have to do with jaguars?"

"Here, let me show you."

Luis took the clear green stones and arranged them into the shape of a cat's face. It looked familiar. Jaguar masks, faces, drawings and motifs are an indelible and frequently occurring theme in Middle America. All the classic civilizations of Mexico had strong jaguar themes in their religion, art and social institutions. The most powerful predator in Mexico, the big cat had long been the object of myth and legend. The classic Maya site of Palenque in the southern jungles of Chiapis state, a spectacular ruin discovered in the 1500's, lists a succession of jaguar kings who ruled four hundred years before abandoning their city to the jungle.

"Okay…what's the story?" queried David, his professional interests piqued.

"Maybe nothing." Luis spread his hands. "It's only a guess…listen." He leaned back into his chair, took another swig of beer, and began. "One year ago…."

A strange story indeed, thought the professor, fifteen minutes later. An ecoterrorist had been sabotaging manufacturing plants along the northern border. He had destroyed equipment and bridges and bombed the factories themselves, killing, perhaps inadvertently, innocents in the process. A jaguar insignia left at the scene identified him as the perpetrator. Then one week ago a female diplomat had been abducted from the Vista Train five kilometers west of here. A kidnapper had called, identifying himself as the Jaguar Man, and claimed to be holding the woman captive. He gave a list of demands—including stopping the proposed Aguila Dam and Reservoir—or the diplomat would be killed. He had given no time frame, but the feds believed this event to be related to those along the frontier. Luis and others had been assigned the case months ago, but as yet the investigation had turned up little.

"These were recovered from the remains of a burned shack in a small town called Dolores, close to the first bombing incident." Louis extended a large hand and rearranged the stones. "They were in a partially burned leather bag, and this," he pointed to a pendant-shaped teardrop, "was worn by a young female destroyed in the fire. The police found other items, but they don't tell us a thing."

"What does the burned house have to do with the jaguar character?" The professor reached for the stones.

"A profiler from Mexico City says our terrorist is a loner harboring a grudge against someone. In this case, the factories polluting the northern states so badly. In the burning case, the factory owners had been watching this suspect closely. His neighbors in Dolores had some interesting things to say about him, too. Seems as though he's some kind of shaman or medicine man from around here in this Copper Canyon area. Has an oriental look to him, but he's definitely an Indian, probably a Tarahumara. He ran lots of shit on the factories, did some threatening and even tried to organize the workers into collective bargaining units." Luis snatched one of the stones that caught his eye and turned it over and over in his hands. Satisfied, he replaced it on the table.

"There aren't many witnesses. A midwife claims she delivered a baby in his house the night of the fire. Says the wife died giving birth, but that the baby was alive when she left. We think he set the fire that burned the house and killed the baby." Luis spread his arms wide and shrugged. "But why? What's the motive?" He frowned and sat up straight, then leaned toward David like a conspirator, his bushy eyebrows arced in question. "Have you seen some of the shit holes they've made up there?"

"No, but I've read about it." And the professor had; American companies, their greed unharnessed and culpability minimized, had flocked to Mexico's northern desert states. Scores of *maquiladoras*, some quite large, had sprung up along the frontier. Thousands of poor Indians from Mexico City, Guadalajara and rural farming areas arrived each month to feed the burgeoning labor demands of the factories.

Already fragile desert soils and ecosystems had become disrupted and despoiled on a scale unforeseen and not believed possible ten years ago. David had read horror stories describing the destruction and pollution; boomtowns constructed of cardboard boxes, rusty corrugated roofing panels, and scrap lumber trucked across the border from the States had sprung up overnight. The instant squalor had become magnified and encouraged by the Mexican Government's indifference. The factories need laborers; how they got them, where they come from, and the conditions in which the workers lived were of no consequence. The only services the *maquiladoras* provided were profitable ones: buses to transport the workers (for which they charged), and stores near the factories filled with high-priced goods. In this way they recaptured the worker's salaries, and more in some cases, by extending credit. The workers were trapped in permanent, chronic debt to the company, the New World's latest version of owing your soul to the company store.

Now the Mexican government planned to build a dam downstream from two canyon rivers emptying into a large alluvial basin surrounded by mountains. It was a massive hydroelectric project that promised to supply a growing demand in the northern states for electricity. Big business hailed it as a make or break project for the Mexican economy and environmentalists were condemning it as an unconscionable tragedy.

"You never said what you're doing here," Luis interrupted the professor's philosophical musings.

"I'm on sabbatical, but I'm mixing it with business. I'm doing some preliminary investigations in the area of the proposed hydroelectric dam your terrorist wants stopped. Can't say that I blame him, really. I have a small grant to find evidence of any prehistoric sites in the basin that will be destroyed when the reservoir is filled." The professor reached for a tube to extract a map. "Are you familiar with the project?"

"Yes and no. Never heard of it before this kidnapping, but everyone else apparently has. More electricity is needed to power the factories. But frankly, David, I'm against it." The *federale* spread his arms and asked, "How many damn factories do we need anyway? Why don't they build some on the other side of the border?"

"You know the answer, Luis, politics. Plain and simple...politics."

"How long you here for?"

"Alexandra leaves for Mexico City in a few days, but I have to spend a couple of weeks investigating the flood plain of the reservoir site. I have a small cabin down in Batopilas Canyon. It's close and convenient to my work."

"Sounds like a big job." Luis stood and walked to the stone wall, his broad shoulders and torso set firmly on long, strong legs. "Heights make me dizzy." He glanced quickly at the vista, then stepped away from the ledge and turned to David.

"Listen. Why can't Alexandra go to Chihuahua with Angela for a week or so? You can get some work done and show me around down there. I need to investigate a couple of leads on that diplomat's abduction last week."

Not a bad idea, thought the professor. When Alexandra left for Mexico City, it would be a good opportunity to do some archaeology as well as spend time with Luis pursuing a little police work. He was reminiscing one of their previous adventures when Alexandra and Angela appeared on the patio with more Coronas, sliced avocado and chicken sandwiches.

Alexandra readily agreed to travel with Angela to Chihuahua, and David half listened to their patter. Luis seemed preoccupied, occasionally rearranging the clear green stones on the table, or retrieving the gold pendant for closer examination. It occurred to David that he might be able to help Luis with the jewelry. The professor had already sent several river core samples to a colleague at the University of Chihuahua. Perhaps an Electron Activation Analysis could be done on these stones as well? The results could be ready in a couple of days, and the report might reveal from what area of the United States or Mexico the turquoise had been mined, as well as the type of gem the clear green stones were. Luis thought this to be a great idea, but appeared reluctant to part with what little evidence he had. Finally the professor's assurances won him over. The *federale* kept one of the clear green stones, a turquoise piece, and gold pendant, but sent the others along with Alexandra to Chihuahua. The decision made, his mood lightened and he joined in the conversation, becoming his usual animated, voluble self.

The professor, on the other hand, was intrigued with the jewelry and slipped into silent conversation with himself. The stones came with a story and he intended to extract it. Considering them within the context of murder, sabotage and kidnapping made them even more intriguing. It might mean leaving the comfort of the cabana for the rugged Chihuahua canyon country, but at 52 how many adventures did a man have left? He caught Luis' eye and raised his Corona in a silent toast. Luis answered in kind, raising his bottle and nodding in affirmation. Partners again. So be it. Tomorrow they would begin.

The Kidnappers Argue

The kidnapper and his accomplice were brothers: Martin, the elder, a Jesuit priest, and Mike, the younger, a shaman in the tradition of their father. Fr. Martin stared at his brother, but Mike avoided his look and studied the distant canyon floor. They sat on a rocky crag overlooking the canyon and Tarahumara village below. A *fiesta* appeared imminent, as the caves shed their inhabitants and a crowd gathered around a blazing fire in anticipation of the party. Hidden from the eyes of the Indian revelers below, the conspirators sat in a mutual brooding silence beneath wispy clouds strung thin like taffeta through a blue sky. A gentle wind stroked the canyon rim, caressing the leaves on stunted hickories and urging an ancient copse of pines to whisper in concert.

They had argued again, much like the last three meetings, and finally called a truce. They couldn't agree and so a sullen, aggrieved silence shrouded the protected ledge until the priest, impatient and angry, stood to leave.

"It's the right thing to do...believe me...I'm sure." He looked to Mike, expecting agreement, but received no acknowledgment. "I said I'm leaving...and listen..." he waggled a finger at his brother, "stay out of the mine and away from the woman. Don't talk to her. It's too dangerous. Feed her...look after her until I contact you...but don't mess with her. It could ruin everything. You hear?"

"What do you care if...."

"Don't touch her!" the priest nearly yelled. "Don't even talk to her." He turned to go, looked back and frowned in disgust, then moved hastily down a path toward the distant valley.

Mike sat another thirty minutes, watching the preparations below, mulling over the implications of the kidnapping. So—his brother didn't believe he understood, did he?

When Martin had phoned the American and Mexican Consulates in Chihuahua to make demands, no one had bothered to respond. They didn't give a damn. Martin was the one who didn't understand. Why couldn't he see it? Something different must be done. Mike knew he should never have gone along with his brother's crazy ideas. He thought of leaving, but then Martin appeared below as a black robed, sandal-clad priest. This raised a chorus of approval from the Indians, and they surged to welcome him. The priest shook hands all around, then pointed toward the river to five men carrying heavy loads. Tied to a pole and carried on the shoulders of two Indians, came a squealing, thrashing pig. Three stout Indian males with red headbands and cotton pants followed the trussed pig. They slowly but carefully transported three large crocks of corn beer—the *tesquina*—for the *tesquinada*.

Mike thought again to leave, but felt compelled to stay and enjoy the activities vicariously. The preparations were familiar to him and brought a smile to his face, recalling other pig roasts and other *tesquinadas*, and so he relaxed and watched, momentarily forgetting the argument and the woman. He knew the majority of the festivalgoers and began to review their names and relationship to each other while the pig was prepared.

The canyon, actually a Tarahumara village, had walls pocked with caves. Formerly abandoned mines, the caves now served as homes for the Indians during the winter months when the wind blew too cold to live high above on the canyon rim near Creel. Campfires issued smoke in wispy black strings that became a hovering gray cloud halfway up the canyon. Discarded articles were strewn up and down the canyon floor, and small children sat on piles of refuse, digging and exploring for who knew what. One man's trash was another's wealth, and the Indians continually turned the rubbish pile inside out, recycling its contents.

A hungry fire blazed in the canyon's center, and the men placed the pig nearby on a large flat rock. A plastic five-gallon bucket was positioned strategically under its neck. The priest talked as he whittled a corncob to a sharp point, telling stories to any who would listen. The Indians milled anxiously about, everyone anticipating the death of the hog and the beginning of the *tesquinada*, the *fiesta*.

The priest eyed the sharpened corncob. Satisfied that it would do the job, he spoke to the crowd as if teaching or directing them, and then said a short prayer. He held the dagger-shaped cob close to the pig's neck, pausing for effect, building tension so that the production unfolded with appropriate drama. Even from above, the tension in the canyon seemed palpable, and

Mike unconsciously held his breath, awaiting the death stroke.

Suddenly Fr. Martin plunged the corncob into the pig's neck artery, and it squealed in protest, jerking violently and lurching to gain its feet while the men held it firmly. They turned the animal so that its blood spurted toward the bucket, and with each beat of its frantic heart, it pumped its life into the plastic container. Gradually its movements became feeble, and then it lay still. With a final twitch it relaxed, its soul gone, a gift to the gods. Everyone cheered! A masterful stroke, completed with expertise and on the first try.

The serious work of preparing the pig began, but then two women began arguing over the bucket of blood, and the mood of the crowd turned somber. Finally, the priest intervened to mediate the dispute by encouraging them to share and the festivities began again. The pig was disemboweled with a sharp hunting knife, sliced stem to stern, and its entrails distributed to eager hands. Two men with double-edged razors scraped the hog's pink skin, shaving every visible hair from its body, including the ears and between its toes. Laughter echoed through the canyon as men and women alike lined up to sample the *tesquina*. Satisfied of its quality, they began to imbibe corn beer and prepare themselves for a serious celebration.

When the pig's body lay clean shaven and washed inside and out, two men flayed it and trimmed out the fat to throw in a large iron pot hung over a blazing fire. Within minutes the fat had rendered into lard. Next they removed the hog's inner layer of skin from the hide and cut it into still smaller sections. Rinsed clean again, these pieces were thrown into the boiling lard. People crowded around the kettle as the redolent aroma of cooking pig flesh wafted through the canyon. Within minutes large sheets of steaming *chincherones*, fried pigskins, circulated among the crowd. They greedily feasted on the rinds, stuffing large portions into each other's mouths, smacking their lips in delight and chasing it with *tesquina*.

Fr. Martin, meanwhile, circulated among the revelers, looking to engage a group in conversation. He gestured to punctuate his words, then pointed to the pig to emphasize some aspect of his statement. A few faces turned serious and attentive, but others frowned and walked toward the *tesquina* pot, shaking their heads in disgust. The priest moved from group to group, explaining as he went, and soon the ambiance succumbed to somber disgust. A few muttered to others and glanced about furtively, feeling guilty and uncomfortable, disillusioned with the priest and his ridiculous ideas.

Mike sat far above, well hidden, yet able to clearly discern the events below. He had witnessed it all before: his brother attempting to proselytize the Indians by using self-serving analogies and maneuvering them to participate in his "Instructive Reenactments." Martin used the phrase to deceive and coerce the Raramuri to abandon their religious beliefs by reenacting a biblical scene using the Indians own spiritual and historical leaders in key roles in place of biblical characters.

Although attracted to the beer and roast pig, the Indians edged away from Martin. They were loath to participate, finding it difficult to abide heresy of their traditional beliefs and not wanting to encourage the silly priest. Most black robes were devils—this the Indians knew—but Fr. Martin seemed harmless and friendly, and he always brought something to share with them. The other priests behaved like self-righteous, grasping toadies of their God, all of them completely ignorant of Raramuri culture.

Mike aimlessly tossed pebbles, deep in thought, nurturing a rising discontent. Why did his brother even bother? He tossed a final pebble and frowned. They believed Martin to be a fool, and laughed and made jokes about him. Mike shot a final malignant look at the distant priest and rose to go. But then he recalled his brother's admonition. "Don't talk to the woman. Don't touch her!" This stoked his anger. *Why not?* he argued silently. What difference did it make? Besides, she was scared to death. He could see it in her eyes: stark terror and a passive, helpless stare. She believed she would die. *But that isn't the plan, damn it!* he thought angrily. *That isn't the plan at all.*

Martin had assured him that she would be released, and that she would be traded to her government for assurances to not build the reservoir. But more than a week had passed and they had heard nothing. Both governments were ignoring them. *No one cares*, he thought bitterly, and now he found himself in the biggest mess of his life. He never should have listened to Martin, never have agreed to such an outrageous plan.

A frown fixed his face and his hand moved to scratch a sparse beard. Mike thought again of the pretty brown-haired woman. He still remembered her frightened expressions and whimpering cries as she rode the burro through lonely, cactus-crowded canyons beneath the pale luminescence of a full moon. Except for a groan, she hadn't uttered a sound when they had sewn up the cut over her eye. She had stared wide-eyed and unfocused into the darkness, her mind's eye intent on an image that had held her mute and distant. What had she seen? Her own death? Had she imagined herself to be somewhere else? Had her soul fled temporarily, then returned when it was sure the body remained intact?

Mike understood matters of the soul. As an apprentice shaman to his father he had learned much about the spirit world and had traveled it extensively. As an adult, he still adhered to the ancient belief system of Tarahuamara and lived a Spartan, traditional lifestyle. Sometimes he ate datura or peyote to give wings to his soul and explore the spirit world with its surreal landscapes and uncertain realities. It was nearly impossible to give the soul wings when awake, and one could normally only succeed with the help of the soul medicine. If she could do this without the medicine plants, he held her in awe.

After they had stitched the cut, the woman's soul had returned and she had protested loudly as they dragged her through the narrow mine shaft leading to the central room. Upon removal of the blindfold, she had the expression of someone stricken to the core of her being. A quiet terror had seized her, and the vacant horror in her eyes still haunted him. He wanted to reach out to her—to touch her face and stroke her eyes. He wanted to assure her that all would end well, and that she could trust him.

An urgent desire to comfort her lifted him from his seat on the rocky crag. He stretched languorously; ignoring the festivities below, then began to thread a path leading up and over the canyon wall. He must run six hours to reach the mine, and he began to pace off the distance with a slow jog. A four-legged companion joined him—a black female jaguar—and together they picked up the pace, striding in unison across the canyon rim. Shouts of surprise and recognition rose from the canyon floor when the celebrants caught sight of his silhouette, but he ignored them, his mind's eye focused on the face of his pretty captive. A sense of necessity gripped him and he spoke to the black cat, urging her to keep up.

Two hours later the jaguar began to falter, and so Mike slowed to a near walk, but soon they ran west again. A red-orange haze extended feathered wings from its fiery corona, as the sun grew tired and melted into the distant horizon, enclosing him in a dying blaze and pulling him toward an uncertain destiny.

Luis Rents a Truck

A pale yellow sun struggled to breast the eastern Sierra Madres while a chilled October wind stroked the canyon walls. The wind hesitated, then gusted and swirled dust and grit from the railroad's gravel bed into the professor's eyes and mouth. He spat in protest and rubbed his burning eyes until they watered. Alexandra pushed at her billowing skirt and held a straw hat to her auburn hair until the wind relented.

"I wish you would come," she complained. Her dark brown eyes flashed disapproval while she held her jacket together with her hands, giving the impression that she hugged herself. With her back to the wind and her shoulders hunched, her petite body shivered. She appeared miserable and unhappy.

"It'll only be a week or so and I'll have all the data and photos I need. Luis will help."

"Luis will slow you down," she said with certainty. "He'll run you all over looking for that poor diplomat and you won't get a thing done. I'll come looking if I don't hear from you in three days," she threatened benignly, shaking her finger at him.

"You're wrong," protested David. "Luis just wants me to show him the *barrancas* and the new dam site. I won't get involved in his investigation."

Alexandra looked doubtful. "What about these rocks?" She held them aloft.

"Those are not rocks. They're pieces of turquoise and some kind of gemstone. Think of them as part of your valuable Mexican heritage."

She sniggered. "Oh sure. Just like all those boxes in the basement. What's his name again?" Alexandra often played dumb when irritated with her husband.

"Professor Atunez, Fidelio Atunez in the Department of Anthropology in

Chihuahua. Don't forget now. Drop them off at the university this afternoon when the train arrives. I'll call in a couple of days for the results."

"Be careful, *querido*." She offered her cheek for a kiss, but he reached instead to embrace her and kissed her full on the lips.

She pulled away, embarrassed, looked to see if anyone watched, then leaned forward to whisper.

"Stay out of the cantinas!" she admonished.

"Alexandra, I...."

"Luis has the sense of a salamander. Be careful." She gave him a wan smile, and then stepped on the stair leading into the Vista Train.

Luis arrived with Angela, his long gray coattails blowing in the breeze. The *federale* hefted his wife's suitcase onboard, then joined the professor outside to wave and make promises of good intent. They vowed to call their wives regularly, watch for snakes and take it easy.

The train whistle blew and the men stood impatiently in the bright sunshine of a cold morning, waving goodbye as the blue and white Vista Train began a slow chug through the mountains and down into the flatlands. The professor felt a pang of regret. He would miss Alexandra. At 52, he longed for the comforts of home and his wife's companionship, but so many years of field archaeology had created a work ethic that resulted in restless discontent unless he was working on a project all the time. *Aww...well*, he thought, He would be done soon enough.

He turned to Luis, who already walked away, his heavy boots slapping the gravel as he approached the lodge parking lot. Luis paused beside a group of heavily clothed Tarahumaras unloading their baskets, toys, and trinkets and said, "Come on, *gringo*. I hired a car to take us down to Batopilas Canyon."

It's starting already, thought David. He's making plans without consulting me. The professor made a mental note to be firm with Luis, or they wouldn't be able to work together, even if only for two or three days.

"Luis, don't start making decisions without including me. I have things I need to...."

Luis waved off his objections as so much donkey fodder and boisterously pounded his friend on the back while telling of their plans for the day. David found it difficult to share the *federale's* enthusiasm, but tossed his travel bag over his shoulder and accompanied Luis, listening to his gregarious chatter.

"First I want you to show me the town, David. Then I'd like to stop at the precinct house to check in with Colonel Cedras...."

"Wait a minute!" said the professor, alarmed. Luis had stopped alongside

31

an old blue Chevy truck that appeared to have died of cancer and been resurrected as an advertisement for a salvage yard. "This is it? This is the car you rented?" David stared, aghast. They'd never make it. It was a death trap.

"Don't worry," Luis assured his reticent friend, "you know how tough Mexican cars are," and he jerked on the driver's side handle several times before it released with a clunking protest.

It looked to be an early 60's model, and the ground showed clearly visible through the rusted floorboards. A cracked spider web decorated the windshield from a head butt, and the inside door handle was missing.

"It'll do," Luis insisted, cranking the engine several times before it coughed, sputtered, then lurched toward the canyon rim where a narrow, paved mountain road connected to the Camino Real, the old mining road leading to the bottom of the Batopilas Canyon. A monolithic concrete statue of Jesus stood above the northern cliffs watching their progress.

"Luis…take it easy, okay?" The professor had a bad feeling about this, and he began a search for missing seat belts. He settled for a firm hold on the seat with his left hand and the door's window lever with his right as Luis maneuvered the truck on the winding asphalt to Cusarare.

The *federale* moved the steering wheel side to side, then muttered, "Damn ball joints must be worn out." The truck strayed from one side of the road to the other, barely staying between the lines as the slack steering wheel turned with little resistance.

"Keep it in low, Luis."

His friend ignored the comment, shifted into second and experimented with the steering some more.

"This thing got brakes?"

"Sure." Luis pumped them several times for the professor's benefit. "We'll get a better truck from the precinct house down in Batopilas. I called ahead…told them we'd need it for three or four days."

"Luis, I do have field work to complete, remember?"

"Sure, sure...but you can show me around for a day or two, can't you?"

"Just get me to Batopilas in one piece and I'll do anything."

The truck did well until they rounded the first curve. A large rock had fallen onto the road, and they nearly crashed before Luis swerved to the right. The distant canyon floor loomed suddenly closer and the professor felt his heart thud dully.

"Jesus, Luis!" he yelled. "Go around the other side. There's a sheer drop-off over here." Luis jerked the steering wheel again, barely missing the rock

32

and scaring his passenger badly.

"Slow down, damn it!"

"Easy, David. I've driven many a mile in old cars." Luis began to talk about his old Mercury convertible, Angela's Chevy Impala, and every car he had ever owned. Meanwhile, the professor's eyes hurtled to the canyon floor, a sheer drop of thousands of feet. The road precipitously hugged the mountain wall like a ribbon, barely wide enough for two cars to pass at once. It had no shoulder and no siderail for emergencies.

While steering with one hand, Luis began to point out things while he drove. "Look at that Indian climbing down the cliff," and, "See those green streaks? Those are veins of copper."

"I know, Luis. Keep your eyes on the road."

"You sound like Angela, *gringo*."

"Quit calling me *gringo*. I've lived in Mexico nearly twenty-five years."

"You'll always be a gringo if you weren't born here, David."

"Fine, Luis. Watch the road, okay?"

They passed a string of Tarahumara dressed in heavy cotton pants and colorful headbands. The Indians toted large rope sacks of baskets and pottery to sell to the Vista Train passengers when the train stopped at Divisadero. Luis pumped the clutch and shifted into third.

"How long will we be in Cusarare?"

"That's up to you. You're the *federale*. It's just a tourist town. Talk to the *policia* and ask around, but we need to be off in a couple of hours if we're going to make Batopilas by evening."

"What's in Batopilas?"

"My cabin. It's just a jumping-off spot at the end of the Camino Real. It's quaint. Dilapidated houses and abandoned mines give Batopilas the feel of a ghost town even though it has an old church and a few hundred people still living there. During the 1800's, it was a boomtown until all the silver veins dried up. The famous Potosi mine is nearby and the whole area is just kind of wild and overgrown."

"Just like Mexico City, huh?"

"Yes, with thousand foot canyon walls instead of concrete buildings."

The professor tried to ignore Luis' driving and concentrate on other things. Did his friend have a chance of finding the diplomat? The story made little sense as far as David could see. One year ago turquoise jewelry and unidentified gemstones had been recovered from a burned house in a *maquiladora* town hundreds of miles to the north. Incidents of sabotage had since been committed by an ecoterrorist, and now a U.S. diplomat had been kidnapped. How could it all be related? Especially the stones—how could the stones be connected to the terrorist?

"Luis, do you think you'll find word of your diplomat down here?"

The *federale* shrugged. "Who knows? I don't even know if I'm on the right side of the mountain range. One thing I am sure of is that everyone in these small mountain towns knows everyone else's business. If someone knows anything, I'll find out."

They traveled in silence, but then a break appeared in the hemlock forest and David's eyes focused on the faraway canyon floor and walls. He saw the rugged terrain and visualized its treacherous surface: beautiful but deadly. He stole a look at Luis. *City Boy*, he thought. If lucky, Luis would discover nothing and go home to Angela and the clean streets of Chihuahua. If events turned bad, the trail led into dangerous canyon lands and a thousand ways for a greenhorn to die accidentally. Roads were practically nonexistent. Instead, hundreds of Indian trails webbed the mountainsides, only a few telephones could be found, and the area had virtually no medical facilities.

"Luis, you'll need a guide if you go into the barrancas. This truck won't take you most places. Anyone hiding a diplomat will be well tucked away in the mountains."

"That's what you're along for, buddy."

"I've got my own agenda, Luis. Remember?"

"Hey, don't worry. We'll just play it by ear a couple of days and see what happens. You're starting to get a little soft in your old age, *gringo*. What did you tell me about a lifetime of wheelbarrowing dirt and climbing pyramids? Lighten up, David. I'll have you back in Alexandra's bed in no time."

The professor began a slow burn while he ruminated over the *federale's* words. Luis didn't take him seriously. It was more of the same old macho crap. David had spent a lifetime doing archaeological fieldwork from the jungles of Guatemala to the Chihuahua highlands, and knew his business well. *Luis*, he thought, *if you're lucky you won't suffer from anything more than snakebite. If not, a grizzly'll eat you.*

Luis and the Professor Celebrate Death

Two hours later the truck wobbled into the town of Cusarare and an ongoing festival. It was The Day of the Dead, a national holiday, and the dead were everywhere. Skeletons with fiendish smiles had been painted on store windows and hung from the gazebo in the town square. Small children with skull-painted faces romped and played dead games while tourists watched with amusement. Prominently displayed outside the Federal Police Station, a skeleton rode a bicycle, and the majority of *policia* had been steadily drinking mescal or brandy most of the day. A national holiday in which the spirits of the dead visit the living, *El Dia de Los Muertos* usually lasted weeks.

Not a productive day, bitched the professor, and not likely to get any better. He had spent the last hour dutifully following Luis around Cusarare. They had stopped at a trinket store so Luis could buy a skull key chain for his grandchild, and stopped to chat with merchants in the outdoor market. Most knew nothing of the kidnapping, and the *policia* only a little more, but everyone was willing to talk and speculate endlessly.

Sitting in the shade of a gazebo, David watched mounted, six-gun toting lawmen and *vaqueros* in etched silver-tipped boots as they listened to the joyful, upbeat tempo of blazing trumpets and rhythmic guitars. The *mariachis* moved the crowd to dance and sing-along to old favorites. The professor tapped his foot and smiled. A colorful, lively scene out of colonial Mexico, it was a heck of a lot better than following the gregarious Luis around.

The *federale* had a talent for conversation and a finely honed intuition about people, but the professor yearned to leave for Batopilas and his cabin. Cusarare had become a tourist town, and David thought it unlikely that Luis would discover anything of value. But as an archaeologist, what did he know about criminals? He wouldn't worry about it, he decided, and began to move his foot in rhythm to the *mariachis* again.

"Great day, isn't it?" Luis surprised him from behind.

"Luis! It's about time. Have you rescued the diplomat and shot the kidnappers yet?"

"Very funny, David. I take it you're ready to leave?"

"It's scary around here with all these dead people. Let's go."

As they began their descent into the canyon, the sun hung low in the sky. Soon it sought solitude and hid behind the western canyon wall. The terrain changed and the pine, hemlock, and jacaranda became sparser. Luis moved the Chevy's steering wheel in a constant arc as he followed the blacktop. He drove slower, occasionally sighing, and seemed to be deep in thought.

"Are you afraid to die, professor?"

David considered the question. How many times had he thought of death? How many times had he been close to death? How do you answer such an introspective question?

"I have a healthy respect for death, but Americans don't dwell on it or celebrate it."

"In Mexico we are taught not to fear death. You must have *macho*." Luis shook a fist for emphasis. "Even as small children we are not sheltered from death."

True, thought the professor. Death in Mexico was viewed differently than in any culture he had studied. Its ancient civilizations had long traditions of human sacrifice, and millions had died during The Conquest and the subsequent revolutions.

"Yes," replied David, "that's because your *macho* ancestors willingly allowed themselves to be sacrificed at the great temples and pyramids." The professor gave him a mischievous look. "It's a form of natural selection."

Luis returned the look—aware that the professor had baited him—waited a moment, then took the bait. "And what does that mean?"

The wily academic set the hook. "Survival of the fittest, Luis. Only those smart enough to avoid the sacrificial stone lived to pass on their genes. Only the smart, scared ones stayed alive." This wasn't strictly true, but it would give the *federale* something to think about.

"Unh," Luis grunted, trying to decide whether or not he had been insulted. He pumped the brakes to slow for a curve then replied, "Well I'm here, so my ancestors must have been smart."

"Or scared," insinuated David.

Luis shot the professor a surprised look and saw the grin on his face.

"That was a shot, *gringo*," he accused, "you set me up."

"You'll get me back."

Luis did. David had to endure a laymen's dissertation on the value of macho for the next seventy miles while the *federale* slowly navigated the truck around hairpin curves, potholes and fallen rock. They crossed several canyons and drove through small ramshackle hamlets and Tarahumara villages, all interspersed with orchards and thick forests of oak and hemlock. Filled with natural wonders, the canyons had eroded rocky crags, wind-sculpted arches and boulders, and curious umbrella shapes. They crossed the Basihuare and Urique rivers on sturdy, but aged bridges and watched their waters boil away in torrents, to cascade into distant gorges and chasms.

The drive was fatiguing, and Luis hunched forward onto the steering wheel when they started the dizzying descent into the huge Batopilas Canyon. Halfway down, the truck began to missfire and die repeatedly.

"*Pinche* truck!" Luis cursed and slammed his fist to the dash when they were reduced to coasting downhill into the town.

"We're out of gas," accused David, irritated.

"He told me he filled it a couple a days ago."

"A couple of days ago!" said the professor, incredulous. "The gas gauge says empty."

"It doesn't work, but we'll make it. It looks all downhill from here."

His nerves already frayed, the professor clenched his jaw and remained mute as Luis coasted the antique truck into town. It would undoubtedly live to ride another day, but David no longer felt sure of his own prospects.

The truck rolled into the town's only Pemex station, which had long since closed its doors, and they stood outside to stretch and shake off their fatigue. But this did little good. The professor felt emotionally drained and irritated at Luis. Alexandra had been right. He should have declined this adventure for the security and familiarity of his books and field work.

"Hungry, David?"

"No…tired. Let's find a ride to my cabin." He turned and led the way into town. They walked past the ruins of the San Miguel Hacienda, formerly the grand ranch house of a rich mine owner, but now weedy and covered with carpets of cascading bougainvillea that poured from the roof in brocades of red and purple. They crossed the Rio Batopilas Bridge and ambled through the mile-long town of stuccoes with red-tiled roofs lining the banks of the river. The air was soaked with the rich the aroma of fruit-laden trees and ancient palms stretched to the sky. The climate seemed balmy compared to the highlands of Creel on the Canyon rim, and so the professor removed his jacket.

David had grown fond of Batopilas and enjoyed the bucolic countryside. It moved at a slow pace, and he was unsure how it maintained its economy. Rumor claimed that much of its money came from smuggling contraband and opium on heavily laden mule trains that traveled weeks over tortuous mountain trails to the seacoast on the Gulf of Baja. From the gulf, it was loaded onto boats at Topolobampo, a small port city in northern Sinaloa state, and shipped across the Gulf of Baja to La Paz on the Baja California coast. From La Paz, it traveled to Tijuana and was dispersed in a hundred ways throughout the United States.

No taxis were to be found, and the professor didn't remember ever seeing one in Batopilas. The sounds of a party grew louder with each step. Luis stopped in front of the El Perdido Otra Vez Cantina.

"Let's stop here, David. I'm hungry."

Skull-faced mariachis exited the cantina, but continued playing as they walked. A portly matron with a heavily mascared face shooed a steady stream of revelers from the cantina.

"It's closing, Luis and it's late. Come on," begged David.

"Don't worry," said Luis, leaving the professor in the midst of mescal and beer-soaked fiesta-goers while he approached the cantina's entrance. *Policia* with machine guns watched warily as he approached the proprietor. The heavily made-up woman attempted to shut the cantina's cedar plank door in Luis' face, but he wedged a boot inside the jamb. He extracted some paper money from his wallet and waved it at the woman. She smiled, but declined and tried to push him away. Quickly, he flashed his badge and spoke earnestly to the woman who frowned, but listened. She glanced again at the badge, snatched the money from his other hand and opened the door.

The professor's mouth fell slack. He couldn't believe it! Had Luis lost his mind? Alexandra had warned him to stay out of cantinas, and here he stood, on the verge of an unwanted adventure. She would kill him if he followed Luis inside.

"Come on, David," waved the *federale*, "they have decided to reopen."

"Luis, I…."

"Come on." Luis waved again and stepped into the cantina. The *mariachis* turned and followed, and the tipsy patrons cheered as everyone reversed directions for the cantina.

Why me, Lord, thought the professor. He sullenly climbed the stairs and pulled open the door, then stepped into an open, tree-filled courtyard surrounded by square tables. Three of the building's interior walls had identical doors, evenly spaced apart. The bar, jukebox and bathrooms lined the fourth wall and immediately became a hub of activity. While he stood appraising the situation, David noticed several young women going in and out of the rooms. Clearly visible fourposter beds stood inside each room. The professor's eyes grew wide with understanding. Luis had bought their way into a whorehouse! This could not be! He walked to where Luis sat, already engaged in conversation with a pockfaced, Indian *puta* named Lasa. Someone plugged in the jukebox, and the professor argued with Luis for several minutes before agreeing to one drink. Luis promised—only one drink and a snack and they would go.

Meanwhile, the *policia* had returned and the *policia* captain stood arguing with the painted matron who had taken the bribe. The professor anxiously watched, his anxiety rising. Frustrated, the captain snapped his fingers at an underling, who promptly pulled the plug on the jukebox. They argued again and finally the matron (madam?) extracted money from her cleavage and handed it to the captain. The jukebox played again and two cans of Tecate appeared on their table next to a grinning sugar skull. The professor stared at his friend, mouth agape. He would owe Luis one for this. The *federale* winked, then waved one of the girls to sit next to his friend.

Macho *indeed*, thought the professor. *David, keep your mouth shut next time.*

Meanwhile, *policia* with machine guns arrived to stand near their table. The professor tensed, ready to bolt. His face turned scarlet as a pretty, but the rotund *puta* tried to engage him in conversation.

"Luis, I don't like this," he muttered, looking at the machine guns.

"Relax and quit worrying. They're working for us. They're protecting us," replied the *federale*.

From what? thought the professor. *Certainly not the putas. What I need is protection from Luis.*

David quickly drank a beer and ordered another. Every half hour the policia pulled the plug on the jukebox and more money changed hands between the madam and the captain. Luis laughed and joked with the *puta*, drinking can after can of beer before finally telling her no and going to seek out the captain.

Both putas quickly lost interest in the embarrassed academic. "Why are you so serious?" they asked him.

Seeing no money forthcoming, the *putas* left, and Lasa, the pockfaced whore, went to flirt with one of the *policia*. They, too, disappeared into one of the bedrooms, leaving David to his beer and grinning skull while his machine gun-toting protectors began to look bored.

The professor broke off a piece of the skull's parietal bone and chewed and sucked. It was made of cane sugar and he snapped off several more pieces, letting them slowly melt into a syrupy glop before swallowing. Then he began to order brandy.

Luis and the captain huddled in a corner like conspirators, and then Luis began to write on his pad. A lead? wondered David. Crazy job being a cop; you get information in strange places and work awful hours. Luis would probably write off this whole escapade. The taxpayers would pick up the bill.

Two hours later, the professor sat in the back of the *policia* car while Luis and the captain told police stories. The captain knew the professor, even though they had never met, and he took them straight to the professor's cabin under the eastern escarpment of the canyon wall south of Batopilas. The captain shook hands with them, offered a final swig from a half-empty brandy bottle, and then slowly drove back toward town. Red tail lights bobbed and jerked in protest as the car bumped and swerved over the cobblestone streets.

"Luis," said the professor, "not a word of this to Angela or Alexandra, or I'm a dead man."

"Kind of fitting, isn't it, *gringo*?"

"How's that?"

"Today is the Day of the Dead—get it?"

The Nightmare

A sullen, oppressive darkness shrouded the cavern. If Ruth stared, she could see dark oval areas on the distant walls, the cave's many passages. Unfortunately she didn't know through which she had entered, blindfolded and stumbling, to arrive in this large dark room. The air felt warm and humid and a faint odor of sulfur emanated from the cave's hot spring while a subdued, sonorous gurgle issued from the spring.

What day was it? she wondered. And how long had she been in the cave? Startled by a nightmare, she had awakened. In the dream, she had been a child again and had gone looking for her white cat. She had walked away from her parent's Ozark cabin in the Boston Mountains of Arkansas and wandered into the surrounding forest searching for her pet. She became lost, and upon sighting a hole in a mountain's side, had approached, fascinated. She entered and followed a narrow passage leading into a huge room with an enormous sinkhole. She shivered, frightened, and turned to leave, but a swarm of bats had swooped down and startled her. She ducked, screaming, slipped in the moist mud and fell backward into the sinkhole! She awoke in a cold sweat.

But this was real, she thought. A nightmare, but real. Her new life as a captive: alone in a cave except for the strange quiet man who came daily to check on her and see to her needs. She reached to touch the thick scab above her eye. The quiet Indian had removed the stitches two days ago. He and another man, whom she barely remembered, had painfully sewn the cut after her abduction from the train.

The passage down into the canyon had been a nightmare, and Ruth could recall frightening episodes when she had hallucinated. A large black cat with yellow eyes had stalked her relentlessly the whole trip. It stayed just on the edge of sight, making it difficult to verify its reality, but it followed closely, its curious yellow eyes never far away. Toward dawn it had disappeared, and she had convinced herself that it never existed.

Sore and stiff, she had arrived completely exhausted. The journey lasted two days, blindfolded and hidden in daylight and a difficult walk and numbing ride at night on the back of a donkey. She could still remember the pale white light of the moon in a star speckled sky the night of their arrival. After temporarily allowing her to see the sky, the quiet Indian had retied the blindfold and helped her climb and walk, stumbling and reeling with fatigue as he guided her inside.

He had been gone two days now—or perhaps three? Time was now an intangible. Initially fearful, her mood had changed to a simmering anger. Patience was not her strong suit. She had food and water: smoked dried meat, probably lamb, and a variety of edible roots and plants.

She had finally convinced herself to swim in the warm bubbling spring after the Indian had told her it was safe. Acclimated to the darkness and less fearful, she bathed daily now. The occasional chirp of bats would hearken their awakening and they would fly around the room while she splashed and bathed, treading water and dog paddling for long periods in order to exercise.

But when would it end? *Why me? Why do they want me?* she wondered. Ruth didn't understand why she had been kidnapped, and was reluctant to speculate on what might happen to her. Only one thought recurred with any certainty, one theme occupied her mind: she must survive. She must somehow make it through this nightmare. Being in the cave had initially terrified her, but she had become accustomed to the insolent darkness and lonely silence of her prison. She must bide her time and wait for an opportunity to flee this hell.

Feeling bored and filled with an uncertain melancholy, she stood and stretched. Her eyes wandered around the room and up the wall to the jagged, irregular hole far above, just below the ceiling. A foot wide and nearly four feet in length, it leaked just enough light to forestall complete darkness, except at night when she sobbed in terror and prayed for morning. A full moon had shed light through the crack when she first arrived, but now its weak luminescence receded nightly as it began to wane. She could see a few stars, but not well, and when total darkness fell, her imagination would push her to the brink of insanity, cowering in fear, sleepless and waiting for dawn.

Her eyes continued to search the cavern until they settled on one of the dark passages. She had once attempted to explore a couple of the tunnels, but had returned to the safety of the large room when she became scared.

What if she chose wrong and became lost? She had no way of marking her trail and no intuitive sense of direction to guide her, so she waited. But this time he must tell her something. She had to know! What was it all about?

The quiet Indian would not kill her—at least not yet. He was waiting for something. When he received word, what then? Would she be released or killed? She shivered convulsively, then told herself—*Quit it! Get a grip, woman. You're not dead yet.*

Ruth's eyes returned to the room's center and she stared at the supplies. She shuffled forward and rummaged until she found the dried meat strips wrapped in cornhusks. She chewed the stiff peppery meat, then extracted a long knobby root from a basket. She broke it into two pieces and chewed the crunchy, fibrous plant. Bland, it had a faint taste of onion.

Her jeans and blouse fit loosely, but she felt well considering her situation. If she got out alive, maybe she could write her own diet book and become famous. *Hah! Gallows humor*, she thought. But then, what else could she joke about? Who else to talk to? God knows the Indian didn't talk much.

She sighed, trying to suppress her restlessness, and decided boredom was her immediate problem. She'd give anything for a good Tony Hillerman mystery. No sense asking the Indian—he probably couldn't read, and it would be in Spanish if he did. He always spoke Spanish. She spoke Spanish proficiently—her job required it—but she longed for a good conversation in English.

Her teeth felt scummy and her hair lay in tangles, so her thoughts returned to the warm pool: her one pleasure in a dark, Spartan prison of rock. She walked to the pool's edge, careful not to slip, and stripped naked. She sat on the smooth water-polished stone, dangling her legs in the water, adjusted her hair, then slid into the bubbling pool. She had never swum naked before in her life and now she did it daily, or whenever the notion struck her. She paddled about for twenty minutes, then dipped to wash her hair and rinse her mouth. Her splashing had agitated the bats, and they began chirping. A few disengaged from the ceiling and began to swoop and glide, turning just short of the wall, blind acrobats in a dark cave.

Then she felt his presence, watching her, noiseless, standing near the supplies in the middle of the room. He had come quietly, stealing into the room like a wraith.

Fear wrenched her gut and she held her breath. What did he want? How long had he stood in the dark watching her swim naked?

In a timorous voice, she called out, "Please go away until I'm dressed. I want to talk to you. Can you please come back later?"

He disappeared. Had he really been there, or did her imagination play tricks? She scanned the cave but sensed nothing, no presence. Where had he gone? Which passage had he used?

Her voice had startled the bats and they began flying toward her, stopping short at the last instant, scaring and reminding her of the nightmare. She looked around the room again, wishing he had stayed, then glided to the pool's edge to wait for the bats settled down. *Oh, God*, she thought. Would she ever get out alive?

The Investigation Begins

The morning began slowly. Despite the previous night's overindulgence and late hours, the professor awakened early to the heavy hooves of a passing mule train. The jingling tack of harnessed mules and the piercing whistles of muleskinners echoed against the canyon walls, energizing an indolent morning and startling him to wakefulness. He wanted to return to sleep, but an insistent curiosity lifted him from bed and pushed him to the window. Six mules free of burden, and two burros led by three mustachioed muleskinners, walked slowly south toward the next valley. To whom or for what purpose he didn't know.

Strange they're not carrying anything, he thought. *It's a waste. But maybe they'll be loaded later.*

Very near his log and plaster cabin, the cobbled road ended and metamorphosed into a myriad of trails and narrow paths leading in all directions: south to the fertile valleys, west into the canyons and mountains of the Sierra Madres, and east into the highland desert of Chihuahua. The trails and roads lay neglected and in need of repair, their surfaces eroded and pocked. One hundred years ago they had borne heavy wagons and beasts of burden, carrying supplies to a large but unknown number of silver and gold mines which dotted the barrancas. Many of the mines were quite remote, with no roads or trails to record evidence of past activity.

Tons and tons of valuable ore had been extracted from the Sierra Madres, and one didn't have to go far to hear stories of famous silver ore bearers like the Potosi' or legends of mines with bloody histories, now lost but still fabulously rich in ore. Worthless maps with suspect histories lay forgotten or undiscovered in old trunks, bank vaults, and even in old tin cans, mortared and cemented into walls by long dead owners.

As he watched the last mule disappear over a small hill, the professor recalled his recent field trips into the canyon country. The prehistoric inhabitants of the canyons and valleys had left behind much evidence of their existence, but most of anything worth studying had been destroyed during three hundred years of intermittent gold rushes, boom towns, natural erosion and weathering, and by the Indians themselves. Legends and reports of ancient civilizations with cities of gold had pushed the Conquistadors steadily north into New Mexico, Arizona, Texas, and California, but to no favorable enterprise. The only classical civilizations lay south in the Valley of Mexico and the southern jungles.

He looked at the wood shelves that held the gleanings of his short forays into the countryside. In the back of his mind he had hoped to find something important, anything that might forestall the building of the reservoir and the inevitable development that would follow. Literally hundreds of archaeological sites would be destroyed. He regretted the lack of funds for professional support staff. In many ways, it resembled the kind of project that he frequently spoke against; an under-funded, poorly conceived, hurry-up-and-get-it-over-with government project that must be completed before actual construction could begin. He didn't even have a transit for surveying or proper transportation. He had purchased a three-wheeled Honda to negotiate the rough terrain, and once left it parked near Rock River. Upon returning, it lay stripped on its side in midstream, the parts probably loaded onto a mule train headed west. He had walked nearly six hours over rough, hilly territory before arriving in Batopilas. Sore and exhausted, he had nearly abandoned the project. But two days of sorting, cleaning and writing in his journal had refreshed him, and he decided to stay on the job much to Alexandra's chagrin.

His subsequent excursions, all overnight camping trips in the barrancas, had been undertaken with rented burros and hired Tarahuamara guides to show him through the wilderness. This slowed his work, but provided him a more certain mode of transportation in the mountains.

The project had not gone as he wished. Many areas of the proposed reservoir would go unresearched and unsurveyed because of no money and too little time. David must return to Mexico City within weeks, and more remained to be completed than had been accomplished. He had just begun to get a feel of what must be done and where to go, and had only recently become acquainted with many of the locals. They had showered him with tips of where to look and filled his ears with legends and stories of secret locations, mysterious people with supernatural powers, and countless mythologies of events and remote places: a bounty of fascinating stories.

The professor felt regret that he would be able to follow up on only a fraction of the local lore.

Luis groaned and rolled over, pulling a wool blanket over his head, which in turn exposed his feet. He sighed, lowered the blanket to his chin, and with one eyeball scanned the room, as if searching for a reason to open the other. Soon both eyes were tracking. He coughed, sniffed, rubbed his eyes, then swung his feet over the side of the bed. He yawned and stretched, and then attempted to stand, nearly stumbling as he did. He hesitated, his face strained, and he loudly broke wind, groaning with satisfaction. He turned to look at the professor.

"Hell of a night, David."

"Hell of a night, Luis."

"Don't tell me you didn't have a good time."

"I didn't have a good time, Luis. I was scared to death most of the evening."

The *federale* sniffed. "It's just business. I got some good leads." He yawned. "We need to get started. Is that coffee I smell?"

Two hours later, their bellies full of *chorizo* and tortillas, they picked up their new vehicle in Batopilas. A vintage blue-gray Toyota Land Cruiser sat parked in front of the office, but Colonel Cedras appeared loath to part with it. He seemed miffed at having to put up with Luis, and curious as to what the federale would be doing. Cedras had received no instructions from Chihuahua and felt deliberately ignored by the regional headquarters. The Colonel loaned the vehicle, but only after Luis insisted that Cedras call Chihuahua to verify Luis' right to requisition it. This put the Colonel in a sour mood, believing himself pushed around by the city boys again, and he didn't bother responding to Luis' good-humored banter.

Luis and the professor headed for the traditional outdoor market so central to Mexican and Indian village life. El mercado was the economic wellspring of the community, and David loved killing time in them. They were the best source of local gossip and cheap goods—for which you were expected to bitterly contest every price—as well as being quick access to traditional Indian crafts. What little money or wealth circulates in Indian villages comes from nearby towns, so the Indians maintain a steady stream of quality, low-priced crafts into the market.

El Mercado San Mateo stank of diesel exhaust, oiled leather, rotting meat, garbage, and the musty odor of mildewed wool and cotton clothing. Luis and David carefully threaded their way through dark, narrow corridors strewn with baskets and pottery. Ducking to avoid a pole of hanging huaraches, they fended off a horde of persistent shoeshine boys, stopping at a butcher's stall for directions to the Joyeria, the jeweler. A row of plucked, pink-skinned chickens hung headless and dripping blood from a yellow polyester line, their claws trussed to the rope, tiny droplets of blood pooling on the floor. The butcher deftly trimmed gristle and fat from a rack of goat ribs, applying the sharp knife with surgical skill, allowing nothing to go to waste as he pared them to his satisfaction. He stopped, flipped them over twice to appraise his handiwork, then peered over the top of his glasses. He pointed with his knife.

"Over there...by the furniture...name's Omar. When you see his teeth, you'll know it's him," and he reached for another rack of ribs. He assessed them critically, looked again at the two men, then ignored them and applied the knife to the ribs.

Teeth? thought the professor. This conjured up many images, not all of them pretty. They navigated the narrow aisle, crossed an open area teeming with customers and arrived at the jeweler's stall. Omar smiled broadly, believing them to be customers, revealing front teeth with a single shiny diamond centered in each. They sparkled in the light and matched the glint of his gray eyes. It had to be him. Obviously not a Mexican, he appeared to be an East Indian or an Arab, though he spoke Spanish like a native.

"*Buenos dias, señores!*" he boomed.

"*Buenos dias,*" replied Luis, grinning in return, unable to take his eyes from the jeweler's mouth. But Omar's smile disappeared and he turned serious upon seeing Luis' badge. He became reserved and diffident, cautiously considering Luis' questions.

"Ever seen anything like this before?" Luis produced the green stone from his pocket.

The professor studied the jeweler and thought he saw Omar's eyebrows rise perceptively as he turned it over and over in his hand. Omar reached for a jeweler's eye to magnify and investigate the translucent green stone.

"Yes and no," said the jeweler, finally. "Yes, I've seen a few, but I don't know where they come from...not exactly anyway."

"What do you mean?" said Luis, seizing the nuance.

"Just that," shrugged the jeweler, "I've seen them before." His face became unreadable and he appeared indifferent. "You see a lot of this sort of thing. It could be anything: chalcedony, quartz, hornblende, malachite or something with copper in it. That's where the green color comes from." He looked again with the jeweler's eye, and then pursed his lips in thought.

"Could it be jade?" suggested the professor.

A hint of irritation flickered momentarily, and then Omar flashed his diamonds at the professor. "You should be so lucky," he smiled. "Especially this stuff, it would be jeweler's quality. No...it's not jade. Trust me," he smiled. "The only place you'll find jade is south in Guatemala and up north in California, Washington, and Canada. None of it's very good quality, though."

He seemed to be knowledgeable and affected the manner of a bored expert, leaving them with the impression that he had forgotten more about gemstones than they'd ever know. In thirty years of archaeology the professor had acquired a substantial knowledge of geology, but he didn't know squat about gemstones, so he readily acquiesced to the jeweler's opinion.

Luis returned the stones to his pocket, then asked, "Anybody else around here in this business?"

"It's a small town, *señor*. There's only so much business a man can do in a place like this." He smiled, shrugged, and lifted his arms in resignation before continuing. "The mines are closed or producing barely enough to stay open. Occasionally someone finds a little something in the streams and rivers west in the canyon country," he pointed, "and the government sends geologists from Chihuahua to survey and do soil assays. But the big finds are all discovered: everything is picked over. I don't know why I stay. It's a poor living for a honest man." He gave the professor a sad smile. "I am reduced to trading with the filthy Indians, and they cheat me badly."

Somehow the professor doubted that. The jeweler looked prosperous, and all Mexican merchants pled poverty and behaved like robbery victims. It was an expected, almost ritual disclaimer commonly heard in the market. No one believed it, but everyone said it or expected to hear it.

Luis looked ready to go, but David was curious and asked, "Do you go into the *barrancas* to trade with the Indians, or do they come here?"

"Both. I have contacts in some of the villages, and I still travel sometimes, but only if I must. As a young man I knew every canyon and cave within a hundred miles of here."

The professor believed him. He had met many like him in Batopilas—the young adventurer or prospector, now old, their dreams dashed with little future before them. But still they hung on, hoping for the big find or the big deal that would send them back to wherever they had come.

"Now my son does most of my running and traveling," Omar continued, pointing to a dour-looking mixed-breed Indian in his twenties. The boy ignored them and looked at the ground. "His mother is Indian," he explained, as if they couldn't tell, or cared to know.

"Tell me," asked Luis, "have you heard anything about an Indian shaman. He's about 35, black beard, tall for an Indian, with a reputation as a rabblerouser who talks bad about the government."

"Everybody talks bad about the government, *señor*," grinned the jeweler. "They're all thieves. Besides…your description fits a dozen dirty, long-haired Indians roaming the canyons looking for datura and peyote. And if he has a beard, he probably isn't a full-blood Indian. Indians don't have beards."

Luis looked at the professor, who nodded agreement. He didn't know why he hadn't thought of it.

Luis warmed to the scent. "This one may like animals," he said, "especially jaguars."

The jeweler waved him off. "They're all the same. I've seen…."

"El Jaguar Feroz (The Fierce Jaguar)," interrupted his scraggly Indian son, suddenly coming to life. "El Jaguar Feroz that walks the Lost Canyons." The boy turned and said something in Tarahumara to his father. The jeweler shook his head, annoyed, and they argued until the boy suddenly stood and walked away. He didn't appear angry, just unwilling to talk anymore. Tall for an Indian, the young man had large hands and feet, and moved lightly on sandal-clad feet, deftly navigating the crowded market. A broad face held a stoic expression, and he seemed to be more Indian than Mexican in his upbringing. He had a feral aura about him, but appeared self-confident. His hair hung long and swayed in rhythm as he departed.

"He's an Indian," said the jeweler again, as if apologizing and explaining the youth's behavior at the same time. "He doesn't know any better."

This the professor doubted. He probably didn't care, and rather than stay and converse with white men, he left, preferring the familiarity and certainty of his own company.

"Who's El Jaguar Feroz?" asked David, curious at the boy's quick, positive reaction. The youth had not hesitated upon hearing Luis' description and had answered with conviction. Why should the jeweler be annoyed that his son volunteered information?

"He doesn't exist, *señor*. It's just an Indian myth; a legend about a holy man who lives with the jaguars somewhere north of here in the Lost Canyons."

"Lost Canyons?" Luis gave him a blank look and turned to his friend for confirmation, but the professor shrugged and looked dumb. He had scoured the maps of this area for months and didn't recall seeing any such thing.

"They're not lost, Inspector, but no one goes there anymore except for a few Indians. There's no record of gold or silver being discovered in the Lost Canyons, and it's a very difficult area to reach." He seemed to reflect on his statement a moment, then added, "Twenty years ago I prospected in that area, but nothing of value can be found there, just some hot springs in the worst terrain you can imagine. If someone did live there, they wouldn't be the kind of person you're looking for. I don't think there are any Indian villages in that part of the canyon country."

Luis had lost interest and began to shift his weight and look around impatiently, but David remained unsatisfied. Something in the jeweler's mannerisms bothered, especially the way he skillfully directed the conversation when he thought it appropriate. It would be wise to check his story or, for that matter, to investigate Omar.

"You are very knowledgeable, *señor*," praised the professor. "We were lucky to find a man such as you to help us."

Omar flashed his diamond-studded teeth in response.

"But we need to talk to someone else who has lived here a long time who can tell us more."

"Look around, señor." The jeweler was suddenly no help at all. "Not too many know or care about what happens out there." He flicked his hand toward the canyon walls. "But good luck." And he turned to walk to the back of his small shop, dismissing his interrogators abruptly by ignoring them.

They turned to go and had not walked more than ten steps when a haggard, dirty-faced woman wrapped in a colorful shoulder *rebozo* pulled at David's hand.

"See *el sacerdote, señor*." She rubbed the back of a blue-veined hand across her sniffling, runny nose. "Yes," she agreed with herself, "see the priest." Her rheumy, red eyes locked with the professor's until he looked away, embarrassed. She tugged on his hand again, so he withdrew a few coins from a pocket and gave them to her.

"Thank you, *señora*," he said, trying to be polite and relieve his embarrassment.

Luis tugged at his other arm, anxious to be off, and they began to navigate the obstacle-filled passageways. David turned to look in the direction of the jeweler. Omar stood at his bench again, his face a mask of anger and his fist tightly gripping the Jeweler's Eye as he glared at the old woman.

Thank you, thought the professor, looking again at the old crone. *That'll be our next stop.*

The noise and clamor receded as they struggled through the din. Luis followed a glimmer of light that steadily became larger until they escaped the oppressive clutter and pungent odor of the market. The professor wanted to tell him what he had seen on Omar's face, but Luis motioned for David to follow and led them toward El Zocalo, the plaza in the center of Batopilas. When the professor caught up to him, Luis put his index finger to his mouth.

"I know," he said simply.

He knew what? "Luis," said the professor, "that jeweler is...."

"...a liar and a crook," Luis finished the sentence. "I know, but we've got to find that Indian kid. Help me look for him."

They both scanned the area, then Luis left to search the stores facing the plaza while David stayed on the periphery of the plaza and watched people come and go. This way they wouldn't miss the boy if Luis inadvertently flushed him while searching indoors.

Casually, but alert, the professor strode along the shady perimeter of the tree-lined *zocalo*, enjoying the potted dieffenbachia, multicolored croton, and blue palo verde, all the while watching for the youth as Luis quickly searched the restaurants, pool hall, and assorted businesses on the park's fringe. El Zocalo is the center of all Mexican towns, a plan brought from Spain and used in every town in Mexico, and the most likely place to find someone or something you seek.

A cerulean strip of sky strewn with wispy white clouds grew steadily brighter. The sun had breasted the eastern canyon wall three hours earlier and it floated high in the sky, bathing the canyon with steady clear light. The professor stood in the shade of the gazebo and observed the animated conversations of businessmen in *guayabera* shirts and watched the preparations of street vendors selling food from homemade carts attached to bicycle wheels. A group of Tarahumara began to set up a display of baskets, weavings, pottery, and children's toys. The Indian men stood around aimlessly while the women worked diligently, preparing their wares and tending to small children at the same time.

Thirty minutes later Luis abandoned his search and motioned for David to join him for coffee on the porch of a small but busy restaurant. Constructed from raw cedar lumber, the wood planking reeked of aromatic cedar. Two long-stemmed ceiling fans turned slowly so as not to disturb the dust. They sat sipping coffee and comparing notes.

"Question is this," said Luis, wiping milk-laden coffee from his mustache with a large finger, "what is he hiding and why?"

"Maybe the stones?" suggested the professor.

"Maybe, but I don't think so."

"What then?"

"It has something to do with the Indian kid. He told us something his father didn't want us to know."

"Like what? Do you think he's involved?"

"With what, the kidnapping? Maybe, but I don't think so. That's unlikely. It's something else. I can't put my finger on it, but I think it's important." He added even more milk to his coffee, stirred it with his finger, then licked it with relish.

"The old woman suggested the priest. What do you think?"

"That," said Luis, "is as good a place as any to begin." He stared at the brown liquid in his cup as if searching for answers.

"You know, David," he began again, "you know how it is in these small towns. A thousand secrets, yet some are well known by many people. You've just got to find someone willing to talk to you. These people know more than they volunteer. The trick is to ask the right questions. Everyone knows everyone else's business, but they have to be careful what they say or it will come back on them. People hold grudges and have long memories. Someone will remember their indiscretion and pay them back. The jeweler and his son may not have anything to do with the kidnapping, but they're concealing something, and this Omar is concerned that we do or don't do something. But what? What is it they don't want us to know or do?" He gulped the remainder of the coffee while looking at David over the cup's rim.

The professor's instincts told him that Luis had read the situation correctly. For all his silly posturing and macho affectations, Luis really did have a good nose for this sort of thing. His questions sat uneasily on David's mind as they left the restaurant and crossed the plaza to the Land Cruiser.

Indeed, thought the professor, *if Omar's being truthful about the stones, then what's he hiding? The myth of the jaguar man and the Lost Canyons? Is the Indian boy really his son? Why was he angry at the beggar woman in the market for telling us to see the priest?* It didn't make sense yet.

Twenty yards from the Toyota, he felt the first wave and jiggle of the ground as a mild earth tremor moved through the area. Luis stumbled beside him, losing his footing, and bent to the ground while the professor grabbed onto his shoulder for support. The quiver ceased as suddenly as it had begun. Luis stood and they both looked around as a sense of panic rose like the ground swell they had felt. Fearful, everyone had run outside from the surrounding buildings and now they stood about. A deafening silence momentarily ruled, then laughter and cries of relief rang out across the plaza. Luis smiled sheepishly.

"I hate those damn things, David."

"Yes, and there's been two or three in the last week. Makes you wonder," said the professor, idly, becoming lost in thought. Small-magnitude earth tremors were a common occurrence in Mexico. The country has several active volcanoes, and the Pacific plates occasionally give way as they continue their inexorable dive below the continent, causing very damaging earthquakes in central and southern Mexico. The professor had survived the Mexico City earthquake in 1985, and the terrible images of destruction, collapsed buildings, buckled roads, and the screams of the injured and buried lay fresh in his mind. He had literally felt hundreds of small tremors in his twenty-five years in Mexico, but knew he would never become used to the hollow-stomach feeling and loss of orientation that accompanied the bigger ones.

Luis slowly guided the Toyota over the cobblestones, moving past rows of stuccoes, around a train of donkeys laden with canisters of raw milk, and finally toward the church. It sat in the shape of a cross, a traditional pattern for churches, with a dome and bell tower the highest point. They parked at the Hotel Mari across the street and walked to the rectory and knocked. An old man, probably the priest, answered the door. Short and gray-haired with sunken cheeks, his eyes hid beneath protruding, bushy eyebrows. He was bent with age and leaned on a cane. He also appeared less than happy to see them. The priest sighed with resignation upon seeing Luis' badge, but invited them in, issuing an instruction to a squat, broad-faced Indian woman to bring tea.

After an hour of conversation, Fr. Leo proved to be no help. He had been in Batopilas himself only three weeks and indicated that he was more than ready to leave. Fr. Martin, the pastor, had left on a four-week religious sabbatical to undergo, all alone, some sort of Jesuit Spiritual Exercises ten miles south in a small cabin outside the town of Satevo. Fr. Leo gave them tea and conversed politely. They learned much about Fr. Leo and his life— including his unhappiness at being sent to Batopilas—and he gave them the impression that serious, unresolved issues existed between Fr. Martin and the church, issues that had led to Fr. Martin's sabbatical. What these issues were, Fr. Leo didn't say, but he seemed relieved that Luis wanted only general information from the absent pastor.

SINS OF THE JAGUAR

"Fr. Martin, bless his confused soul, will be sad to hear that he missed you," Fr. Leo said to David. "He dotes on the Indians and their silly pagan beliefs, and I'm sure he would have enjoyed the company and conversation of an anthropologist." He ignored Luis, and his gnarled hand shook as he sipped his tea, then rattled the cup against the saucer, trying to center it. "No doubt you have much in common," he sniffed disapprovingly. "I personally see no value in learning anything from the *cimmarones*, the wild ones. What do they have to teach us? Nothing…that's what." He answered his own question with the conviction of a dyed-in-the-wool bigot. "It is they who must learn from us. Most of them have yet to join the Christian faith and experience the sanctifying, cleansing blood of Jesus in their lives. They are heathens and their souls are doomed to eternal torment. The Dark Angel will do with them as he pleases." He smiled pleasantly, satisfied with the idea, and looked at them expectantly, waiting for the two sinners in his dark living room to dispute him.

The professor believed he had a pretty good idea of the tone and content of the priest's homilies. Although Fr. Leo would have been outraged at the comparison, he very much reminded David of an intolerant Protestant minister he had heard some thirty years ago at a Missouri tent revival. Perhaps Jesus himself would measure up to the priest's standards of piety, but David doubted that anyone else would.

Luis and the professor made appropriate sounds of sympathy and acknowledgment at Fr. Leo's less-than-profound judgments, and then excused themselves. As they walked to the Land Cruiser, David could see that Luis was exasperated. They had started the day well, but suddenly found themselves without any new leads. The two sleuths sat in the jeep a moment, then Luis turned and asked.

"What do you think, David? Are we both going straight to hell?"

"We'll have a lot of company, Luis. Whose soul do you think he's really worried about?"

Luis ignored the question, put the key in the ignition, and then said, "Any ideas?"

"About what?"

"The Indian kid, the priest. Where do we go from here?"

"What about all those leads you got last night in the cantina?" The professor wanted him to admit that he had been goofing and playing last night—not investigating a kidnapping.

55

"You're right," Luis snapped his fingers. "Let's go."

"Where?" asked the surprised professor.

"To the post office. Where is it, anyway?"

The Town Gossip

The sun disappeared behind the western canyon wall and dark shadows from towering palisades cloaked the town. The professor's wristwatch read 4:11 p.m., and he felt that he had wasted the day chasing Luis and his phantom leads. David struggled to fend off his feeling of impatience, wanting to be done with Luis and the investigation. As the Land Cruiser moved unevenly across the cobblestone streets toward the river, he began a mental inventory of unfinished tasks regarding the survey and mapping of potential archaeological sites in the Aguila Reservoir basin. Tomorrow he would be firm and insist that Luis accompany him, or the *federale* would have to go it alone.

The post office sat a mere two blocks away, but it took ten minutes to arrive. A construction barrier blocked the road and mounds of torn up cobblestone lay everywhere along Calle Reyes, the location of the post office. They had to park four blocks away on the other side of the plaza, near the Camino Real. Luis left the Toyota in the shade of a cypress grove and the professor gave a small boy 10 *pesos*—about a dollar—to keep his eye on the car for them. The boy immediately assumed a proprietary air; his eyes lit up, his chest swelled with importance and he walked with authority, occasionally pausing to lean on the car.

White water rapids from the canyon river hissed and gurgled from behind as they crossed the Camino Real and sauntered toward town. The eastern canyon wall, all three thousand feet of it, stood occluded in the shade of the western mountains, hiding dark green veins of oxidized copper that shone a brilliant green when illuminated by direct sunlight.

As they crossed the highway, three pairs of Indians toting heavy logs on their shoulders jogged by. Luis stood dumbfounded.

"Incredible," he said, stopping to stare at the logs. "Where are they going?"

"Those will probably end up as ceiling beams, or part of a pole barn. Transporting them like that is cheaper than hiring a truck."

"But they're so heavy!" exclaimed Luis.

"It's impressive," agreed the professor, as they watched them jog south along the Camino Real, "but the Raramuri…er…the Tarahumara, are amazing people. They've been trained since childhood to run long distances over mountain trails for hours, sometimes days at a time. They are incredibly fit."

They talked more about the Indians—Luis had no personal knowledge of them—so David fell into a quick lecture about the Tarahumara culture and the mountainous Copper Canyon geography. Luis feigned interest, lost in thought while the professor recalled arcane tidbits about the Indians. He walked a halfstep behind as the professor led the way to Calle Reyes.

An uphill, rugged street, Calle Reyes had large sections torn up to be recobbled. Long fortress blocks of colonial style stuccoes, all set above high curbs and stairs leading into stores, ran in concert on either side. Batopilas had no neon signs. Every entryway appeared virtually the same as the next, yet everyone in town knew the exact location of each business.

They stepped from the sidewalk into the street to avoid three heavily laden donkeys whose tails busily moved a swarm of black flies from one side to the other. A pile of dung lay on the sidewalk and the donkeys scattered it with their hooves, shifting their weight restlessly from one leg to the other, occasionally jerking impatiently at their halter tethers. The donkey's owner, meanwhile, engaged in animated conversation with the clerk at the *abaceria*, the grocery store. The clerk listened politely, broom in hand, poised to sweep the dung into the street when the donkeys left. A shoeless, dirty-faced girl in a drab brown dress stood at the clerk's leg eating a *paleta*, an ice cream bar, and watched Luis and the professor curiously. Unknown in the community, Luis would cause a few stares; many of them bold and obvious, as a stranger is always fuel for speculation in a small town.

They trod another hundred feet, then stopped to look at a large hole filled with muddy water. The workmen stood about listlessly, their pump idle, waiting to be told to work. The professor had no doubt the hole would be there at the end of the week.

The post office always had a few loiterers—men discussing business or politics—and its exterior displayed a facade of dirty white stucco with spiderweb cracks reaching in all directions. Luis politely tipped his white hat to a group on the sidewalk before entering the post office. A single forty watt bulb burned dimly from the room's high ceiling, casting shadows onto faded pink walls. The ceiling's cracked plaster hung loosely, threatening to fall, while an old man pushed a pile of dirt with a broom, reluctant to sweep it into a pan and finish the job early. A thin, balding, hatchet-faced postal clerk leaned lazily on a broken Formica-topped counter and appraised them.

"Yes?" he said, unmoving.

"The postmaster, please," stated Luis, placing both hands on the counter and leaning toward the clerk.

"He isn't in today, *señor*." The clerk looked away.

"Then who's that?" The professor pointed toward an office in the rear where a man stared at them through a plateglass window.

"That's the postmaster, but he's busy today, *señor*. What can I do for you?"

"You can go get him…right now." Luis flipped open his identification for inspection.

The clerk frowned. "*Sí, señor*," he said reluctantly. "I'll see if he can talk to you."

"Wait," said Luis, grabbing his arm, "I'll introduce myself." He motioned for David to join him as he rounded the corner and headed for the rear office.

Luis pushed open the door, exposing the postmaster in an overstuffed chair with his feet on the desktop. He held a green pop bottle of Sidral in one hand and his other arm rested on a substantial stomach. The postmaster, Mario Cifuentes, motioned his head to two vacant chairs. While they seated themselves, he eyed them silently.

"*Policia*," he stated flatly.

"Federal," concurred Luis, offering his I.D., but Mario ignored it.

"What do you want?" he slurred, his question neither friendly nor unfriendly. Barely sober, his florid face hung in wattles around his neck and burst capillaries colored a bulbous nose. A large man at nearly two meters, his stomach stretched a white *guayaberra* shirt at the buttons.

"Information, *señor*." Luis eyed the soda pop bottle. "Do you always drink tequila on the job?"

"It's mescal…and only when I'm at work," he retorted sarcastically. "What information would a lowly postmaster have that would be of value to the *policia*?"

Mario's face expressed little emotion and he showed no fear of Luis' badge. He looked to have weathered many a complaint and numerous political battles, and had probably been the postmaster in Batopilas for twenty years. He belonged to PRI, the country's ruling political party, and his family probably had money. Connections allowed him to sit firmly entrenched in his position; he had little reason to fear the two investigators. And that is what he had—a position, not a job. He probably hadn't sorted mail or done anything postal-related during his tenure as postmaster. He appeared immediately recognizable: a smug, politically connected bureaucrat, much like the other middle-class civil servants in the country—all of them owing their position to the PRI political party.

"Colonel Cedras tells me that you are a very knowledgeable man. He says there's very little that happens in the canyon country that you don't know."

"*Chingada*," retorted Mario, taking a sip from the Sidral bottle. "I could say much the same of Colonel Cedras. He's the one who has federales tracking smugglers and robbing Indians."

Luis let the statement pass without rancor, aware that Mario could easily help if he wished, or obstruct the investigation by not cooperating.

"What have you heard of the kidnapping?" Luis watched Mario closely.

"Nada." Mario glanced at Luis, then at David, waiting for a challenge to his denial.

"Nothing?" repeated Luis' brow furrowed. He moved and sat on the edge of the postmaster's scarred, prerevolution oak desk.

"Who else have you talked to?" Mario took another sip of the mescal.

"The jeweler, Omar, and Fr. Leo."

Mario grunted, gave them a sly smile, and said, "You're hanging out with rough company, captain."

"That so?" said Luis. "Tell me, *señor*, why would you tell Colonel Cedras that the diplomat planned to stay and vacation at the Hotel Mari, but not share the information with me?"

Mario, taking a sip from the bottle, nearly gagged. He wiped his mouth, looked first at the professor, then at Luis.

His jowls trembled. "I saw a reservation card the young lady sent to the hotel and mentioned it in passing to the good Colonel. I'm surprised he remembered." The postmaster shifted his bulk, uncomfortable.

"Anyone else know about the reservation? Did anyone overhear your conversation with Colonel Cedras?"

Mario shrugged, thought a moment, and then said, "The jeweler's son, Ribi, was picking up his father's mail. I don't know...Fr. Martin may have been around. I don't remember." He feigned indifference.

"Okay, then. Tell me of your troubles with Fr. Martin."

Mario blanched. "What the...." He pulled his boots from the desktop and sat up. "What do you know of my...ah...my talks with the good padre?"

"I know they didn't go so good. I know you're accused of opening mail from the Bishop of Chihuahua...."

"Lies!" thundered Mario. "A bunch of damn lies!" His florid face became even more flushed and the broken capillaries on his nose turned dark purple. "Colonel Cedras has no right to talk to...."

The professor watched the drama unfold. Luis had told him nothing of his conversations with the policia last night or with Colonel Cedras this morning. Yet the Colonel had casually implicated the postmaster by revealing a conversation. Did Cedras have a score to settle, or did he want to aid the investigation? Who else knew of the diplomat's impending visit? Mario had already mentioned Ribi, who may have told his father, and Fr. Martin may have known, also. Surely the hotel staff knew, and whom might they have told? David felt a familiar rising excitement that always accompanied a discovery or an unresolved issue. Palpable tension permeated the room.

Luis interrupted the blustering bureaucrat.

"Listen, *señor*. I'm not here to play games. I could easily call the bishop's office in Chihuahua who, I'm sure, would be happy to file another complaint regarding your unscrupulous behavior."

"The issue has been resolved. There's no need." Mario took a deep breath, then a pull from the bottle, grimaced and said, "What do you want to know? I know nothing of the kidnapping. Everyone talked about it for awhile, but it's old news now."

"Then what's the recent news? What's been going on around here? No wait...." Luis switched gears. "Tell me about the jeweler and his son. Then I want to know all about Fr. Martin."

"The jeweler? Omar?" Mario silently reviewed what he knew of Omar and how it might relate to the kidnapping. Was the jeweler planning something that Mario didn't know about?

His arms swept wide. "What can I say? He's a well-known swindler...and maybe more. Depends on who you talk to."

"What does that mean?" Luis scooted closer to the fat bureaucrat.

Mario shrugged again. "I hear stories...stories of Omar occasionally killing an Indian or cheating someone badly. You know, the usual stuff."

The usual stuff? thought David.

"He's a *bandito*," Mario continued reluctantly, enunciating each word slowly. "Omar has lived in or around Batopilas for thirty years. He came from somewhere—Afghanistan, I think—to work as a prospector and a jeweler. I think his family has money, but they all live over there," he flipped a hand to indicate the other side of the ocean, "but they don't have anything to do with him anymore, something to do about leaving a wife and family behind. He's hung on for years, waiting for the big find, trading and cheating the Indians. He's a thief and liar, and it's rumored that he's killed more than one Indian. The Tarahuamara avoid him if they can, even though they joke and tell stories about him. The boy is his illegitimate son by an Indian woman who died giving birth to his second child. The second child died too. Ribi was raised by a wet nurse and schooled at the mission. Sometimes he lives with Omar, sometimes with the Indians. He acts like an Indian, though. Omar uses him as a go-between to trade with the Indians, but he's unreliable. Actually…I kind of like him…as much as you can like an Indian, that is." He took another sip of mescal. "Why do you ask?"

Luis ignored the question. "Why wouldn't he want us to talk to Fr. Martin?"

The postmaster shrugged. "Who knows? The priest hears confessions. He knows a lot people, and there's always a fool ready to confide their problems to him. He is very…how would you say…active with the Indians."

"Active?" Luis' eyebrows arched, quizzically.

Mario hesitated, fighting the impulse to blurt it out. "He's a damn troublemaker, captain. He's a tree-hugging environmentalist and a rabblerouser among the Indians. Not worth a crap as a priest either, if you ask me."

"Why do you say that?" interposed David, interested in anything to do with Indians.

"For one thing he's an Indian himself, or half anyway. I've known his family for years. His mother was a Chinese anthropologist from Los Angeles who came to study the Tarahumara. She got hooked up with the father, a medicine healer, and had a couple of children by him before trying to take the kids back to California with her. The boys ended up living at a Jesuit mission. One of them, our Fr. Martin, eventually became a priest."

"What happened to the other one?"

"He couldn't decide to be an Indian or a Mexican. He lived in and out of the mission—went to the United States for a while with his mother—then returned to live with the *cimmarones*, the wild ones. I haven't seen him in years. He's probably dead by now. Ask the priest if you really want to know."

"Why do you say that Fr. Martin is a rabblerouser?" asked Luis.

Mario grunted in disgust. "He spends more time with them than he does here in Batopilas. Besides…I hear stories."

"What kind of stories?" The professor pressed for more.

"Stories about the good priest participating in their pagan religious rites. He goes into the canyons and pulls them from their filthy caves to preach and tell them that their religion is similar to Christianity. His father was a shaman and taught him all the old Indian lore and rituals." Mario hesitated, reluctant to say more, but the mescal had loosened his tongue. "The bishop is furious with him."

Aha! thought David. Mario had revealed the reason for his dispute with the priest. The postmaster had been reading the bishop's correspondence to Fr. Martin and the priest had complained. The postmaster had gotten his fat ass burned by the Church. As unhappy as they were with Fr. Martin, they were even more displeased with someone reading official mail.

"What else?" Luis demanded.

"What do you want? I've told you everything. One must be careful in a small town, captain. Even a man like you can make enemies very fast. God is forgiving. But Fr. Martin…who knows? He's a man of great passion and believes very strongly in what he does. A priest is more powerful than the government sometimes—you should know that, especially in a small town like Batopilas. Fr. Martin has an opinion on everything, and he's consulted before anything is done in this community. I would advise you to move carefully with your investigation."

Luis chewed his lower lip and considered Mario's admonition. The *federale* seemed reluctant to leave, but then said, "Thanks for the information. Can I assume you'll be this cooperative next time we talk?"

"There'll be no next time, captain. Not unless you can arrange to come when the whole town doesn't know you're here." He started to drink from the bottle but swilled it around instead, looked up and said, "If you're looking for Fr. Martin, he's in Satevo."

"Yes," the professor interrupted. "The old priest at the rectory told us that he's undergoing some sort of spiritual exercises."

Mario snorted. "Spiritual exercises? Not likely. Look for Fr. Martin at the abandoned church. If he's not there, follow the Indians to a *tesquinada* if you want to find him."

They left the postmaster to his dimly lit room and nearly empty bottle of mescal. He never looked up when they turned to go. David followed Luis through the dusty aisle, past the curious clerk and out into the waning light. The Batopilas Canyon was cloaked in a gray, and the professor yearned to return to the comfort of his books in the cabin.

"What's a *tesquinada*?" asked Luis as they strode toward the Camino Real and their Jeep.

"A tesquinada is an Indian celebration. They drink a lot of corn beer and act like Indians." The professor gave him a silly but simple explanation.

"Oh…yeah?" Luis looked interested. "Does that mean that our errant priest likes to party with the Indians?"

"Could be."

"Have you been to a *tesquinada*, David?"

"A few," the professor replied, lamely. He knew where this led.

"Good. You can show me how to act tomorrow when we go to Satevo. I think we can learn more by participating in local cultural events, don't you?" The federale smiled mischievously.

"Luis, you're a conniving troublemaker," mumbled the professor.

"Thank you, professor. I think you're a good detective, also." He deflected the insult and returned a smile. "Come on, I'll buy you a drink at El Perdido Otra Vez."

"What?" stammered the surprised archaeologist.

"We have an appointment with Colonel Cedras at five o'clock." He quickly glanced at David to confirm his discomfort. "You're turning red, *gringo*. But don't worry. The girls don't come out until dark."

Omar Schemes

Omar irritably tapped the lip of the metal bathtub. An awareness that events had occurred of which he had no knowledge lay heavy on his mind. As to what they were he had no clue. He took a sip of ginseng tea and pondered this dilemma while soaking his naked bottom in a tub of hot water and herbs. His legs lay splayed over the metal rim, he idly traced patterns on the water's surface with his finger. That bastard son of his had created some of the problem. He should never have allowed the boy to live. It would have been best to strangle him at birth rather than suffer the disgrace of having your seed turn out so badly.

When the jeweler needed him most, Ribi always behaved like a damn Indian. And every time Omar allowed him to return to the house, the same thing happened. The boy promised to help out, but Omar knew he wouldn't. What he wanted from the boy, Ribi wasn't capable of giving. For one thing, he didn't understand the concept of profit. Why had Allah seen fit to send a businessman a child who had no understanding of the most important thing in life?

Six months ago Omar had sent Ribi into the canyon country with a substantial inventory of goods to trade to the Indians. The jeweler had been quite specific and had given Ribi orders what to buy and what to trade for; a simple task. The boy had returned two weeks late carrying a box of worthless colored rocks—iron pyrite and turquoise, if you can believe it—and a box of toy puppets acquired from the Snake Man in Bone Canyon. Four hundred dollars pissed away.

And now his son had committed a no-no by telling the federale and archaeologist about El Jaguar Feroz. Not that the information wasn't out there—everyone had heard of him. Omar didn't believe any of the stories for a second, seeing them as superstitious nonsense from gullible, credulous Indians promoting the myth. And although he felt pretty sure of El Jaguar

Feroz's real identity, Omar seethed with irritation that his son had inadvertently put those two snoops on the man's trail. He thought their chances of finding him were nil and zero, but nothing was certain, and Omar wanted to get to him before anyone else. He felt certain El Jaguar Feroz knew the answer to the secret he had sought for so many years—the location of the green stones that the *federale* had in his possession.

Omar would have to find out what was going on. Perhaps a call to Colonel Cedras would help? Or, if he became desperate, he could pay that drunken infidel Cifuentes for information. They both owed him, especially Cedras, but the Colonel changed skins like a snake and he could hurt you badly if you weren't careful. Still, Omar might have to call his former partner in crime. Although the Colonel no longer helped him smuggle pre-Columbian artifacts, Omar had heard rumors that Colonel Cedras had a thriving heroin smuggling business.

The jeweler had been mildly curious as to why there had been no movement to investigate the diplomat's kidnapping. But then again, she was only a woman, and he hadn't expected anyone to come looking here, either. Batopilas, a colonial backwater, promised nothing to the adventurer—no terrorists, certainly no night life, and most of the silver mines had long since closed or produced so little as to be barely profitable.

He had nearly forgotten the missing diplomat, as he had been very preoccupied with a painfully swollen prostate. He could care less about the abduction of a middle-aged female, even if she claimed to be a diplomat. The idea struck him as comical. A female diplomat? What does a woman know? Only a country of infidels would allow women to rise above their station. A woman belonged in a man's bed or in his kitchen, and the ridiculous pretensions of Western women never ceased to amaze him.

After standing and bending all day, the arrival of the federale and archaeologist had caught Omar by surprise. He had been suspicious of the professor upon his arrival in Batopilas two months ago, and so had kept an eye on his activities. But the academic had never wandered far from the Aguila Canyon flats and Omar soon lost interest. The American posed no threat to finding the source of the jaguar jewelry, and probably hadn't even known of its existence until his *federale* friend had appeared and Ribi had talked about El Jaguar Feroz. Damn that child, anyhow.

Omar had recognized the stones immediately. They were the property of the old shaman Omar had dispatched to hell. The old man was tough, and had died slowly, but had not revealed the location of the wonderful jewelry he occasionally brought to trade when in need of money.

And now an archaeologist and a *federale* were nosing around. How could the stones be connected to the kidnapping of the diplomat? He should have asked, he realized, and this further soured his mood. He must take care and show no interest or others might realize their true value. Worse yet, the canyons might become overrun with idiots searching for the source vein. He must proceed cautiously. First he would call that bandit, Cedras, and if that didn't produce information maybe he would have to pay a visit to the professor and the *federale* when they weren't home.

A mild cramp followed a twinge in his prostate and he turned his attention to his crotch. He sat soaking in a steaming tub of water in his tiled bathroom—a daily ritual now—fantasizing about the young Indian girl waiting in his bedroom. She had been a good purchase and had learned his tastes quickly. Omar reached to massage his groin, anxious for her to apply the greasy ointment he had purchased from the old woman. The girl had become adept. She would rub the smelly medicine into his crotch and massage his swollen gland until it relaxed. Then she would coax and caress him into an erection, finishing him off with her mouth.

A purely therapeutic procedure, he grinned, amused at his own wit, recommended and prescribed by the doctor. But the doctor had no credentials, and by-Allah she was ugly—a raisin-faced, rheumy-eyed Indian shamaness, the sister of his first house woman and Ribi's aunt. But she knew her stuff. Omar didn't want to know the contents of the potion; he just wanted more of it. The medicine or the girl helped, he didn't know which, and twice in the last week he had experienced spontaneous erections at work when fantasizing about her nightly massage.

"Maria, it's time," he called to her. "Bring a towel and ready the bed. I have special plans for you tonight."

A thin wisp of a girl, barely thirteen, padded barefoot into the room with a towel and jar of ointment. When she bent to help him out of the tub, he slapped her face so hard that it brought tears to her eyes.

"You know better than that," he hissed. "Don't ever touch me without asking first….and take off that filthy dress…I hate that Indian shit you wear."

The small girl dutifully removed her colorful dress and underwear. She waited for his instructions this time, her face a mask of despair and fear.

It's important that you train them right, thought Omar, and even more important that you bend them to your will before going to the bedroom. Tonight promised to be a night to remember.

A Spiritual Exercise

Rapture blazed from Fr. Martin's face as he stared unseeing at a cedar crucifix suspended from the domed nave of the long-deserted church. Built by Indian slave labor in the early 1700's, it had been abandoned upon completion for unknown reasons. A pale luminescence leaked through windows devoid of stained glass, and the rushing white water of the Batopilas River hissed outside. On his knees for two hours now, Fr. Martin had transcended all initial distractions of saying the rosary, prayerfully whispering the third decade of the Sorrowful Mysteries. The repetitive rhythm of the Hail Mary held him enthralled, cloaked in the protective garment of God's love.

Two hundred years of dust and rubble lay virtually undisturbed. Garishly painted statues sat on the altar, and purple berry juice (the blood of Christ), stained the walls. A plethora of fetishes, wooden masks, crowns of thorns, even a cedar cross lay strewn throughout the church. These esoteric representations inhabited the dark enclaves and corners, visible testimony of fierce tangled religious traditions and confused faiths, hopelessly intertwined with indigenous beliefs and Creole Christianity. A bleeding Christ, his face twisted in agony, was painted onto the west wall. Faded now, the image had been "retouched" by vandals to present a more credible Indian deity. Nonetheless, it represented a powerful portrait and symbol of religious syncretism, the blending of beliefs.

Fr. Martin, a Jesuit priest, had nearly completed his third week of The Spiritual Exercises, a system of contemplation and religious disciplines designed by Ignatius Loyola to arouse conviction of sin and its consequences, to inspire an awareness of Jesus' earthly life, and to know His passion and resurrection. If completed correctly, the Spiritual Exercises would instill in the mendicant a constant state of inner calm that would aid in making a critical decision or determining the general path of one's life.

A brilliant individualist, Fr. Martin was experiencing a crisis of vocation. The bishop had on many occasions received alarming reports of Fr. Martin's activities and had twice summoned him to Chihuahua to explain his activities and methods to an incredulous council of theologians. They had listened raptly and with growing alarm as he explained his interpretations of the Gospels and how he used them to proselytize the Indians.

It all seemed quite simple to Fr. Martin. Even a child could understand it. The native religions of Mexico were mirror images of Christian beliefs; you only had to stretch your imagination to recognize it. "Look at the ancient Indian practice of human sacrifice," he told them, "can't you see a spiritual parallel in the church's doctrine of transubstantiation? It is just a form of ritual cannibalism. Read the literature," he pressed, "these people believe in sin, heaven and hell, and the Sacrament of Marriage. These people used the cross of our Savior as a symbol before the Conquistadors came."

To Fr. Martin, Christ's teachings validated a myriad of Indian fables and myths. These stories existed in all primitive cultures, but had been reduced and corrupted to take on a form meaningful only within the context of that culture's belief system. Fr. Martin believed he had the key to translation. He claimed to understand these universal principles and he knew, with a conviction anchored in faith, that God had spoken to these primitives and instructed them. The Church needed a person who understood the Indians and their religious beliefs—someone like himself: half Indian, brilliant and educated as a Jesuit in the finest tradition of academic excellence.

Fr. Martin had become a religious outlaw; this his peers and elders agreed. They had no objections regarding his intent—the Conquistadors had readily built churches on pagan holy sites and encouraged syncretic religious beliefs—but his methods remained questionable and his theology suspect. Besides, this was the twenty-first century, not the 1500's, and the methods of the old church had been condemned. But the Tarahumara remained uncompromising, one of the few unconverted Indian tribes, more than 50,000 of them, still following old religious beliefs and practicing an isolated, traditional way of life untouched by modern society.

This raised many questions. Could Fr. Martin convert the Tarahumara using his questionable methods? Was it ethical and moral to allow him to proceed? Could they turn their backs and see if the Holy Spirit really worked through Fr. Martin, or should they discipline him for his activism and near heretical beliefs? These were vexing times for the comfortable, orthodox elders and they were reluctant to act.

Their response, typically, entailed doing neither. Instead they agreed that Fr. Martin, though intelligent and well-meaning, needed to examine his own life and convictions for the source of his motivation. He would be strongly encouraged to return to Chihuahua, to commence the Jesuit Spiritual Exercises and undergo counseling. Even though he knew the decision to be wrong, he accepted their invitation to meditate, but declined coming to Chihuahua, telling them he knew of a better church to endure this intense period of reflection and meditation.

He had chosen this abandoned 17th century church, and here spent the majority of three weeks meditating, pausing only to involve himself in a critical venture with his brother and to proselytize the Indians.

During the first week, he had reluctantly endured his own recriminations of sin, an area in which Fr. Martin did not feel totally secure. Take, for example, the acts of sabotage he had helped his errant brother plan and execute. This remained a moral dilemma. Surely he could assume these activities in the cause of Christ, couldn't he? Factories destroyed the Indian culture and polluted God's home for man! Everyone would benefit when the factories closed, even the stockholders. It would save them from the sin and damnation that resulted from owning stock in a dehumanizing business.

The kidnapping of the female diplomat—that had been necessary, hadn't it? The end justified the means. The politicians and corporations had no conscience and would stop at nothing to build the Aguila Dam. Thousands would be displaced and homeless, the land spoiled and polluted and an ancient way of life swept from the earth. Fr. Martin's very own heritage! Only God and Christianity could save the Raramuri, the Tarahuamara. Only Christianity could make them aware of their commonality with the rest of the Christian world, and only this awareness could unite and empower them to control their own destiny.

Unfortunately the Raramuri behaved like children and needed guidance. Salvation would come by understanding their traditional beliefs through Christian eyes, and only Fr. Martin could guide them toward this goal. Of this he was certain. As a Christian Tarahumara, it all made perfect sense to him. The church needed to be less orthodox and the Indians more malleable.

So far the Raramuri had shown little interest in his ideas and interpretations of their beliefs. But they trusted him and humored his attempts to reinterpret and reenact their rituals with him as choreographer, especially when he bought the corn beer and sponsored the celebration. It was a beginning. He hoped the bishop would stay out of it, and for this Fr. Martin prayed fervently, seeing an analogy between his work among the Indians and Jesus' ministry among the Jews. Both were ancient peoples with rich traditions, but their religious beliefs needed finetuning and redirection toward the truth of Christianity.

He moved into the fourth decade of the Sorrowful Mysteries, never missing a beat in his prayerful rhythm. The focus this week was Christ's passion, Fr. Martin's favorite exercise so far. Particularly relevant, he believed, in view of his own involvement in helping to kidnap the female diplomat and his persecution by the bishop. Faith was the engine and passion the fuel. Lesser men would have to step aside. Fr. Martin was a man of action.

Luis Decides to Go Alone

A warm morning breeze gusted from the southern fertile valley into the Batopilas canyon, carrying the sweet scent of warm humus and decaying vegetation from the river. Luis lay dozing on his cot in the cabin, but the professor had risen promptly at 6:00 a.m., restless to begin the day. He had passed on Luis' invitation to meet with Colonel Cedras at the El Perdido Otra Vez cantina, opting instead to call Alexandra and report in and, finally, to call Dr. Pascual Atunez at the University of Chihuahua for his analysis of the gemstones.

The results intrigued him; especially within the context of the information he had received on the content of the river core samples sent to Chihuahua two weeks previous. The beautiful green stones appeared to be jadeite, a precious stone. Even more remarkable, they shone almost translucent and near perfect. Although jade comes in several colors and at least one other variety—nephrite, these stones begged attention. Because of their special qualities, they could be worth thousands of dollars each.

This posed a fascinating question: from where did they originate? The Electron Activation Analysis had shown them to be jade, but no known record of any comparable source stone existed. Although jade had been found in southern Guatemala, California, and British Columbia, none had ever been discovered in Mexico, even though there were many examples of pre-Columbian jade in burials and works of art looted during The Conquest. This jadeite did not match the molecular structure of other known specimens, and none were even close to the superior quality of these stones. The professor had once seen a finger ring with a one-centimeter cabochon of Burmese jade, the highest quality jade, which sold for over thirty thousand dollars. The best quality sold for as much as fifty thousand dollars an ounce, an incredible amount. Did these stones come from Burma?

Dr. Atunez didn't think so. One of the river core samples had turned up trace amounts of jadeite. The professor had taken the sample from the Urique River, a tributary that wound through a remote, unpopulated section of the sierras before flowing into the area of the planned Aguila Reservoir. Small streams tumbled out of the higher canyons and into the Urique from an uncharted area northeast of Batopilas which Omar, the jeweler, had called the "Lost Canyons." David had been on their periphery and he recalled that they did, indeed, look forbidding. The Urique River flowed as a series of unnavigable cataracts in a narrow, sheer canyon with thousand-foot canyon walls and perilous crags and sheer cliff faces. Even the Tarahumara would have a difficult time climbing and exploring the area.

If Dr. Atunez was correct, the very first source of Mexican jadeite might lay somewhere in the Lost Canyon area. But it would be nearly impossible to locate as the huge area appeared impassable. It would be like searching for the proverbial needle in the haystack.

Luis' bushy eyebrows and "*Gringo*, I need to give that a think," had carried a strong inference. Did his friend suppose that if they found the jade source they would also find the kidnapper? In the Urique River canyon country? Heaven forbid. If so, she could stay kidnapped. Luis could go it alone if he intended to organize an excursion. The professor would take him to Satevo to find the priest, but that was all. David had plenty of unfinished work and Luis seemed fixed on keeping him from it.

The professor, on the other hand, could think of nothing else. Jade holds a special fascination for archaeologists because it is frequently found in conjunction with religious symbols and works of art. Jade embodies some of the world's most beautiful examples of art. He felt the familiar tingle that always accompanied a mystery, as well as an itch that could only be scratched by searching and finding the source rock. This itch would likely go unscratched, though, because he had no intention of undertaking such a perilous journey, especially with Luis leading an expedition.

As he sat on the riverbank's edge looking down into a boiling cataract, he heard distant laughter and turned to trace its source. On the opposite bank, near a bend in the river, four Indian women in colorful blouses stood with their skirts hiked high, washing clothes. They cleaned each piece individually, hitting it against boulders in the river, then scrubbing it roughly before laying it over rocks to dry in the bright sunlight. Two more women joined the group, and soon more laughter and gossip drifted down the river passage.

Luis straggled from the cabin, yawned and stretched, then called out a greeting before crossing the dirt road and appearing at the professor's side.

"Mighty pretty river, David." He yawned again. "When do we leave for Satevo?"

"Around noon."

"When can you show me where you got that river sample?"

"I can't. It's a two-day hike with a guide and I have to get busy on my own project, Luis. I need to tie up loose ends here, finish packing and ship some crates to Chihuahua. I told Alexandra I'd be done in a week or so."

Luis stood quietly with pursed lips, and David thought he could almost predict the *federale's* next statement.

"If that kidnapped diplomat is still alive, she's being held in that Lost Canyon country you were telling me about."

"How do you figure...."

The *federale* waved him off. "David...it all makes sense. Didn't they find that rock in your river sample?"

"Yes, but that doesn't mean the gems came from the same place."

"Is jade found in other places in Mexico?"

"Not to my knowledge, but...."

"Then it's here, gringo, here in these mountains." He spread his arms.

"It's probably only a coincidence."

"I don't believe in coincidences, David, I'm a detective. We gotta talk to that priest, if we can find him, and get more information on that Jaguar Feroz character. Then we need to organize a trip into that Lost Canyon area."

"Luis, I can't go. I'm sorry, but I can't go with you."

Luis paused a moment, then said, "Then I'll go by myself, David." He stretched unconcernedly, bent to pick up a rock and threw it into the river. "It's okay, *gringo*," he condescended, "dangerous work isn't for everyone. I'll manage somehow. I'll rent some mules, get a guide, you know...." His chest swelled.

Please, Lord, thought the professor, *not the macho act again*. He felt tempted to say something rude, but held back, rising to his feet, turning to go back into the cabin.

"Coffee, Luis?"

"Huh? Oh, yeah...sounds good."

A squeal followed by a splash and hearty laughter resounded through the river channel. The Indian women played joyfully while working hard. Something very appealing in a primitive lifestyle had always drawn David into the field. But it didn't suit everyone. Undeveloped areas with indigenous peoples could be dangerous for strangers and the inexperienced. He thought again of Luis, and then of the towering canyon walls of the Urique River. He shuddered. Luis might get himself killed. David's conscience tugged at him. Should he allow Luis to go alone or not? Damn him and his green stones, anyway. He strode toward the cabin immersed in his dilemma. *Oh well*, he thought, he would go to Satevo and find the priest. He could decide later.

From Hell to Heaven and Back

Will it ever end? Ruth thought, gliding effortlessly through the black water, counting the strokes to arrive at the opposite side of the pool. *How many days now?* Surely they would decide something soon. She continued to ply the water, losing all track of time. How long had she been swimming? she wondered. A half hour? An hour? It didn't matter anymore. Swimming had become a meaningless drill to pass time, and so she glided through the pool, bored and starved for human contact. She would have given anything for a conversation.

Too bad the Indian didn't talk, she told herself. And where was he, anyway? It had been days since she had last seen him, standing quietly in the dark, secretly observing her while she swam naked. She recalled the incident, and her body tingled with electricity. Goose flesh pimpled her skin. Why did he spy on her? Did he want to scare her, or was it merely a vicarious thrill watching a naked woman swim? She really wished he'd come back. It seemed like forever since he'd checked on her and she wanted to talk to someone, anyone—even her kidnapper.

She dog paddled and tread water momentarily, then quietly rolled to her back so as not to disturb the bats. She floated languorously, her arms and legs extended in the shape of an X. The warm water felt luxurious, like satin against her skin, and she opened and closed her legs lethargically, enjoying the soothing comfort of the liquid.

Then a tingle of premonition tugged at her and she tensed, holding her breath. She gasped! There, standing near the supplies in the middle of the room. He moved so quietly, like a wraith stealing into the room, that he always surprised her.

His presence frightened her.

"I'm bathing," she said in a timorous voice.

"I see."

"You frightened me. Couldn't you have waited?"

"I won't hurt you." He stood with his back to her, seemed to hesitate as if contemplating leaving, but turned toward the pool. "I'll leave in minute. Are you well?"

"Yes, but don't leave…not yet. I want to talk to you." She started to get out of the hot spring, then stopped.

"You speak English!"

"Yes…a little."

He's different today, something has happened, she thought. A pang of fear tugged at her gut as she lifted herself from of the pool.

"Be a gentleman and turn your head."

"I won't hurt you."

"You keep saying that." She dressed quickly, aware that he watched her every movement.

"Do you have a name?"

"Call me Mike. You probably can't pronounce my real name."

She struggled into her clothes, and her wet skin resisted the heavy cloth of her jeans. He continued to watch, but made no move to interfere.

"Turn me loose."

"That isn't possible…not yet."

"Why? What do you want me for?" she pleaded. "I'm a nobody. I'm not worth anything to anybody."

"Your feelings of personal worth and your value as a political hostage are different. We will soon know if you have value to your government."

At last, she knew why. She was a hostage for some unknown political cause, a lamb to be nurtured or sacrificed—depending on whom? On what?

"You must be crazy. I'm just an Honorary Consul. I fill in for the real actors. Nobody will negotiate a deal for my life. You grabbed the wrong person."

"We'll see." But the confidence had vanished from his voice. He hesitated. "Would you like to go outside?"

"What?" she gasped, stunned. "Go outside? Oh…please don't play with me."

"Come here. Let me blindfold you."

"Where are we going?" A dart of fear stabbed her vitals. Maybe she shouldn't go? Did she have a choice?

"Come on…I won't hurt you," he coaxed.

She finished tying her shoes and quickly pulled and fastened her hair into a ponytail. She took a deep breath and walked to him, trembling with anticipation. Fear? *No*, she decided, *he won't hurt me.*

He attached the blindfold, then began to slowly guide her, arm firmly grasped in his large hand.

"Lower your head…more," he instructed, pressing lightly as she ducked. "Stay low until I tell you to stand."

He led her slowly but steadily until they exited the tunnel on hands and knees. Bushes and limbs scraped and rubbed her at the cave mouth, pulling on her as if reluctant to allow her leave. Still holding his hand, she slid and stumbled to the bottom. He led her a short distance, stopped, and repeatedly turned her in a circle. She became dizzy, lost her footing and nearly fell before he came to her aid.

"It's okay. Here…." He untied the blindfold. She steadied herself, and then looked up. The moon hid momentarily behind quick moving clouds, then glowed brightly, its soft luminescence casting shadows among the boulders. She turned at the familiar sound of rippling water and saw the sparkling reflection of moonlight on a percolating stream flowing from a large bubbling hot spring. Steam vapors, thin stringy tresses, wafted into the sky before disappearing into the gloom.

When she turned to him, he had quietly moved away to sit at pool's edge. She, too, walked and stood next to the pool, her hands on her hips.

"What's going on, Mike? Why am I here?"

"Sit down…there," he pointed. He looked at the moon, then at her, and began his story.

Ten minutes later she sat riveted and numb, unable to move, her mind taking it all in as she listened to his rambling narration.

Incredible, she thought, and stupid. It would never work. This Indian and his brother were naive beyond belief and they would surely fail. Didn't they know any history? Had they no perspective? Two powerful governments would not stop a multibillion dollar hydroelectric project for her. She was nobody. On an importance scale of from 1 to 10, she would give herself a 2—maybe. These two would surely lose and probably be killed in the process—and she might die because of their stupidity.

They endured an awkward silence, each conversing with themselves in quiet introspection. Finally, unable to remain quiet, even though it might hasten her own death, she succumbed to an overwhelming urge to relate how the real world worked, how powerful individuals and businesses determine government policies and world economies. She sighed and began, speaking earnestly and relating all she knew, talking as if her life depended on it.

When she finished, he frowned and said, "I know all that."

"Then why?" she exclaimed. "Why, if you know it won't work?"

"It might work and it's important that a man live his convictions. It's important that my people and their way of life not pass into history unnoticed because of a new generation of Conquistadors."

"Mike...."

"My people are simple and credulous and are powerless before government and big business. We are treated like children and condescended to. We are never consulted...we are wards of the state."

He stood, and with an enormous sigh, said, "Look around."

She did, and in the gloom saw a huge circular cliff face. No...wait...there were shapes beneath the mountain! The shadow of the cliff's overhang hid something.

"What is it...?" She walked toward the cliff wall, stopped and peered intently into the obscure area below the ledges. A growing excitement held her breathless as she surveyed the wall. A cliff dwelling! An ancient cliff dwelling—and probably undiscovered.

"What is this place?"

"It's my home now," he said with conviction, "and five hundred years ago, the home of my people until the Spaniards came and enslaved them in the mines. No one but my brother and I know of it. My father discovered it many years ago and passed the secret on to us."

"But how...."

"It's completely hidden. We're in a small box canyon. The dwellings are not visible from the air and a landslide covered the entrance hundreds of years ago. It is a holy place." He looked around with a proprietary air. "The spirits of my ancestors dwell here, and they hid this place so the Spaniards couldn't destroy it."

"But why would they do that?"

He ignored the question and slowly shuffled along the perimeter, seemingly deep in thought. Then he sat again and began tossing small pebbles into the pool. "Tell me about yourself."

"Huh?"

"Tell me about your life, Miss Honorary Consul."

"Ruth."

"Ruth. Tell me about yourself or we must go back inside."

Oh no! She couldn't bear it again. Everything seemed so beautiful outside—almost a paradise after the cave.

"What do you want to know?" She felt strangely attracted to him, and so she stood close, almost wanting to touch him, to beg him not to put her in the cave again.

"Something important. Tell me about your family."

So she told him everything, purging herself of failures and unrealized dreams: school, marriage, her dead child, bitter divorce and unhappy job in the Foreign Service.

He listened quietly and said nothing, and a bittersweet silence crept into the small canyon as she silently considered her life story. Although things had not worsened since the death of her child, they had not improved much either. But she had never given up, always believing that if she worked hard enough she could fix it—until this. Now she thought of dying on a daily basis. She had even considered suicide the first two or three days when first placed in the cave. Death would have been a respite from the constant anxiety and terror, but the horror had diminished and she felt stronger, emotionally and physically. Lately her biggest enemy had been uselessness and boredom.

Ruth stole a glance at Mike and her eyes grew wide, astonished to see a glistening, moonlit tear streaking his face. What in the world?

He wiped the tear with a hand and turned to her. "I had a baby once, too," he began, then stopped, hesitant to inflame a festering memory.

She moved to him intuitively and sat at his feet. Without thinking she laid her head against his leg, trusting him, starved for affection and feeling vulnerable, unwilling to have it all end so soon.

"It was after I left school in Chihuahua. I was studying anthropology when I met this girl. We fell in love and moved to Nuevo Leon so that I could get work at the factories…the worst mistake of my life…."

Mike talked for an hour. She sat enthralled, raptly hanging on every sentence while he talked of his wife, their life and the pollution by the factories and the hellish conditions of the *maquiladora* towns. He stopped briefly, as if reliving the experience, then told of his deformed baby and dead wife.

"I couldn't let it pass and I can't let it continue to happen. If the dam is built, it will happen to others, too. I'd rather die than submit. I'm a man and someone must lead the fight. The Raramuri have grown weak from the constant intrusions and temptations of modern society. Our children forget our religion and leave their families for the northern factories. When the family is gone, we will all die. Someone has to fight."

A comfortable silence filled the void, and she still sat at his feet with her head against his leg. A gentle, cool breeze caressed her and she looked first at his face, then above into the sequined sky. The moon had glided behind the canyon rim and shadows grew long, threatening a blanket of darkness before the dawn. He looked at her face, staring boldly, and his hand reached to fondle her hair—an intimate gesture committed without guilt: a natural, casual act of affection.

Ruth let the hand stroke her, surprised to feel herself responding to his innocent caresses. She felt attracted to this gentle, strong man and had difficulty seeing him as a terrorist and kidnapper. The time for anger had passed. She liked him, she decided, if such a thing was possible, and she turned to look him in the eye.

"What are you going to do, Mike…with me I mean?"

"No one's going to hurt you." He frowned, then said, "I need to talk to my brother. We've got to find a way out of this. I don't think this will work either. I need to go and see him…he'll know what to do."

"Who's your brother? How will he know what to do?"

"He's a smart man, but he's made a serious mistake this time. I'll leave tonight and find him. I'll be back tomorrow," and he stood as if to go.

Ruth gave him a shy look, confused at her attraction and feelings of affection for him, wanting to touch him again, yet reluctant to make the first move.

"Mike," she said in a small voice, "did you kill those people at TexMex Chemical?"

His shoulders sagged, and his face bespoke guilt and many hours of agonizing introspection. "It was an accident. We thought the building would be empty when the bomb went off. My brother calculated wrong and we feel badly about it. But we couldn't let it stop us, we had to continue the fight." Grief tinged his words.

"An accident?"

"Yes, I've never hurt another man in my life. I'm a healer…a *curandero* for my people." His face sagged with the weight of the memory.

"Mike," she said in a tremulous voice, feeling emboldened, "it's okay if you want to touch me." She sat feeling vulnerable, afraid that he wouldn't. Then he smiled for the first time.

"I won't hurt you."

"I know. I trust you." She put her head on his shoulder and his strong arms gathered her to him and held her until she returned his embrace, holding him tightly and trembling with desire. She felt his strong hands began to roam. He lightly stroked the small of her back, then trailed a finger up and across the nape of her neck before drawing a line down her spine. Tingles of pleasure erupted behind his touch and she shivered, burrowing her head into his chest.

"Ruth," he whispered. When she looked into his eyes, he sought her lips, hungrily pulling her to him like a devouring incubus.

She felt lightheaded. *Oh my*, she thought, allowing herself to be guided. His shoulders felt like marble, and when he held her tightly, she gasped for air.

"Careful," she admonished, pushing away, "you're too strong."

"I'm sorry…it's been too long, I…."

She reached for him, and with one smooth motion he rolled her to the ground. She allowed him to expose her breasts, and the chill night air caused her nipples to contract into tiny stones. He moaned and she pulled his head to a breast while looking at the blanket of diamonds twinkling in the sky. She felt warm and alive again, and her body began to respond to his restless embraces.

They quickly stripped and began to explore each other's bodies, tenderly touching and caressing until their movements turned feverish and urgent. Her long legs parted and he knelt between them, lightly stroking her inner thighs with callused hands while staring into her eyes. His tumescence was much in evidence and he hesitated, trembling with desire, waiting until her eyes revealed readiness.

He mounted her, beginning slowly, then moving urgently, succumbing to his passion and nearly drowning in ecstasy as he closed the gap and arched his hips into her. He shivered and she sighed. An inherent feeling of rightness, of having finally arrived swept through them as they began the primal ritual of lovers. They moved in rhythm, careful to bring the other along with them as they soared toward their pleasure.

She had willingly delivered herself to her captor, the days of terror and demented acceptance eagerly cast aside. Now she focused on his strong body and urgent movements as he guided her toward oblivion. Her eyes, liquid pools of passion, reflected pinpoints of light from hundreds of blinking stars in the satin sky. Her mouth took the shape of an 'O' and a low, guttural moan welled from deep within as her cataclysm arrived, thrilling and melting her like a foaming ocean wave rushing across an expanse of white sand.

Mike stiffened and called out in a language she didn't understand, then collapsed within her embrace.

Passion exhausted, they lay in a tangled embrace, staring at the sky. The heavenly blaze had begun to wane, and night was fleeing dawn like a thief stayed too long.

"Are you going to put me back in the cave?"

No answer.

"Tell me, Mike," she raised herself on one arm and turned to face him. "Tell me."

"I must," he sighed.

"I won't go anywhere! I promise," she pleaded.

"I have to. There's too much at stake."

She cried with frustration and her chest heaved with emotion as she thought of the dark, dreary cavern.

"I hate that cave!" she shrieked. "I hate it!"

"It's not a cave, it's a mine."

"Whatever. Why don't you just kill me and get it over with! I hate you too. You're the cause of this!" she accused.

He reached to comfort her, but she pushed him away and reached for her clothing. He hesitated, and then dressed also.

"When will you be back?" she asked, her voice heavy with sullen anger.

"Tomorrow night if I run."

"Run?" She looked askance.

"All the Raramuri run."

"For how long?"

He shrugged. "It doesn't matter. However long it takes."

She appraised his tall, muscular body.

"Nobody can run that long."

"Any Tarahumara can run for hours, sometimes days, without stopping," he stated flatly with no hint of boasting. "We're taught from small children to run races in the mountains over long distances. It's nothing really."

She had already quit listening, and could only think of the mine. Her spirits plunged and granite despair gripped her as she considered the cave and its damp, rocky floors and walls. Her eyes held pools of tears when she turned to him, but an inchoate anger rose from within.

"Let's get it over with," she said coldly, tossing him the blindfold, steeling herself for the inevitable. "I don't care if you ever come back."

He looked at her, paralyzed with indecision, feeling helpless because of his mission, yet guilty for having to leave her in the mine.

"Do it, Mike," she said more softly, her anger failing, "and please hurry back or I think I might kill myself."

A Run Across the Canyon

A carnival of dark shapes stretched from the eastern canyon wall, shrouding the ancient ruin within the umbrage of dawn's first light. A dim gray strip appeared on the horizon. It brightened and gained luminosity and color, until a coral haze spread its wings over the Lost Canyons, burnishing the mountains in a golden mist.

The old female jaguar, her black mottled fur tattered with age and scarred from a feral life in the forests and canyons, sat on her haunches, waiting patiently for her friend to arrive. She yawned, tired from being up all night, but reluctant to lie down in the shade of the cliff dwelling without first seeing him again. Her friend would soon reappear and she could lie down. The jaguar knew the old mine well, but stayed outside, aware that she could not go inside as long as the young man's female lived there. The mine's entrance hid behind a grove of mesquite and scraggly bushes, and the jaguar remained close by, ever alert to the unwanted intrusion of a wandering puma or grizzly bear.

Her ears twitched. She heard the rustle of his feet and turned expectantly. Seconds passed and Mike came into view, stooped and bent from the cave's shallow passageway. He straightened and pushed aside the brambles and thicket, half walking and half sliding down a hill of rubble. He looked quickly to the north where she sat. Her ears twitched in recognition, and she turned completely around twice before laying down.

Mike, the younger brother of Fr. Martin and El Jaguar Feroz to his superstitious brethren, stood beside the bubbling spring in the center of the ruins. A thin cloud of mist floated above the warm water. The overflow rolled downhill to slip beneath a narrow but tall pile of boulders that covered the former entrance into the cliff dwelling. If not for the small stream of escaping water, nothing would call attention to the large pile of rocks, an unremarkable stone barrier in a rubble-strewn canyon.

Mike's bearded face appeared rigid and grim. He stood with slumping shoulders, slowly peeling the bark from a green twig, his emotions at war. He looked at the smooth rock surface around the pool and visualized Ruth's soft, satin skin and the pressure of her thighs as she hugged him with passion. He had tasted the forbidden fruit and now felt confused. He couldn't quite wrap his mind around it. How would allowing the woman into his world, his Eden, change his life? Martin had warned against touching her, but Mike was vulnerable and had succumbed to the pretty, helpless diplomat. The sharing of stories and the passion of their lovemaking had deeply moved him—changed him. The burning anger he had nurtured after the death of his wife and baby now ebbed like the disappearing stream at his feet.

Discontent and sadness had come to visit him. Suddenly everything had reversed. He had been able to remain focused up until the kidnapping. The fight against the factories and government was right. "A crusade is a righteous cause," Martin had declared. His brother's zealous ideas had goaded Mike along, pushing him into an alliance that had planned and executed acts of bombing and sabotage. Now the cause seemed unimportant. He could only think of Ruth and the hurt in her eyes. She had cried when he left and said she hated him. He wanted to go to her. He wanted to save her and keep her for himself.

Again he recalled Martin's voice. "Don't listen to her and don't touch her," he had admonished, but Mike's loneliness had been his undoing. It had been a year since he talked to a woman, or even considered seeking female companionship. Why had he not felt this way before? What was different about this woman? She welcomed him, her loneliness and vulnerability as great as his, and they had been drawn like moths to the flame.

The horror of the factory towns and the importance of his dead wife and child now seemed an abstraction. What's more, Ruth's assessment rang true. Martin's scheme to stand two governments on their head by blocking the building of the Aguila Dam and save the cliff dwellings now seemed inspired fantasy. The world didn't work that way. Though probably too late, he must tell his brother that everything had changed, that Mike wanted out. Martin could return to his Christian nonsense and leave Mike out of it.

But then what? he wondered. Mike had lived as a small child with his Indian father and later spent three years in California with his Chinese mother. None of these situations were bearable, so he had gone to live with his brother at the Jesuit mission for five years. This, too, became unacceptable as Mike always felt out of place and not accepted by the disapproving priests. His circadian rhythms were out of sync with civilization. While Martin thrived at the mission, Mike had left at sixteen to live among the *cimmarones*. He felt lost, a man with a foot in two cultures, but accepted by neither.

His early twenties were spent living in much the same fashion as his father, a lonely shaman removed from his people, wandering the lost canyons and living an aboriginal life. He fed his body by hunting and gathering a cornucopia of wild plants and animals. He took medicine from plants and sustained his spiritual needs by ingesting peyote and datura, seeking visions in the dream world.

His sole friend during this period had been the jaguar. He had discovered her as a cub, trapped in a snare set by a hunter. Dying of starvation and thirst, her leg broken, Mike had released her from the trap and set the leg. He had nursed her back to health and watched her grow large and supple. A wild animal by nature, yet she had decided to stay close and form a bond with the quiet man. She would leave for days at a time in the beginning, but would always return, eyeing him from a distant crag on the canyon wall or waiting in the shade of the forest for him to appear. Then she began to run with him, seeking his company and sharing the sheer joy of moving through the canyons.

When he returned to the Copper Canyon area he found her living and hunting in the same area as before. The cat welcomed him back in her own way—by choosing to live near him. Rarely playful, she acted as an equal, not as a pet. They were companions and friends. Mike knew that others saw their relationship as strange, probably even bizarre, and Martin rarely passed an opportunity to disparage him his pet. But the cat made a good companion and did not suffer from the numerous flaws of human personality.

Mike avoided people and had grown accustomed to spending time by himself. But after a while loneliness had driven him to his brother who in turn had directed him to the university in Chihuahua. Within the year he had met Lisa Medina and quickly lost interest in school. They had married, moved to Nuevo Leon and lived a hellish existence for two years.

Last year's sabotage had begun as righteous revenge cloaked in the validity of a just cause. But now only hollowness remained where a reservoir of passion had fueled his anger. The woman had temporarily quenched his thirst and calmed his fervor. Now he must confront Martin with the folly of their enterprise, and it must be done soon. But Satevo lay thirty miles southeast over rugged, punishing terrain. It would be difficult, even for a young man in peak physical condition. Though early morning, it would take most of the day and part of the evening to run to Satevo. He must begin immediately, but first he would eat.

Mike entered a nearby dwelling and took a basket from a cache of supplies. The room contained a mix of implements and household items; jeweler's tools, cooking vessels, strips of leather and other items needed to maintain his solitary existence. With basket in hand he walked toward the rocky barrier that blocked entry into the small box canyon. He scuttled over its top, and then walked a few minutes until he spotted what he sought—a stand of Madrone trees in a small grove of pine and oak. He plucked the silk cocoons of the Madrone butterfly pupae from the tree limbs and dropped them into the basket until they lay in a substantial heap and near to overflowing. The Madrone larvae, called Iwiki by the Indians, are fatty but high in protein.

He returned to the cliff dwellings and sat listening to Iwiki pop and crackle in a small fire. He tossed a few into his mouth and then mixed the remainder with thin corn gruel. The Jaguar watched with interest and occasionally sniffed, but otherwise showed no interest in his meal.

Mike ate quickly. He rehearsed of what he must say to Martin, then thought again of Ruth. He was tempted to go inside and bring her out again, but knew he shouldn't. No matter what she promised, she would try to escape and become hopelessly lost in the canyons. She would surely die. A snake, a mountain lion, or a bear would get her if she didn't fall and break a leg. No, she would have to wait for his return. He remembered her threat of suicide and a sudden urgency seized him. He stood and stretched, put out the fire and scattered the coals with a cup of water, then put his cooking implements away.

The jaguar's head came up. Interested, she watched Mike's hurried preparations. She yawned, tempted to return to her slumber, but when he prepared a small hip pack and stretched in anticipation of his long run, she stood also, stretching and yawning. When he sat by the gurgling spring the jaguar joined him, standing silently while Mike sang a familiar song. Finished, he took one last look at the cliff dwellings, then breasted the rock barrier and walked downhill to a clear narrow stream that swirled and cascaded endlessly until it reached the larger, more turbulent Urique River on its southern journey.

A jagged patch of light blue sky framed a pale magenta orb as the sun crept high above the narrow canyon. The mountainous rim looked barren except for occasional stands of hemlock. He looked up and down the river, then decided. Rather than follow the winding stream with its waterfall, sheer cliff faces and numerous natural barriers, he would jog to the eastern mountain wall and slip through the narrow crack that led to Rock Canyon, an hour's run east. From there he would scale the eastern escarpment of the Urique canyon wall and run a winding path south on the canyon crest for a few hours. Then he would descend and climb again through a series of narrow canyons for another three hours before a final ascent into the Batopilas Canyon and a mere three hour run to Satevo as it turned dark.

It had been a week since his last run to Satevo to meet Martin in the old church by the river. Running felt good, and he immediately assumed a familiar pace, jogging easily alongside the stream. The current flowed narrow, fed only by the natural springs in the area, but it had a broad bank on which to run this time of year. In the spring it would become a swollen rushing river, pushing against the canyon walls, but now its banks provided a gravel turf at a slight incline on which to run. Behind him, the jaguar picked up his easy rhythm and ran steadily with him, never varying her stride as she kept pace with the tall, muscled man.

Two hours later the jaguar reluctantly followed him up the nearly sheer Urique Canyon wall, then again loped alongside when he chose to run a winding path along the canyon rim for several hours. Here the sky stretched big and blue and endless, and the sun shone like a brilliant diamond in a domed top, issuing light like a beacon into the Copper Canyon.

When he began the dizzying descent into the smaller canyons, the jaguar sat high above, watching his steady progress down into a canyon, then up the other side and out of sight. Though remarkably fit, the old cat panted with exhaustion. She sat with her tongue lolling to the side, exhausted and breathing rapidly, then lay down, her ears twitching alertly. Finally she rose and walked behind a boulder to lay in the shade. The afternoon shadows had grown long—just the right time for a nap.

Luis and David Miss the *Tesquinada*

A warm breeze tickled the river canyon while a slate colored haze crept menacingly across the sky, deepening and lengthening the shadows from the western canyon wall, casting a somber pallor over the river valley.

In a hidden ravine perpendicular to the river, small-scattered campfires smoldered along both cliff escarpments. The fires created hazy, wispy clouds of smoke that hung like a ceiling over the narrow canyon. Groups of three or four Indians, some in dirty white robes, others with their skin painted white, loitered impatiently by each fire. They drank *tesquina*, a fermented corn beer, and munched on tamales and dried goat meat. They ate and drank in a restless silence while Fr. Martin moved from group to group, speaking earnestly and with great animation as he explained and cajoled his sheep to complete his own choreographed performance of a biblical scene. The Tarahumara avoided his eyes but listened, unable to ignore his persistent, pestilent behavior.

The Indians had tired of his charades and were anxious to drink in earnest. Irritation clearly showed on the face of a few, and others listened but remained stoic as a wave of passive resistance swept through the rock ravine. Didn't the crazy priest know when to quit? They had done their part, allowed themselves to be choreographed and directed in this new, yet somehow familiar, reenactment of Jesus feeding the masses. Father Martin, garbed in a black robe, sandals, and with his rosary swinging from a rope belt, had played the role of Jesus. But the breaking of loaves and fishes held little meaning for the Indians. Fr. Martin's distributing the tortillas and *tesquina* did not appear miraculous. It was welcome, but not a miracle. The Tarahuamara wanted to do some serious imbibing and their patience grew thin. When would the priest's enthusiasm wane? When would he see that they had had enough?

The Indians trusted and respected Fr. Martin who, after all, was a holy man. Although tainted by wearing the garb of the white faces, he spoke their language at least as well as they did, and was very knowledgeable about all things Tarahumara. If not for his chronic disapproval and biblical charades, they would like him even more. But this trait he shared with all white faces: disapproval and ignorance, and hopelessly out of touch with the spirits and supernatural beings that inhabit the Tarahumara canyon country.

But the *tesquina* purchased by Fr. Martin from the store in Satevo tasted wonderful and the Indians began to refill their plastic cups and gulp it with relish. Before long smiles appeared on faces with sagging facial muscles, and an occasional guffaw would invite more laughter. Soon everyone ignored the scraggly, bearded priest and sought out other campfires for friends and relatives.

Fr. Martin, reluctant to have his production end prematurely, had cornered a small group of empty-handed Indians who were slowly edging away from him, moving surreptitiously toward the beer. Finally, one grabbed the arm of another and they left abruptly for the *tesquina* pot, leaving one hapless disciple in the priest's clutches. Deserted by his friends, he shot furtive looks at the *tesquina* pot, then jerked his arm free from the priest and went to join his friends. Enough, the look on his face said, time for the fiesta.

Fr. Martin cast about for a new victim to bore with scholarly discourse, but everyone ignored him, busy with drink and talk. The reenactment forgotten, fragments of conversation echoed through the ravine; "ten goats and a blanket," from one group, and, "it took him three days, but he ran it to death near the lost canyons," and, "she had big breasts and a child on each."

The priest stood at the ravine entrance looking back into the shady recesses, a lone figure with no real friends and no certain commonality with the Indians. Anyone else would have been embarrassed, but Fr. Martin smiled, satisfied at his labor. It had gone well, he assured himself. The ideas had been introduced and explained. Although the Indians had behaved indifferent— even oblivious—he knew the drama had made an impression and that his brethren would think about this great work today—especially Fr. Martin's portrayal of Jesus. God would see to it. The seeds of Christianity could take root only within the fertile ground of imagination and inspiration. And he had given an inspired portrayal of Jesus, this he knew. Today's reenactment could only aid the eventual conversion of these innocent *cimmarones*.

Pausing to consider his next move, he became aware of barely audible steps crunching the gravel floor along the distant river. The steps grew louder and a voice joined the rhythmic fall of feet, so he moved quickly toward the noise. Whoever approached walked too noisily to be Tarahumara, and he wanted to redirect the path of the intruders so as not to embarrass or startle his disciples in the barely visible ravine above the river.

Fr. Martin exited the narrow canyon and walked briskly toward the river, his mind fomenting with worry. Who could it be? *Federales*? Smugglers or traders? Possibly even representatives from the bishop's office coming to check up on him? No, he assured himself, no one would know where to look or how to find this place. He continued walking downhill toward the river. Upon reaching the bank he turned right, moving around a wall of rock and boulders, advancing along river's edge.

The voices drew near and two middleaged men rounded a gravel-strewn bend near the riverbank. Both were large but the taller, younger of the two wore the blue-gray uniform of a *federale*. They seemed to be arguing. Fr. Martin tensed. Why would the *policia* come to this out-of-the-way place? Looking for smugglers? Perhaps they sought one of the Indians in the ravine above the river?

Fr. Martin shouted a greeting and waved as he strode with purpose toward the two startled men. The federale turned to say something to his companion, and then stopped short and waited. The older of the two appeared at the young man's side, but the *federale* ignored him and watched intently as Fr. Martin approached.

"Are you lost, gentlemen?" inquired the smiling, black-robed priest as he stopped in front of the professor and Luis.

"I would ask you the same," retorted Luis. "Might you be Fr. Martin?"

"The same and only, I hope!" The priest extended a hand in greeting, warily appraising the two, his mind barely removed from the biblical reenactment of a few minutes previous. "Are you looking for someone?"

"You," said Luis, his eyebrows arching. He offered his badge and I.D. to the priest and introduced David.

"Fr. Leo told us that we would find you meditating in the old church. We stopped there first, then asked around town. An Indian boy at the Pemex directed us this way...to a *tesquinada*, I believe. Isn't that right, David?" He turned to his companion for confirmation.

"Yes, he did," agreed the professor, who looked intently at Fr. Martin.

The priest ignored the staring archaeologist and focused his attention on Luis.

"You looked for me in Batopilas? Why? How can I be of service?" The priest looked at the professor, then again at Luis.

"We have a few questions," said Luis. "I've been told that you know everything that happens in the canyon country."

"An exaggeration, *señor*," protested Fr. Martin. "A priest knows many things because of his position in the community and his work among the parishioners. Are you looking for someone?" he repeated again.

"A female diplomat kidnapped last week on the train," said the federale.

Fr. Martin seemed unruffled. "The female diplomat? I first heard about it myself only a few days ago. We care little for politics or worldly affairs here in the canyons. Kidnapping, murder and politics are not part of the daily diet in this part of the world."

"How long have you been in Satevo?" queried Luis.

"Nearly three weeks. I spend most of my days meditating and praying," explained Fr. Martin. "Did Fr. Leo…er…discuss my situation with you?"

"Somewhat," replied Luis, "though I must admit it isn't really clear."

The professor continued to stare at the priest.

"Do I have dirt on my face, professor?"

"What? Oh…sorry. Just thinking," replied David. He looked at his feet. "You look familiar."

"I don't believe we've ever met," said Fr. Martin. "I haven't seen you in church, have I?" The question hung like an accusation.

"Uh…no…probably not," said the professor, embarrassed. "Maybe I've seen you around Batopilas."

"Tell me about your brother," interjected Luis. "When did you last see him?"

Fr. Martin coughed into his hand. "My brother, *señor*?" He hesitated a moment. "Not too many people know I have a brother. Who have you been talking to?"

"Have you seen him lately?" insisted Luis.

"Sometimes," replied the priest, his eyes casting about for a place to stay. He paused, put off by the question. "He comes and goes. Mike is like a river stone, never staying in one place too long and pulled along by the current of others. What does he have to do with anything?"

The *federale* ignored the question and extracted the blue-green stones from his jacket pocket. "Ever seen these before?"

Still the professor stared, and so Fr. Martin ignored Luis' hand to glare at David before looking at the gemstones.

"Green rocks," said the priest, shifting his weight from one foot to the other. "Are they valuable?"

"Have you seen these before, or any like them?" repeated Luis, impatiently.

The priest hesitated and looked away again. "Possibly. Who knows? Where do they come from? Are they important?"

"Fr. Martin, why is it you avoid answering my questions?" Irritated, Luis jerked his hand back and pocketed the stones.

"Your questions are meaningless to me. I'm afraid I can be of little help. I thought you were looking for a kidnapped diplomat, but instead you ask me silly questions about my brother, who is practically a cimmarone…and about these silly rocks." He gestured to Luis' pocket. "Frankly, gentlemen, you waste my time. God calls me to prayer. Good day."

He walked between them as if dividing the waters of the Red Sea, ignoring them as he passed, moving at a steady pace along the river until he turned out of sight and headed toward Satevo. Fr. Martin never looked back. Their audience with him had been terminated. Now he must consider this disturbing development and seek guidance from the Inexhaustible Font of Wisdom. He would pray for grace and strength in the face of adversity. He would ask God to give him strength to follow through with His inspired plan. Fr. Martin thought it a marvelous plan, given to him as a gift by God during the passion of prayer. He had been charged with a serious mission and must not fail.

While he paced off the distance into town, he recited the rosary, counting the beads as they hung from his rope belt. He felt better immediately and the monotony of the prayer gave him a comforting, familiar response to the ignorance and adversity of the policia and his lackey archaeologist. Hail Mary, full of grace...

"What the…." Luis mumbled, watching the retreating figure of Fr. Martin.

"Can he do that?" asked the professor.

"Do what?"

"I thought you were a policeman. Can he just walk away like that?"

Luis clenched his jaws. Clearly etched frown lines revealed an inchoate anger. "Damn!" he exploded, turning to David. "You were no help. What the hell were you staring at, anyway?"

"He looks like the gemstones."

"Ehh…?" Luis glanced at the river bend, then again at the professor. "You okay, *gringo*?"

"When you put the stones together what do they look like, remember?"

Luis' bushy eyebrows twitched. "A jaguar?"

"Exactly!" exclaimed the professor. Luis frowned and looked askance. "You've spent too many hours in the sun, David. He's half Chinese...he looks like..."

"...a jaguar." The professor finished for him. "Broad forehead, slanted eyes, beard, hell of a probocis...."

"There's no connection," insisted Luis, "and the beard looks like shit...never did like beards. Something seditious about beards."

"...and did you notice how he avoided answering all your questions about the brother...."

"Mike?"

"...yes, Mike. And I'll bet you a bottle of brandy that he's seen those gemstones before."

Luis mulled it over. "You may be right," he agreed, reluctantly. "He damn sure avoided answering any questions, didn't he?" he restated rhetorically.

"Why did you let him get away like that?" pressed the professor. "I had a couple of questions I wanted to ask."

"He's a priest, for Christ's sake! I can't arrest a priest. What's he done besides be an arrogant asshole?" Miffed, Luis threw up his arms.

"Let's get back to Batopilas," said David, moving toward the river path and Satevo. "It looks like rain and I want to call Alexandra before dark."

Luis wavered, frustrated, digging his heel into the gravel. Finally he followed, catching up within a few steps.

"David, I'm going after that brother of his. He knows something, that's for sure."

A carpet of thick gray clouds mirrored their mood, oppressing their spirits and sealing them in the canyon as they trekked the river valley.

"David," said Luis, hesitantly, "I think he's involved...with the kidnapping, I mean. That priest and his brother are involved somehow."

"A priest? Hell that's crazy, Luis!"

"I know...I know," agreed the *federale*. "A priest. But you mark my words...he's involved. You're right about that jaguar stuff, the stones, the brother...." He stopped and exclaimed, "David! Do you think the brother could be that Jaguar Feroz character?"

A jagged stab of light pierced the clouds and illuminated the gurgling creek. The professor turned to face Luis and reflected light from the stream danced furtively across his eyes. A knowing smile tugged at the corner of his mouth.

"Luis, if he looks anything like that priest, I'd be surprised if he wasn't the Jaguar Feroz."

A black day, thought Fr. Martin, putting distance between himself and the duo that had questioned him. He glanced at the sky to confirm the presence of slate colored clouds, then again to the graveled stream bank. The sun had retreated behind an impenetrable wall of thunderheads, and the canyon walls enclosed and oppressed him as he paced resolutely toward the larger river, the Batopilas and its broad valley. He could hear the distant confluence of white water hissing and gurgling where the busy stream entered El Rio Batopilas and flowed inexorably to the sea. The sour smell of sweat and his own rank odor grew strong beneath his clerical garb. The humidity accompanying the weather change soaked his clothes, causing them to cling and bind as he fled the federale and his academic friend.

While he walked, he considered their questions. One thing was certain— they knew something. How much he couldn't be sure, but they had ferreted out good leads somewhere, he could tell by their questions. While he had been meditating and praying these three weeks, pausing only to work among the Indians, those two had been in Batopilas prying into his personal business. They had acquired information in his absence that would never have been volunteered had he been in town. With who had they talked? Colonel Cedras for sure, he thought sourly, that was a given. But who else? He began to assess who might have provided information or tried to hurt him in his absence, but the list grew long and he realized that he had made many enemies over the years. They may have even talked to that lazy, drunken snoop of a postmaster, Mario. Damn his meddling eyes!

Fr. Martin should have insisted that Mario be removed. The audacity of that sinful cretin! Reading personal and official correspondence from the bishop, then whispering his saccharine secrets to other loose tongues in town.

Fr. Martin withdrew a monogrammed St. Francis Xavier Church, Batopilas handkerchief from his belted robe and wiped his beaded forehead and absently scratched his beard. He might need to change plans. What had gone wrong, he couldn't imagine, but matters could only worsen. Once the threads of the tapestry unraveled, it fell to pieces. The fabric lay ruined and must be replaced. He must contact Mike and they would arrange to move or dispose of the female diplomat. It didn't really matter which to him. He would pray for guidance, then act upon God's will.

He wadded the handkerchief and haphazardly tucked it into his belt. But the hanky hung precariously, then silently fell to the ground when he turned to go, lying unnoticed near the smooth stones of the creek.

He followed the trail north toward Satevo and the Batopilas canyon, moving through groves of jacaranda and scattered agave. A stand of mesquite impeded his path and he moved around its eroded, exposed roots. The trunk grew squarely in the path and tree limbs arched up and over the bank, extending shady arms into the creek bed. Flickering streaks of lightning wove through fluid gray clouds, presaging the rumble of thunder as the wind mustered strength and pushed the storm northeast into the canyon country. Gusts of moisture-laden air swirled into the canyon as a trio of dust devils rushed toward the creek and expired. The dust settled in the stream and began a short journey to El Rio Batopilas. The troubled priest marched stoically onward.

The professor spotted the handkerchief first and stopped to retrieve it. St. Francis Xavier Church, Batopilas it said.

"He lost his nose rag."

"No...he's lost his mind," retorted an irate Luis, reaching for the handkerchief. "Let's take it back to him."

"It's going to rain, Luis."

"I can see that. Can't you move any faster?"

"Hey...I'm fifty-two years old."

"What about all those years wheelbarrowing dirt and climbing pyramids. You said...."

"I lied."

Luis chuckled, slowed his pace and seemed to relax. "How far do you reckon it is to Satevo?"

"Another hour...maybe more," puffed the professor.

"We might not make it." Luis looked doubtfully at the gray and black patchwork sky. "Come on...move it, David. I'll treat you to a beer if we beat the storm."

Fr. Martin picked up his pace, driven by nervous energy, silently absorbed in his dilemma and becoming anxious at the unresolved issues. Why had they asked about Mike? Very few people knew of him. A recluse, his brother never mixed with others and avoided the company of peers. If he had friends, Martin was unaware of them.

Just like father, he thought with disgust—a peyote-eating mystic and incurable romantic, an anachronism from times best forgotten. *Worse, he's a pagan*, the priest reminded himself. Mike still believed in Tata god and his wife. He believed that Diablo and a host of malevolent beings lived under the streams and at various levels of the Tarahumara universe. Although devout in his own way, Mike's spirituality was based on fear and the avoidance of polluting acts. He believed in dreams and wandering souls and that rainbows caused illness, and that the evil of others could cause sickness and steal souls.

Absolute nonsense, said an annoyed Fr. Martin to himself, sure that Mike knew better. His brother could read and write and had studied in the Jesuit mission as a child, and had been an above average student. Why had he abandoned the knowledge rich traditions of Western civilization to opt for the traditional pagan lifestyle of their father? When one could study Kant, St. Augustine and Jesus why seek spirituality in medicinal plants and the oral traditions of Tata god and his wife with their endless battles with Diablo? Western philosophy was a treasury of ideas and inspiration, whereas Tarahumara religion remained the poor cousin of ignorance.

Fr. Martin grimaced. Relations with his family, dissatisfying at best, were a chronic source of embarrassment. In a country where social aspirations and mobility were defined by family position in the community and even the church itself, Fr. Martin always found himself suckling the hind teat of opportunity, his brilliance and abilities ignored in favor of those from better families. His recognition of the problem caused him to push harder, but this only caused others to put space between him and themselves and to sniff disapprovingly at his presumption of equality. But even though his brother embarrassed him, he loved Mike, the only real family Fr. Martin had. He tolerated his pagan nonsense, while insisting on Mike's respect as an older brother does of the younger, with Martin acting the role of the knowledgeable, experienced sibling and the putative head of their family.

Although they were partners in crime, and both wanted to do away with the tyranny of the factories, their motivations were singularly different. Mike, a traditionalist and shaman, wanted to protect the cliff dwellings, his only real home and the home of their father. Fr. Martin, however, wanted it all. He wanted the energy source of the factories strung along the U.S. border strangled because the new dam would bring more power and factories. God's green earth and His most precious creation, man, would quickly descend into a mire of exploitation and greed if the reservoir were built. Thus the two brothers had formed an unholy alliance, each using the other as a means to achieve their own end, both pursuing a flawed approach.

But now an enemy assailed their alliance and Fr. Martin asked why and wherefore? Nothing had gone as planned. The bishop harassed him constantly and the kidnapping had not been taken seriously—until now. And whom had they sent to investigate? A *federale* and an anthropologist. It just didn't make sense. Fr. Martin believed that he had committed an incredibly audacious act and dealt a powerful political blow to the proponents of the Aguila Reservoir. Instead, the two brothers now found themselves as the perpetrators of ill-conceived acts.

Mike, a simple man, was still sorting through the debris of his life: his dead wife and child and his aboriginal lifestyle. Fr. Martin, on the other hand, had suffered one professional slight too many. Church politics had dulled his genius and his halfbreed parentage continued to burden his life. In response to this oppression, he had become more strident and reckless in his theology. His ideas and methods had crossed the boundary of compulsion to obsession. He behaved erratic and deluded, lost in a relationship with the only person who would listen, the only one that took him seriously—God. The priest veered away from the river and selected a shorter route to town. He scrambled over gravel foothills at the canyon's base and darted through a very narrow crack in the canyon wall, navigating a boulder-strewn passageway in near darkness. In ten minutes he had cut an hour from his trip, emerging south of Satevo. He walked the eastern foothills to avoid the town's people and any unwanted conversations. Suddenly a tremendous Crack! and thick jag of lightning stung the ground like God's staff striking the earth. Startled, Fr. Martin glanced south and saw sheets of wind-driven rain powered by dark thunderheads sweeping into the valley. He raced for the abandoned church near the river, his sandaled feet flashing beneath his black robe as he exhilarated in the race. He ran fast, like a black wraith fleeing the sun, and anyone who might be watching could see that the good Father had, as yet, outrun his destiny.

Cain and Abel

The chirping of disturbed bats and the rustle of their wings descended from the darkness above the dais. Mike sat quietly behind the ancient altar and below the domed ceiling of the abandoned Jesuit church. He felt tired from his long run through the rugged canyon country and annoyed that his brother had disappeared. Although absent, it was obvious that Martin had made the church his temporary home during the Spiritual Exercises. Much of the church's debris had been organized into piles of rubbish; pieces of fallen plaster and rotten wood shards still littered the floor. Numerous fetishes and charms left by the Tarahuamara had been gathered into a pile by the church entry, which stood absent of its thick cedar doors. Mike surmised that his brother intended to toss them into the nearby stream, finding them offensive, idolatrous representations of native ignorance and therefore more foul than the other piles of dirt. Gusts of moisture-drenched air swept through vacant window frames, swirling dust and redistributing the priest's rubbish piles as chaos would have them.

A bolt of lightning and crack of thunder caused a reflexive jerk. He stood and looked through a window and watched the incoming storm. The clouds heaved and roiled as violent wind currents contested to push the storm onward. The sky ranged from slate gray to blue-black, and bulbous water-laden pouches hung from the underside of the cloud mass, threatening to discharge their load at any moment. From the eastern bank of the river a low hiss whispered from a copse of soaring hemlock and turned into a moan of protest as pine boughs bent and strained against blustering currents. Looking south toward town, he saw slanted curtains of water issuing from the sky. The tempest blew north and seemed to gain strength as it approached the church.

He returned to his seat on the floor, content to wait out the downpour. With nothing to do, he began to rehearse all that he intended to say to his brother. The journey from the ruins had gone quickly, primarily because he had obsessed on his captive and spent the interminable hours totally focused on her. He could still visualize Ruth last night in the ruins—naked, an ethereal silhouette in the soft light of the moon. Then he would recall their lovemaking, remembering the feel of a breast or the curve of her thigh, totally immersed in fantasy. When he ran southeast out of the Lost Canyons toward Satevo, he had begun a silent rehearsal of what he would say to Martin, steeling himself for the confrontation that would surely follow.

Now he felt bone tired, like a mule worked hard and stabled without food and water. His pungent body odor stung his nose and the humidity felt oppressive, making it difficult to concentrate on what must be said to Martin. Mike had hoped to confront him immediately and be done with it, but that hadn't happened. Meanwhile his resolve wavered and doubt ate at him like moths in a chest of woolen garments, creating holes in the strands of his logic and leaving him with an acute sense of dread. Arguing with Martin, a nearly hopeless task, rarely ended satisfactorily. The priest's sharp mind and withering tongue intimidated everyone. The jaguar man found himself wishing the confrontation over so that he could return to Ruth and the canyon country.

Mike looked to the wall and stared at the painting of the agonized Jesus. The image seemed to shimmer momentarily, to be replaced with Ruth, offering a coy smile, her arms outstretched in welcome. He stared, mesmerized, allowing the fantasy to hold him, when suddenly his brother's head flashed by a window. An instant later Fr. Martin appeared panting in the doorway. He began searching for his handkerchief, then sensing someone's presence, looked to the front of the church.

An observer would have difficulty telling the two apart in the face. Martin, one year older, had a slighter build. As a young man he had been hard and strong like the other *cimmarone* youths. As an adult he had maintained an acetic Spartan lifestyle, and inactivity and his black robes gave him an amorphous, oval appearance. He shared the same broad forehead and nose, Mongolian eye-fold, and sparse beard as his brother, but his eyes carried a spark of fire. His quick movements and ability to challenge others with his eyes bespoke a keen intelligence. It contrasted markedly with the quieter, less abrasive demeanor of Mike who appeared more weathered and rugged, a wandering, untamed spirit inhabiting the lonely canyons.

Fr. Martin gave up the search for his handkerchief and wiped his brow with a wet sleeve. He glanced again at the storm, then turned to his brother.

101

"What are you doing here? I told you to stay at the ruin."

"The cat will watch her while I'm gone."

This caused the priest to jerk, repelled at the idea of a jaguar protecting the woman. He grasped the rosary at his belt with one hand and crossed himself protectively with the other.

"It's unnatural...that beast is a succubus. You'll burn in hell for consorting with that animal."

Mike ignored his protests. "What have you heard?"

"What?"

"What have you heard?" Mike stood to face his brother.

"It's too early to...."

"It's been two weeks. They don't care."

"It takes time to sort out...."

"No." Mike stepped down from the altar onto the church floor. "It didn't work."

"Of course it'll work. You must be patient." Fr. Martin walked toward his brother. "Why are you here? I told you to stay with the diplomat. My plan..."

"Your plan is a failure...just like the others."

"What?" The priest's look of incredulity became a frown. Unaccustomed to challenges from his quiet brother, the priest put his hands on his hips. "What is it, Mike? What's going on?"

"Nothing...it's just that...I think that...well, we need to do something different. The kidnapping isn't going to work. It was a mistake."

Fr. Martin reached for his rosary and gripped until his fingers turned white, fighting an urge to scream at the ignorant simplicity of his brother's statement. He walked to his right and stopped to face the painting of Jesus. He stood motionless, pausing for effect.

"Christ never made a single mistake in his life; he was perfect."

"You're not Jesus, Martin."

"Don't blaspheme!" The black robe swirled as he turned in anger. "It's His plan!" He pointed at the primitive painting. "It's our only hope of forestalling the Aguila Dam, of protecting the innocence of our people, or of hiding the ruins and you know it. If the dam is built, fifty thousand Raramuri will disappear in ten years and the whole area will be overrun and polluted by builders and tourists searching for another Eden to despoil."

The priest's face turned livid and he seemed to grow in stature as the force of his conviction and the venom in his words struck Mike like a whip. But the younger brother had heard it all before and he let the words and emotion cascade from him with practiced indifference.

"No," Mike said again, shaking his head, "if they wanted to trade, they would have said so by now."

"What do you know?" said Fr. Martin, striding within inches of his younger brother. "What have you been doing? The *policia* are looking for you."

"They're looking for the wrong man, aren't they?"

"What does that mean? You helped with everything. You....."

"I gave you the floor plans to TexMex Chemical."

"You helped blow up...."

"No!" Mike protested. "No I didn't! I didn't make the bomb, you did. Your bomb killed those men!"

"Then why did you give me...."

"Because you swore to sabotage their machinery, not kill people!"

"It was an accident." Fr. Martin's face sagged, stricken with guilt. He clasped his hands, and then reached for his rosary. "You supported me. You...."

"I went along, that's all. I went along with all of it. I acted like a fool."

"You can't just quit," pleaded the anguished priest. "We're in the middle of this thing." Fr. Martin shook his fist. "The *policia* are asking questions." His eyes narrowed in anger. "You're like a child. You think you can quit anytime you don't like the game. Well, you can't. You're part of a grand plan and it must be played out!"

"When did you talk to the *policia*?"

"An hour ago."

"Where?"

"Dulce Barranca." Martin motioned with his head. "They have the stones from Father's jaguar pendant and they were asking about you."

Mike kicked at a pile of debris on the floor while he considered this surprising development. A twinge of fear tugged at his gut and his skin felt electric. A shudder wracked his body, then a blast of wind-driven rain battered the south wall of the church and water poured through the windows in cold torrents, causing Mike to jump aside. After two hundred years the roof had gapping holes. In places, only a skeleton of rafters and beams remained. Within seconds, the ancient roof sprung hundreds of leaks, so they moved onto the dais beneath the domed ceiling and its belfry.

Mike turned to face his brother, his jaw clenched in anger. "I want out. It's over."

Fr. Martin sneered contempt. "So...this is the extent of your commitment."

He waited for a reply, but Mike looked at the floor. "The great revolutionary," disparaged Fr. Martin, "committed only to himself."

Mike raised his head to meet his older brother's mocking eye. A blistering rancor festered as he remembered previous arguments and his brother's mocking and taunting, his holier-than-thou posturing and condescending statements, a lifetime of being talked down to. His fist clenched and he wanted to strike his brother's smirking face.

"…no guts, huh? No commitment?" The ridicule continued. Then it stopped. A cunning gleam shone in Martin's eye when he surmised the reason for his brother's coming.

"You talked to the woman," he accused. "She sent you."

"No. She…."

"Yes!" yelled Fr. Martin. "You touched her…you had sex with her! The little slut turned your head with her…."

Mike hit him, knocking his older brother to the ground for the first time.

"Don't say bad things about her. I…I love her. We…." He stood above Martin, his tongue a heavy stone, his mind seething with unexpressed emotions.

"It won't work, you fool." Martin rubbed his jaw. "She's using you." He sat up, looking at Mike's angry face. "You're too different, don't you see? She's from the city. She's educated and spoiled. You're…." He searched for the right word.

"…an Indian," Mike finished for him.

"Yes! Damn you! An Indian. She's using sex to manipulate you."

"No."

"Yes…and it's worked, hasn't it? You think you can keep her, don't you? Do you think she'll stay when you take her out of the mine? What has she promised you, a…."

"…it's not like that. You don't understand.

"What don't I understand? What are you going to do, turn her loose? How long before we're both in jail or dead if you do? You're pathetic." His voice dripped condescension. The priest attempted to regain his feet and his dignity. "I'm going back with you. We need to talk about…."

"No," Mike interrupted.

"What do you mean no? You can't possibly understand the consequences of…."

"Stay away, Martin." Mike planted himself firmly in front of his brother, his fists clenched. "Stay away. You're not welcome anymore. Leave us alone.

I'm done with you…don't try to find me again. I'll make my own mistakes." He turned to go.

"Wait, Mike," the priest begged and attempted to follow. "Let's talk. I'm sorry."

Mike bolted for the door as a crash of thunder shook the air. He darted into the storm with Fr. Martin pursuing, calling out and pleading as Mike ran for the river channel. The wind howled a warning and rain stung the priest's face, pummeling him with a constant fury. Fr. Martin anxiously ran alongside the river, searching up and down its steep bank, calling loudly and shouting promises into gale force winds.

Stunned by the turn of events and unable to find Mike, he abandoned his search and turned toward the church, his shoulders slumped in defeat, his feet heavy with the realization that he may have lost his last family member. Alone now, his brother, the last of his relatives, had disowned him.

Initially shocked, then saddened at Mike's sudden change, Fr. Martin realized that the plan had indeed unraveled and would surely collapse. If Mike released the woman, she would bolt for safety. Fr. Martin's role in the kidnapping would be discovered. He was a dead man, betrayed by a craven brother, and all because of a woman, a slut probably, who would do or say anything to escape. She would betray Mike, just as Mike had betrayed Fr. Martin. But she must not be allowed to escape. There must be a way to prevent her from implicating him in the kidnapping. He must act before it was too late.

He stood in the rain like the madman he was, trembling and soaked, totally oblivious to the howling winds that sought to push him back toward the river. He resisted, deep in thought, his mind focused on the problem of Mike and the American diplomat. What should he do? He walked hesitantly toward the road, and when he drew near, a blue Toyota Land Cruiser with one headlight breasted the hill. The headlight shone on his face momentarily and the car slowed as it approached. It stopped and the window came down.

"Nice day for a stroll, huh, padre?" shouted the gray-suited *federale* into the storm. He extended the lost hanky to the priest. "We're headed for Batopilas…could you use some help?"

The priest hesitated, looking first at Luis, then at the professor. Suddenly he knew what he must do. Fr. Martin smiled and accepted the handkerchief.

"Yes, thank you. God must have sent you. I'm sorry about our encounter earlier." He paused, then leaned toward the open window. "I have shocking news regarding my brother, and I'm afraid it isn't good. As sad as it makes me, I'm obligated to tell you that Mike kidnapped the diplomat. He was just here and we argued." He gestured vaguely toward the church. "If you could drop me off at St. Francis in Batopilas, I'll share the whole dreadful story with you."

Luis and the Professor Argue

Gusting winds from the violent winter storm made travel on the winding asphalt road to Batopilas a perilous endeavor. Yawning chuckholes and fallen rock studded the road, so Luis pulled over to wait out the rain. Besides, the priest told a good story and Luis wanted to watch Fr. Martin's eyes when he talked. A man could learn much watching someone's eyes, but the Land Cruiser's rearview mirror didn't get the job done. The distraction of the storm and having to drive made it impossible. Luis stopped and parked in the lee of a grove of hemlock near a sturdy, onelane bridge that extended over a deep ravine. He turned in his seat to face the priest.

Fr. Martin presented a cogent scenario of what had probably occurred. The stones had belonged to their father and had been handed down to Mike in the form of an elaborate pendant. They had been designed to represent a jaguar and set onto a silver mount. Their father, now dead, had been a shaman and *curandero*. Like many practitioners of the old religions he had shared a special fascination with the jaguar, as did his youngest son, Mike. Fr. Martin verified that Mike did in fact keep a "pet" jaguar and was known as El Jaguar Feroz to the *cimmarones*, who had difficulty believing it also. The priest said the word "pet" with obvious displeasure.

Mike had once lived in Nuevo Leon, near La Frontera, and worked in one of the chemical factories. He had lost his baby and wife during childbirth, become mixed up with the wrong crowd, and had probably been involved with the factory bombing and other ecoterrorist incidents. Mike had returned to the Copper Canyon last year, but Fr. Martin claimed to have only seen him sporadically and swore he had no prior knowledge of Mike's intention to kidnap the American diplomat. Indeed, Fr. Martin had just learned of it thirty minutes previous upon finding Mike waiting in the church. Mike had come seeking help, but had left angry when Fr. Martin refused and insisted that

Mike release the young woman. The priest believed he knew where Mike kept the diplomat: a remote area of the Lost Canyons within the ruins of an ancient cliff dwelling.

"What?" the professor nearly gagged. "Where did you say?"

"I said cliff dwellings, in the Lost Canyons."

"There aren't any cliff dwellings in Mexico."

The priest smiled condescendingly. "Oh yes there are, professor. I've seen them myself. Mike and I played there as children, although I don't believe they've ever been discovered. Actually…it's sort of a family secret. Our father showed them to us when we were young, and Mike has lived…."

"Are you acquainted with the prehistoric Anasazi Indians of Colorado and New Mexico?" interrupted David, excited at the possibility of undiscovered ruins.

"Well, I've heard of them, but I don't know…I saw a book once…." The priest appeared to be searching his memory.

"…I mean the kind of cliff dwellings that the Anasazi lived in, the kind with mortared stone," coaxed the professor.

The priest took a moment, then said, "Yes, I'd say so. As a matter a fact, they look almost the same. Anyway…." and he turned to Luis, who frowned; irritated that David had interrupted Fr. Martin's narrative. Luis didn't give a mule's ass about cliff dwellings—crime was his passion.

The Toyota sat passively and endured nature's onslaught as gusting winds blew sheets of rain against it, resulting in a constant metallic roar inside the car and zero visibility outside. The professor sat rigid and slack-jawed, trying to assimilate the priest's incredible assertion. It couldn't be, he argued with himself. The nearest Anasazi sites were five hundred miles north in southwestern New Mexico. David had spent one summer nearly thirty years ago as a graduate student, assisting the excavations at the Gila Cliff dwellings. No known Anasazi archaeological sites existed in the Sierra Madres this far south. He had spent his last twenty-five years immersed in Latin American archaeology and felt embarrassingly unfamiliar with archaic archaeology in the United States. Still, he mused, was it possible that the Anasazi realm had stretched so far south? He ignored Luis and the priest and pursued his own line of thought.

The Anasazi had lived in Colorado and New Mexico and were the last of the archaic civilizations to arise in the Southwest. Although similar to their southern cousins of the same period, the Hohokam and Mogollon in Arizona and New Mexico, the Anasazi were very different. All three cultures shared the same triumvirate of food—maize, beans and squash—as their primary means of subsistence, but the Anasazi also shared cultural traits with the eastern archaic cultures. Their corn was of the indented variety. They had stone-lined ceremonial pits, known as *kivas*, which had no corollary elsewhere, and they had built sensational cliff dwellings utilizing mortared stone, mud, and logs to construct cities on the face of cliffs. Their descendants were the modern-day pueblo dwellers in Hopi and Taos.

Even though the chances of the dwellings being Anasazi were slim to none, David experienced a familiar tingle, the premonition of discovery, a possibility that he could make a major find. The importance of discovering archaeological sites in the flood basin of the Aguila reservoir paled in comparison to finding what, in essence, might be a new civilization.

"I'm going," he said abruptly. "When can we leave?"

"Huh…?" said Luis. "Just a minute, *gringo*. I'm talking to the good padre about the stones and…."

The stones! remembered the professor. How could he forget the jade stones? The gemstones could be another reason the ruins were located in such a remote place. The jade deposits could easily be nearby.

"Let's go," he said, anxious to return to his cabin and books. "I need to look up some things."

"Keep your pants up, David. It's storming like an angry virgin out there," then Luis winced, abashed at the inappropriate reference in the priest's presence. But when he looked up, the priest stared out the window.

Fr. Martin sat in silence, oblivious to David and the *federale*, getting his lie together and planning how to move these two new pawns on his chessboard. Some things hadn't changed, he reminded himself. It was of utmost importance that the Aguila Dam not be built. The professor's reaction to the cliff dwellings had surprised the priest, and he intuited immediately that he could use the cliff dwellings and the professor to his own benefit. The cop, however, stared constantly, sizing him up. What was he thinking? The *federale*, he realized, would have to be dealt with carefully in order to execute the scheme that he, as yet, had not finalized. Fr. Martin couldn't see the end, but the glimmer of a plan had begun to coalesce. Amazing, he thought, how God continued to guide him to say and do the correct thing. It would all work out, and Fr. Martin had no qualms regarding his role. Mike had left him for the carnal bed of a slut. He had betrayed Fr. Martin, and therefore God's Plan, and could no longer be treated with consideration. Sad, but true. He would have to deal with his brother as needed. Whatever was required to achieve The Plan must happen without prejudice. Of course Fr. Martin would somehow save him if he could, but if necessary Mike would be sacrificed like the woman. It was basic philosophy, he reassured himself; the needs of the many, in this case fifty thousand Tarahumara, far surpassed those of the individual. Mike's obsession with saving and preserving the ruins were nothing in comparison to the needs of the Raramuri.

Luis stared at the priest until Fr. Martin gave him his attention.

"The worst appears to be over, captain." Fr. Martin squinted to see through a foggy window. "I'm anxious to return to St. Francis. I need to make a few calls, explain to Fr. Leo my intention to interrupt my meditations in Satevo, and make ready to find my brother."

"Yes," agreed the professor. "And I'm coming along to see…"

"Listen! Both of you." Luis' face grew mottled and set into a frown as he sought to assert control. He looked sternly at David and then Fr. Martin.

"Padre, like it or not you're a material witness in a string of crimes ranging from murder to kidnapping—all of them punishable by firing squad. Whether you're aware of it or not, you can't come and go anymore until these matters have been resolved."

"Surely you don't think that I…."

"Padre, you're not going anywhere or doing anything without my approval."

"Come on, Luis," pleaded David, "Fr. Martin has offered to show us the way to the ruins and his…."

"The ruins don't interest me," snapped Luis. He turned to the priest. "I'm looking for a murderer and kidnapper, and you're telling me he's your brother. You've described a dangerous man. We're not going to just mosey in and have a friendly conference while David here digs up potsherds at the ruins."

"Aw, Luis…." began the professor, objecting to his friend's treatment of the priest. "Nobody said we were planning a picnic, but Fr. Martin is offering to serve as a…."

"Enough!" Luis' large hand made a chopping motion in the air. "I'll decide if and when we go on this trip, and if you even go."

"What!" The professor bolted upright in his seat. "Luis, you can't be serious…." but a withering look from the *federale* shut him up, and he clenched his jaw while Luis directed his attention to Fr. Martin.

"Captain, I understand your concerns," insisted the priest, "but I know my brother and he's not a violent person."

Luis laughed. This confirmed his opinion that priests were all the same—sheltered ninnies looking for good and downplaying the evil of men when convenient.

"...really, captain," continued the priest, "Mike has never even shot a gun before."

Luis waved off his objections as so much donkey fodder. "Bombings and kidnapping qualify as violent acts, padre. Just sit tight and don't make any plans. I'll give it a think on the way to town."

Luis started the Toyota and hit the wiper switch. Everyone used their shirtsleeve to wipe fog from the windows. Lighter outside now, the tempest had blown through, leaving a steady downpour to rinse the road of broken twigs and leaves. Luis put the car in gear and it lurched onto the blacktop. Each man fell into silent conversation with himself, interpreting events and sorting issues according to his own agenda.

Luis, who should have been delighted with the sudden turn of events, fell into a black, near angry depression as he considered the priest's truthfulness and the professor's lack of caution. Did Fr. Martin want to appear altruistic, or did he see this as an opportunity? And why was the professor acting like a defector ready to jump ship?

While Fr. Martin and Luis took turns watching the other's eyes in the rearview mirror, David stared unseeing at the blacktop, his synapses engaged in academic recall and deductive reasoning processes as he bit into the problem of the cliff dwellings and began to worry it like a dog with a bone.

Luis drove carefully, stopping for low spots in the road that channeled small streams, and once had to utilize the car's four-wheel drive to cross a small landslide of mud and rock that had collapsed from a projecting hip of a limestone rock. Normally a twenty-minute trip, the ride back to Batopilas lasted nearly an hour. Finally the rain became a light drizzle and the southern sky turned lighter, seeming to swell and push the clouds north.

Two miles from Batopilas, Fr. Martin said, "Captain Alvarado, I hope you're not planning a large expedition of *policia* to accompany us into the canyons."

"Why so?" asked Luis, peering into the rearview mirror.

"Mike will know of our approach long before we arrive and have plenty of time to escape. You'll never find him if he does—believe me. I can't guarantee the safety of the woman if you choose to go with a bunch of *policia* or the army. You'll lose both of them."

Luis strained to watch the road and the rearview mirror at the same time. What Fr. Martin said made sense, but Luis sensed that he was being manipulated. How? Intuition told him that priest wasn't telling the whole truth. Was he omitting information to achieve a desired outcome? When comparing the priest's earlier treatment of them in the small canyon with his present eagerness to assist, it didn't set well. Luis knew he had missed something important, and didn't want to make decisions without having the facts at his disposal. Believing that liars eventually contradict themselves, he decided to be patient and play the priest along.

"What do you suggest?" he asked, his tone void of interest.

"I know the Lost Canyons, captain. I'm an Indian—remember? Three men can move quickly and quietly in a fraction of the time a large contingent can. Besides, I don't think you have a chance of recovering the woman without me along to talk to Mike."

"Why's that?"

"I'm his brother, I'm an Indian and I understand him. I can't promise you anything, but he's always listened before and followed my advice."

"Look!" pointed the professor, "pull in."

"Huh...." Luis slowed at the curve near their cabin and turned into the muddy driveway. "What is it? I thought I'd take Fr. Martin...."

"The front door's open. Someone's been in our cabin."

The rain had diminished to a fine mist and so the professor rolled down his window and craned his neck for a better look. The screen door hung by one hinge and the front door gaped wide open. "Maybe the storm...."

"Not a chance, David. Padre, wait here." Luis parked the Toyota and drew his .45 automatic. "Stay back a minute, David." The federale approached warily, stood to the door's side, then leaped into the cabin with his gun gripped in both hands. A quick look revealed the cabin to be a mess, but empty. He waved at the professor to join him.

"Dammit," muttered David, looking at the debris, "why would anyone...."

"Who knows?" answered Luis, looking past the door and out into the yard to make sure Fr. Martin remained in the car. Luis held up a hand to tell the priest to stay put, then slowly inspected the mess. Then he walked and stood in front of the professor, his hands on his hips.

"David, if you don't quit interfering with my investigation, I'll tie you to a bed in that pimpled-faced whore's room at the cantina and call Alexandra to come and get you."

"What? Hey...look at this mess." The professor, angry and confused, shot Luis a malevolent look.

"That priest is a stranger to the truth, and you're making everything worse," accused Luis.

"How's that?"

"You're encouraging him with that archaeology stuff."

"Everything he says makes sense to me. Hell...he's a priest. Why would he lie about it?"

"Who knows? But he's feeding me wet cow patties and giving you candy...all that talk about cliff dwellings. My gut feeling is that he's a skunk and my gut is usually right." Luis moved a few items aside with his boot, then kicked a few stones.

"Don't kick my rocks, Luis." The professor bent to retrieve them, but hesitated, remembering something. He walked instead to his desk. The drawers hung ajar, some emptied onto the floor, and papers lay strewn everywhere.

"They're not here," he said.

"What isn't here?"

"My notes."

"The floor's covered with your papers."

"I left them here, under the desk lamp." He pointed to the kerosene lantern.

"What papers?" Luis feigned interest, but continued to look around the room.

"My notes on the core sampling from Dr. Atunez. Why would anyone want them, Luis?"

"Who knows? Still a lot of miners around here. Could be someone wanting to know what you've found."

They rummaged some more, looking for the notes and straightening the room. Luis checked again to make sure the priest remained in the Toyota.

After awhile, David said, "He's right, you know?"

"About what?"

"About how just the three of us should go."

"I don't think so. We'll need radios, backup personnel, dogs, a week's worth of supplies...."

"You won't get any credit for it."

"Ehh?" This stopped Luis cold. "What do you mean?"

"Is this an important case?"

"Hell yes! A kidnapped American diplomat, are you kidding? Why...the man that solves this case will be able to name his ticket."

"Then forget it."

"Huh…why?"

"How many bosses do you have?"

Luis' mustache and eyebrows twitched and he shifted his weight uncomfortably. He began to understand. "Why do you ask?"

"How many, Luis?"

"Two or three."

"How many bosses do they have?"

"Two or three."

"How long do you think they're going to leave you in charge? You think they'll let you take credit when there's so much to be gained?"

Luis' forehead creased into worry lines as he considered the truth of his friend's words.

"Luis, I'm sorry about that back there." The professor motioned vaguely toward the road. "I'm going to find those ruins one way or another, whether I go with you or not. I don't have anything to lose. But tell me, what are you going to do if they boot you off this case, send in the army and get to the ruins and find nothing?"

Luis didn't hesitate. "I'll be cleaning latrines in the Chihuahua penitentiary."

"Exactly," agreed David.

"But I don't trust that damn priest!"

"Who do you trust more? Me and the priest or your bosses in Chihuahua?"

David knew it to be an unfair comparison. Luis had risen through the ranks the hard way, beginning as a street cop in Mexico City, having to pay his sergeant $10.00 a day just to keep a job. The sergeant, in turn, had to give his boss money to keep his job, and so on. Despite Luis' early introduction to graft and bribery on the mean streets of Mexico City, he was basically honest and possessed above average intelligence. Cream rises to the top. Eventually he had been promoted to detective and given a salary that supported a family. But Luis was intimately familiar with La Mordida, the bribe, and the corrupt machinations of the *policia*. Occasionally one had to be smart instead of honest, and this might be one of those times.

Without answering he walked to the desk and picked up the professor's maps, found one he liked, and then looked at David.

"We can report this burglary to the policia later. Tell that infernal priest to come in and go over these maps with us. We need to make a plan."

Introspection and Flight

A faint glow in the southwest signaled the storm's departure. Angry with his brother and anxious to return to the ruins, Mike had jogged nearly an hour before giving in to the storm's fury and taking shelter in an old mine. He passed the time in dismal silence, rehashing his argument with Martin and watching in awe as the thunderstorm hurled bolt after bolt of lightning into the broad Urique valley.

Upon leaving the church in Satevo, he had run like a demon in pursuit of a fleeing host. But now, in retrospect, the meeting with Martin had ended the way he had expected: badly, but successfully. Mike had made it clear that he and Ruth were no longer part of Martin's crazy scheme and that his brother was now the odd man out.

Their separation would be spiritual as well as physical. Mike had no intention of seeking out Martin ever again. To feel binding blood ties people must have commonalties that go deeper than parentage. They must have shared experiences, a religion in common and a similar view of the universe. Martin, as far as Mike knew, shared nothing in common with anyone—even the other Tarahumara. Mike had lived his entire life around Indians and Christians, and in his opinion Martin couldn't claim affiliation with either. Though oblivious of it, Martin was the lost soul. Mike had always felt uncomfortable around his brother and had long suspected that something was not quite right about him. Even as a precocious child, his brother's well intended but holier-than-thou pronouncements and opinions had gotten on everyone's nerves, especially their father who had gradually, then quickly, put space between himself and his oldest son.

Instead he took Mike on his forays into the canyon country, leaving Martin with their Chinese mother, who simmered with unhappiness and thought of abandoning them all for a warm bed and steaming cup of oolong tea. When she did finally leave with her cardboard box of anthropology books, notes, and tape recorder she took Mike with her, leaving Martin for her feral husband to raise. But this arrangement proved temporary as Mike soon deserted her and Los Angeles for the uncivilized, but familiar surroundings of the canyon country. Martin's departure for the Jesuit mission and Mike's staying with their father until his murder three years later on an ill-fated trading venture had only widened the rupture in their relationship.

Small gray thunderheads, the remnants of the winter storm, moved steadily along, trailing behind the larger, angry mass that roared northward into the Lost Canyons. He could hear the distant crack of thunder and see veined lightning in the storm mass. The Urique River, now burgeoning with the storm's runoff, hissed and crashed vigorously as the white water rushed toward its destination in the Gulf of Baja.

The urge to go struck him, and as he stood at the mine's entrance surveying the broad valley and making plans to return to the ruins, he suddenly felt energized. Ruth awaited him, and she would be his new life. He would put aside his involvement with Martin and long nurtured grief over his dead wife and child. Like his parents and his bizarre upbringing, these remained unresolvable issues in his life. The ruins were his home and he wanted to be near Ruth.

He stretched and retied his sandals in preparation for the long run north into the Lost Canyons. The storm traveled fast, and so he could run without danger of overtaking it. He must move quickly while the gray light of evening allowed him to climb the precarious, sheer cliffs and ford the full streams. The ground would be sodden and treacherous and it was imperative that he depart in order to arrive by morning. His stomach growled in protest, but he ignored it. A lifetime of living off the land in a rugged, unforgiving environment had hardened and conditioned him to small inconveniences. For sustenance and strength he would feast on the memory of Ruth.

He inhaled deeply as he jogged toward the river. The ozone-enriched air, ideal for running long distances, allowed him to quickly gain rhythm, his long muscular legs effortlessly moving alongside the serpentine banks of the Urique. The sun moved behind the western cliff face and it became dark, but he never varied his pace, and within the hour he had arrived at the confluence of three streams. He must now climb the devil's spine.

He chose the stream on the left and jogged onward for a short distance before leaving its well-worn water trail for a path into the mountains. He would return by way of Rock Canyon, he decided. As he ran, he sang a rhythmic chant that would give him strength and help pass the time. He flitted through the canyons like a ghost: gracefully and with little effort, just another shadow along the trail; and then he disappeared, swallowed by the night, a free man escaping his past, intent on his future.

Ruth Falls Asleep

"Excuse me while I kiss the sky." Ruth mouthed the words silently, laying on her back while watching the white orb creep slowly past the jagged slash in the mine's ceiling. The warm spring behind her gurgled faithfully as she lay reminiscing poignant moments of her youth. But Jimi Hendrix and memories of 1967 were what she had least expected. It seemed an eternity since those raucous years. But now the words held special meaning, and she treasured and repeated them again as she looked at the small patch of sky and recalled the quiet joy of other nights spent stargazing.

Ruth had only the mine, a few supplies, the stars and the warm spring to occupy her. Inevitably she found herself recalling events and conversations from her childhood, the happiest, most carefree time of her life. One memory led to another, and so on. She shouldn't be so self-absorbed, but what was the alternative? An ignominious martyrdom? The slow death of insanity with each excruciating moment an eternity? She coped the best she could, trying to keep it all together in the face of terrible adversity. She had received no training in the Foreign Service that would have prepared her for this ordeal. She passed time playing mind games, recalling the best and sometimes most unexpected memories, then switch to construct behavioral paradigms and unrealistic scenarios for the actors in the drama of her kidnapping—anything to maintain her sanity. Early on she had begun repeating to herself, "I must survive."

The jagged opening, nearly thirty feet above on the western wall, leaked a pale fluorescence. Within the hour the light would dim as the moon continued its journey, and the slash would turn gray and finally purple. Laying perfectly still on a cloudless night she could see a handful of stars on a satin background and fall into a subtle pattern of recall, remembering pleasant times spent at bonfires, games and picnics.

Now, as the starlight grew stronger, she recalled a memorable night in 1967. Eighteen years old, she had allowed a boyfriend at Oklahoma State to convince her to leave the dorm and camp out in the Wichita Mountains. Unlike these paltry night sparks, she remembered the wonder of really seeing stars for the first time, far away from the city lights that prevent one from seeing them so well. It had been almost frightening; millions of blinking sequins, so close, covering the earth in a suffocating blanket of diamonds, stretching as far as the eye could see.

It had been the first time she made love outdoors under the stars, and her memory of that night remained vivid. She could still smell the campfire and taste the wicked deliciousness of her passion whenever she relived the guiltless abandon of youth's first love. Tonight, with eyes closed, she would imagine herself there, feasting and savoring the memory like a delicate morsel, consuming it slowly and reluctantly.

When she had exhausted this vein, she moved to her most recent: last night with Mike under the stars in the ruins. The passion was there, but this memory was painted with confusion, fear and anger. Remembering wispy tendrils of steam rising into the cool crisp sky, she visualized twinkling stars against a velvet background as Mike's lean body, gripped in the climax of passion, flexed hard against her and turned to iron. Her legs opened reflexively, then drew together tightly as a rushing tingle coursed through her, causing her to moan with pent-up passion.

God, she thought, *what's happening to me?* She began to whimper and then sob, and clouds moved in to smother the moonlight, leaving her in darkness with a malignant fear that grew each moment until the light reappeared. She choked back her self-pity and lay quiet, stoically enduring the darkness, hoping the cloud would pass. The distant rumble of thunder and occasional flickers of lightning warned her of an approaching storm. She drew deep breaths to calm herself, readjusted her bedroll and wadded-up coat that served as a pillow, then resumed her uncomfortable position. To pass time, she would concentrate on the storm, the first such occurrence since her kidnapping, and therefore something new to occupy her. With a purling spring providing a muted background, she listened and watched with rapt attention. Although her window to the outside was small indeed, the storm promised to be large. Her imagination would provide the panorama and fantasy to remove her from the cave and place her outside. There she would experience cold wind and feel stinging rain on her face amid crashing thunder and lightning flashes.

The tempest raged, tugging at her senses and pushing her to maintain the fantasy, to feel alive and not buried within this mountain. But then she grew tired and a familiar feeling of hopelessness enveloped her. She closed her eyes in silent prayer, knowing full well that He couldn't hear her in the mine. Some nights she would steel herself and repeat over and over, "I must survive this, I must survive," like a mantra until falling asleep. But last night's encounter with Mike had cursed her with hope, and she prayed the Our Father over and over, eventually succumbing to fatigue and falling into a fitful sleep, dreaming of 1967 and the Summer of Love.

She had won for now. With terror and the fear of death as recent memories and hopelessness and despair her only companions, she continued to fight. She would not die an ignominious death. She would live another day.

The Journey Begins

Luis, David and Fr. Martin agreed on one day to put personal business in order before leaving. This, of course, resulted in a flurry of activity as well as an unexpected realization: a mutual awareness that they were all engaged in deception because they had entered into a conspiracy of silence regarding their true intentions.

Luis would report to Colonel Cedras that he was following up on leads that would take him out of town a few days. The professor was riddled with guilt because he had called Alexandra and detailed only the part of the plan that would cause her the least anxiety: that Fr. Martin would guide them to an unknown archaeological site and that they would be gone several days. Fr. Martin had revealed nothing but had agreed to meet the other two for lunch at the Pepita Plata, the Silver Nugget, to finalize plans for an early departure tomorrow.

Alexandra had been happy when David called, but became laconic and shared no enthusiasm when he explained his plan. With a heavy sigh and long silence that revealed her true feelings, she accepted his explanation, knowing her husband well enough to see that she could not change him. She filled him in on her activities in Chihuahua, since she was staying at Luis and Angela's, but made it clear that she would return to Mexico City if he didn't show signs of finishing his work. Everything was fine, she supposed. Dr. Atunez had called with a message concerning seismic activity in the northern sierras and would David please call him? This perked his interest but Alexandra could remember nothing else of the conversation, and the professor couldn't call the university until Monday. He mumbled the usual endearments and she responded in kind, and then he softly cradled the phone. David paid 40 *pesos* to the *farmacia* clerk for the phone call, then lingered aimlessly, looking at the shelves and feeling guilty for evading the truth with

Alexandra. He kept reviewing the conversation until he had assured himself that his motive was pure and that he hadn't really deceived her. Looking at his wristwatch, he remembered that he had unfinished errands. He exited the *farmacia* and loitered briefly on the sidewalk, watching the activity in the *zocalo* while deciding his next move.

The dense fog from yesterday's storm had quickly dissipated, leaving a heavy dew of lustrous diamonds on carpets of yellow grass and glistening boulders. The air felt thick with humidity but smelled fresh, and the sun was just cresting the eastern canyon wall, burnishing gold the red tile roofs of the colonial town.

Leaving the *farmacia* behind, David crossed the square and walked briskly over the cobblestone toward El Mercado Batopilas, the local outdoor market. Although he had equipment from previous field trips, he needed a new rock hammer and wanted to purchase an additional fifty feet of rope and several twine baskets. Light weight and portable, the baskets expanded to carry large amounts of almost anything: rocks, pots, cloth, etc. If half of what the priest claimed proved accurate, David suspected that he would return with more than he could carry.

He smelled the market long before seeing it, and upon rounding the corner he saw that it pulsed with activity. It was Saturday, and Tarahumara matrons in colorful *rebozo* scarfs and red headbands had staked claim to the sidewalks surrounding the plaza to display their traditional crafts; pottery, sandals, dolls, blankets, beadwork, toys and more. Merchants from up the Camino Real in Cusarare and Creel had arrived to buy in bulk and transport their purchases by train to Chihuahua.

The market rippled with movement as people talked, argued, laughed and bartered. Children ran through crowded market aisles. Stalls and shops overflowed with goods, and David ducked his head and moved carefully as he navigated the maze from memory. He stopped first to see Omar, the jeweler, as several questions had come to mind regarding the geology and source rock in which gem stones are found, and he wanted to question him about the Lost Canyon area of which Omar had claimed familiarity. The same rheumy-eyed old woman informed him that Omar had "gone prospecting again. Had a fight with his boy," she cackled. "Can't get that Ribi to do nothing."

Disappointed, but in a hurry, David forgot Omar and went to find a rock hammer and rope at the *tlapaleria*, the hardware store. His list of items was short. He already had a compass, cooking utensils, medical kit, tent, and an assortment of backpacks: depending on his needs, the terrain, and his projected length of stay in the field.

After making his purchases, he returned to the *farmacia* and bought aspirin, iodine and six rolls of film for his small 35-millimeter field camera. He had no mail at the post office, and saw that the hole in the street contained rainwater and that it was still surrounded by lethargic admirers. Realizing that he was ahead of schedule, he stopped at the corner *abaceria*, the grocery store. He consulted his list, then purchased tortillas, beans, four large sheets of beef jerky, powdered potatoes and eggs, a tin of instant coffee and a pound of sugar. He also bought a roll of white labeling tape and box of plastic sandwich bags, which were ideal for sorting and storing small artifacts. He looked at his watch and smiled. It said 12:00 noon. He could pack in less than an hour and be ready.

Luis and Fr. Martin, seated in a restaurant, were enduring a strained silence when the professor plopped his purchases on an adjoining table. "I could eat a donkey," said David, feeling jovial. He joined his fellow conspirators at the table. "Better have lunch now, Luis. You'll be eating tree bark and insects in a few days."

"I'll eat the donkey before I'll resort to eating leaves and bugs. Which reminds me," he turned to Fr. Martin. "You said we'd need a donkey."

"Yes, and I'm sure we can get one the day before we set out on foot. We can load the Land Cruiser here and drive nearly twenty miles of the distance. I know the area well, and the Indians in a village near our departure point are my friends. It would be best to get a donkey there and leave the car for safekeeping." Fr. Martin smiled expansively, trying to win Luis' trust.

Luis was not impressed. Why doesn't he shave that beard? People with beards were lazy or had something to hide. He reached for his map tube. "Any roads to this village?"

"None you'll find on that map, but the Land Cruiser should be able to make it. I visited the town two weeks ago and everything looked good. Some of the roads are little more than paths, but if we go slowly, we'll do okay. It'll save us a couple of days," he added.

"Let's do it, Luis," encouraged the professor.

"Hold your pee, *gringo*." Luis turned to the priest. "Listen, Padre...." He hesitated, as if deciding, then said,"...I know you're going to be our guide and resident expert on your brother, that jaguar character. But," he thrust his head closer to the priest's face, "for some reason I'm still having trouble trusting you."

"Luis!" The professor looked pained, embarrassed at his friend's lack of tact.

"Shut up, David."

"Please…please," Fr. Martin held up his hands. Turning to the professor, he said, "It's okay, Dr. Wolf. I understand the captain's reticence. After all, Mike's my brother and he's kidnapped a woman that he's keeping in a place known only to Mike and me. I understand," he assured them, suavely, "…but I'm sure I'll demonstrate my trustworthiness soon, and I look forward to having you both as companions."

"Yeah, well…I hope so too, believe me." Luis appeared unmollified. He found Fr. Martin's eloquence and abundance of self-confidence to be irritating, and the *federale* had decided it was all a front to cover something ugly about the priest.

Still eyeing Fr. Martin, Luis stretched and leaned his chair back on two legs. To the professor, he said, "Got everything we need?"

"Yes, and then some. I…."

"Padre," Luis interrupted, returning to the priest. "What did Fr. Leo say? Everything okay?"

"Fr. Leo is out of town since yesterday morning and will not return until sometime this afternoon. Confession is at five o' clock."

"So…are you going to have any problems?"

"I think we should leave now."

"Not possible," retorted Luis, eyeing the priest suspiciously.

Fr. Martin shrugged. "Just an idea.

"Luis, that's not a bad…." David started to voice support for the priest, but Luis held up his hand to squelch any dissent.

"Why? What's the hurry?" He looked at his watch. "It's 12:33 now."

"Because I don't wish to have the well-meaning Fr. Leo or the bishop involved in my business at this point. I do have a personal life aside from the church. Mike is my last living relative and this is a very personal matter." Fr. Martin's slanted eyes seemed to narrow even more, and he looked accusingly at Luis. "Tell me, captain. Do your wife and supervisors know what you're planning? Did you tell Colonel Cedras where you're going?"

Luis met his stare momentarily, then turned to the professor, who appeared to be recalling his own conversation with Alexandra. David looked pained, but threw in his lot with the priest again.

"We can be ready in an hour, Luis." The professor stood and pointed at his purchases. "I've got everything I can think of."

124

"Padre?"

"I've a small bag, captain. I travel light." He smiled, condescendingly. "I'm an Indian, remember?"

Luis took a deep breath. "Okay, damn it. Let's do it."

Ruth Sees Her New Home

After a night of tumultuous dreams—some wistfully nostalgic, others harsh and frightening—Ruth lay spent and unrested, her mind addled with stress. Her emotions moved like a restive sea and she couldn't easily separate memory from fantasy, or reality from the surreal. Being awake or asleep in the mine was not an act of will, only a different plane of perception. After days of terror and sleepless nights filled with nightmares, her despair was mirrored in the black walls that surrounded her. Finding the resolve to say, "I must survive," then believe it was not an easy task. Her spirit was nearly broken, and she lay on the mine's floor like clay on the potter's wheel, ready to be reshaped into a useful vessel. She must pick herself up and face the uncertainties of the day.

Her consciousness slowly drifted, hesitant to move forward yet reluctant to fall back into the chaos of a dream cycle. She resisted awareness, then capitulated, and lay passive but knowing. Her eyes closed, but her mind conscious, she became aware of the soothing gurgle of the hot spring and the bone deep ache of her body on the hard floor. She groaned and shifted her weight, reluctant to open her eyes. To what? she wondered. What time was it? Would she see the blessed light of day filtering through the tiny crack above on the wall, or would she find the blackness of eternity?

Just as she decided to return to sleep, he called out to her.

"Ruth."

Her eyes flew open. Had she dreamed his voice?

"Don't be scared…it's me…Mike."

"Mike," she said in a tremulous voice, excited that he had returned. "Where are you? I can't see you."

"Here…beside you." A dark shadow sat just a few feet to her right.

"I can't see you." She struggled to sit up. Her eyes focused slowly, and she felt disoriented. From above, a sliver of light with floating dust motes shone through the mine's natural window.

Mike stood and extended a hand. She accepted, letting him pull her to him. She hesitated a moment, feeling unsure. When he reached for her with both arms, she succumbed, feeling vulnerable, realizing that she had wanted desperately for him to return.

"Told you I'd be back by morning. I missed you...I worried about you." He stroked her hair. "I'm back," he repeated. "It's okay."

"Outside," she whispered, her head on his shoulder.

"What?"

"I want to go outside...please." Her voice quavered.

"Of course...here, take my hand." He maneuvered her toward the second passage on the left.

She stopped and pulled her hand away. "You forgot the blindfold, Mike."

"No, I didn't. That's over now...no more blindfold."

"It's over?" She searched his face for a clue, but the darkness hid his emotions. She didn't know whether to believe him or not.

"Yes...here...you'll need some help." He reached for her hand again, and helped guide her through the narrow passage. "Watch your head." He lightly pressed on her shoulder.

"I'm afraid," she said, resisting.

"It's okay. Just don't turn loose of my hand."

Like a fearful child, she gripped his hand with both hers, then stepped quickly to keep up.

"Only a little further," he encouraged.

The passage was darker than the cave for most of the walk, but then became lighter as it sloped upward. The floor was blanketed with gravel. She released one of her hands and reached to touch the wall, finding it smooth and damp. Soon they were hunched and leaning against it for support, having to turn sideways as they moved toward a small jag of light.

On her hands and knees now, she followed, stooping to avoid hitting her head until finally they arrived at the opening. He exited first, moving aside a wall of brush that covered the mine's entrance. She followed, scraping her hands and elbow before scooting through the opening.

She gained her feet and straightened with difficulty. Her back ached from sleeping on the mine's floor, and a terrible weariness rested in her bones. Unaccustomed to light, she shielded her eyes and squinted painfully as she looked around. She gave Mike her hand, and using her other to block the sun, allowed him to guide her down the slope and into the ruins.

Finally her eyes adjusted and she looked about keenly, seeing it all for the first time in the light of day. She remembered it being different. Without moonlight to obscure and entice the imagination, its aura of mysteriousness and romantic fantasy had disappeared. But it was still amazing, she thought, seeing a cliff dwelling beneath a huge protective overhang. Mountains with sheer cliffs on three sides prevented entry into the narrow canyon, blocking visibility from above and providing a near impenetrable barrier. A wall of rubble with only a stream flowing beneath it blocked visibility and entry from the east. The hot spring seemed much larger than she recalled, and now she could clearly see holes or entries leading into the mountain on both sides of the cliff dwelling. Large piles of rubble lay like small-eroded hills, and several stone and mortar constructions lay between the spring and the cliff dwelling. The dwellings hid beneath the base of a huge mountain, snuggled beneath a shady, protective overhang of rock. Built from stone and mortar, it stretched nearly sixty meters end to end.

A long-absent feeling of enchantment lifted her spirits, and she walked to the spring and climbed on top of a large boulder from where she could view the whole canyon. The air smelled delicious after last night's storm and her skin tingled beneath undulant rays of warm sunshine. After so many days of darkness and sensory deprivation, she was experiencing everything acutely. Chirping birds, especially the song of a nearby meadowlark, brought a smile to her face, the first real joy she had experienced in more than a week. The sun was a brilliant white orb above majestic groves of hemlock, vigilant sentinels guarding the ruin's perimeter on three sides. The trees cast long shadows across the mountainsides and floor of the hidden valley, creating a menagerie of shapes when the wind bent their large boughs.

A slow trickle of happiness flowed into her soul and a wan smile hung loosely on her face. Never had she enjoyed so little so much, and in her diminished capacity even the monotonous activity of a nearby trail of ants gave her joy.

"Want to see the rest?"

"Huh…?" She turned and clearly saw her champion for the first time in the light of day. Taller than she remembered, with shoulders wide and well-defined, he stood lanky with long rippling muscles. His broad face and slanted eyes were dark and weathered from countless hours outdoors. His hands were large and callused and his feet were strapped into a pair of rawhide sandals with tiretread soles. A soiled shirt and dirty pants hung loose and ill-fitting from his large frame. He lowered his eyes and looked away when Ruth's eyes sought his.

"The ruins...would you like to see more?" he repeated, seemingly ill at ease.

"Yes," she replied, "that would be wonderful." She stood and stretched again, breathed deeply with evident joy, reflected a moment, then turned to Mike.

"You said it's over. Does that mean I'm not a prisoner anymore?"

"Yes. Come on," he offered her a hand. "I'll tell you about it while you look at our new home."

A familiar feeling of dread drenched her. "Our new home?" She stood numb and uncomprehending, and a shiver shook her. Oh...God! Was he the savior or the warden? She wanted an answer now, a clue, a nuance or gesture that would let her know what to expect. But she must bide her time and not panic; she would be patient and try to adapt.

"Yes...beautiful, isn't it?" he continued. Smiling, he took her hand and gave her a gentle pull, already talking and explaining, leading her toward the dwellings. He seemed excited, and so Ruth acquiesced and followed, but she offered no encouragement and very little interest in the ruins, and after a while he noticed her remoteness.

"Are you hungry?"

"I don't know...yes...maybe." She forced a smile.

"It's been terrible, hasn't it?" His eyes darted to the floor momentarily. "Look...we can do this later." He spread his arms expansively. "I'll get some food and maybe I can show you later, okay?"

He led her to a stone oven in the shade of the overhang. A well-used campfire with large stones surrounded a cooking pit. Tiny embers still glowed within and she surmised that he had returned last night and sat by the fire thinking of her and making plans for her life.

She allowed him to take the lead and offered no resistance. Though sick to her soul with the implication of "our new home," she found it difficult not to see him as her savior. He seemed gentle and sincere and didn't act like a terrorist, and her situation had improved too dramatically to not be grateful. True, he had helped kidnap her, but he acted remorseful and had released her from that hellish mine. She lived!

She must feel her way through this new dilemma and make the best of a changing situation. She would assume that she was still a prisoner, albeit a thankful one, until an opportunity to escape presented itself. In the meantime,

Mike was her ticket to freedom and she would not offend him. Indeed she would do anything to please him—anything. She might just survive. She could finally hope again.

Ruth watched the quiet Indian work, her eyes occasionally straying to an item or oddity that caught her attention. She even viewed the ruins with new interest. She felt stronger, and the urge for activity bubbled within. With the exception of several swims a day in the hot spring, she had done little but focus inward, imagining trivial concerns as significant and allowing reality to fester into the surreal. She stood and walked toward Mike, who climbed up a ladder into one of the dwelling's rooms.

"I want to help," she called out.

He returned with a twine sack slung over his back and shimmied down the ladder.

"I said I want to help," she repeated. "What's in the sack?"

"Not much...corn flour, atole mix, salt, a few pans and stuff."

"Let's see." She reached for the bag. "Tell me what you want and I'll do it. I used to be a Girl Scout."

"A what?"

"Never mind. Just give me the...." Ruth saw the jaguar. She dropped the bag and yelped. He spun around to follow her eyes, but saw only his cat laying in the shade. The jaguar's eyes narrowed and her ears jerked upward. Aware she was being watched, she stood and stretched and yawned, exposing shiny white teeth in a gaping mouth. Ruth looked at Mike, opened her mouth to scream, but fainted instead.

"Ruth!" Mike whispered urgently, dipping his headband into the spring and wiping her face. "Ruth, it's okay...she won't hurt you. She's...."

"Oooh," She moaned, then jerked, and her eyes flew open. She reached for him. "Cat...there's a big lion!"

"No, no...it's a jaguar...somewhere...she's here somewhere. You scared her." He reached and helped her to her feet.

"Scared her?" she repeated, incredulously, taking deep breaths. "Let's go." She jerked at his arm, frantic. "We can't stay here. It's too dangerous." She looked to where she had last seen the jaguar.

"It's okay." He smiled. "I know her. She's...."

"Her? That big cat? What do you mean?" Ruth hugged herself and looked. "Do you have a gun?"

"A gun?" A look of revulsion crossed his face. "The cat...it's a jaguar...is a friend. She lives here. It's our home, but she would never hurt...."

130

"You have a pet jaguar? Tell me you're lying, Mike. No one has a pet jaguar."

"She's a companion, not a pet. She's lived with me on-and-off for years." He frowned, seemingly disappointed with her reaction.

Spooked, Ruth continued to look about, but the jaguar had disappeared. Within moments her fear ebbed and was replaced with cautious resignation. Her life was like a roller coaster. What next? She had to get out of this place.

"So...Tarzan has Cheetah and Jane and you have me and your jaguar," she said acidly, but smiled to soften her sarcasm.

"Tarzan and Cheetah?" he repeated with a blank face.

Oh, Lord, he's not pretending, she realized. "Never mind. Don't plan to go anywhere without me, because I don't want to end up in that thing's stomach."

"Oh...there's no chance of that," he chuckled. "She would never hurt you. She has been protecting you since we put you in the mine. She keeps pumas and snakes out of the area."

"Pumas? There are lions here?"

"Pumas...yes...sometimes...but only a few. You don't need to worry."

But Ruth worried. *Snakes, lions, jaguars! What's next?* Did they have cannibals and head hunters in Mexico? She moved next to his side and took his hand. "I do feel safe with you. Just stay close, okay? This is all so crazy for me." She felt suddenly vulnerable and her eyes began to tear. *No!* she told herself. She couldn't cry. She must stay strong or she would never make it out alive. She steeled her face and tried to act unafraid.

But Mike had seen her fear and pulled her close for reassurance, longing to touch the body that had inspired his fantasies and held him enthralled ever since the kidnapping. He believed that her spirit had become sick in the mine and wanted to help heal her.

"Sorry," she sniffed, quickly wiping her eyes. "I'm a little on edge. Sometimes I think I'm going crazy." She leaned into his chest and his arms encircled her protectively. She felt overwhelmed. Two weeks of fighting a hellish captivity with demented stoicism had taken its toll. The floodgates opened anyway, and she began to sob pitifully.

"Ruth, what have I...."

"Just hold me...please?" she whimpered, continuing to cry, letting it all out as he stroked her hair and murmured endearments.

Finally, with her well of tears dry, and the emptiness and fear that had ruled her life the last two weeks pushed aside, she stood on her tiptoes and gave him a quick, coy kiss. She had remained strong and in control, and she had survived the mine.

"Thank you, Mike…for…everything…I mean…." she didn't know what to say. What did you say to someone who had kidnapped you, but then maybe saved your life? How could or should she thank him? She had every right to be angry. Instead she felt foolish and thought her statement of thanks awkward.

She glanced and found him staring at her. And then he reached and pulled her to him again. She saw hunger in his eyes and knew that he had no intention of consoling her. He wanted to devour her. Mike placed his hands on her hips and lowered his head to kiss her. It was a good kiss, long and passionate, and she allowed herself to be swept along by his ardor. This kiss led to another and his hands roamed freely. His body stiffened with urgency, pushing him deeper into a wallow of passion.

But it just didn't feel right, and Ruth began to demur. She was attracted to him; his rugged good looks and hard body were physically appealing, but her body wasn't responding. He was moving too fast, and she couldn't recall the passion of two nights previous when everything had seemed magical.

Mike moaned and the front of his pants swelled expectantly.

"Mike, no…I'm not ready." She turned away.

"Ruth…." His voice was stretched tight with passion. "What's wrong?" He burrowed his face into her hair and breathed deeply.

"It's just not time…yet. Later…maybe."

"Did I say something or…."

"No, it's me. I just…give me some time, okay?" She pulled away, but smiled, feeling abashed. "Let's talk some more, eat…show me the ruins. Don't hurry me…please?" She straightened her clothes, embarrassed..

"Sure," he said reluctantly, a sheepish smile on his face. "Is it that you don't like to…."

"No…no." Her face turned scarlet. "I'm sure we'll do it…soon. I just need more time. Here," she changed the subject, "give me those pans. Can Indians really light a fire by rubbing two sticks together?"

The afternoon sun shone brightly, warming the chilled mountain air, bathing the hidden canyon with a weightless splendor that revealed its stark emptiness. They had eaten and talked like good friends, long and openly, savoring the conversation. Mike spoke with a simple eloquence, his ideas and stories devoid of the guile and double entendre so common in her world. She found it refreshing, and occasionally startling, to hear him talk of life, love, sex and religion with such candor and from such a different worldview. An Indian and totally unsophisticated, his beliefs regarding religion seemed nearly absurd to her. She listened anyway and tried not to show her chagrin, realizing the vastness of the chasm between their worlds.

The tour of the ruins took nearly two hours, and more remained to be seen. When the jaguar appeared, Ruth quickly joined Mike at his side. But it gave them little notice, sometimes raising its head when they drew near, and once rising to go for a drink from the pool. Mike carried a ladder from one home to the next, pulling it up behind them as they climbed to the next level.

The rooms appeared unchanged, probably much as they were four hundred years ago when the Indians had dropped what they were doing and abandon them. But not all were empty. Some contained skeletons, and these they avoided as Mike asserted that wandering souls might become angry if they entered. Pottery, metates for grinding corn, tools and various pieces of crude furniture sat as they had been left. It felt eerie searching an empty city without knowing the evil that had caused everyone to abandon it.

Several rooms on the bottom floor held food and tools gathered by Mike and his father over the years. One had been converted to a workshop. She expressed surprise to see pieces of jewelry in various stages of preparation strewn about the room.

"You make gold jewelry?" she asked, amazed, turning a large pendant with a green translucent stone over and over in her hand.

"My father taught me. Lots of Indians make jewelry. It's a way of expressing our...."

"But this is gold, isn't it?" she interrupted, astonished at the intricate engraving and the luster of the stone. Suddenly it registered. "It's a gold mine isn't it? This town is here because of the mine."

"Yes," he admitted, reluctantly, "but no one knows. Discovery of gold would mean the destruction of this place. The greed of the white men...they would tear this place apart...turn the mountain into small stones."

Incredible, she thought. A gold mine, and probably worth billions. Ruth looked at Mike, who studied her in turn, and she realized that he had read her mind.

"It's our secret," she assured him, careful not to say anything that would cause him to mistrust her. "I'll never tell anyone."

"Never?"

"Never...I swear it."

He seemed satisfied. "I thought so. Most white people don't understand the spiritual or ritual value of gold and gemstones. They want them for wealth and power. My father taught me to capture the souls of spirits and represent the beauty of nature in jewelry. Jewelry should be a mirror image of a spiritual manifestation. You must be able to look and see at once that it represents a sacred idea."

Wow! she thought. The Indian was a deeper thinker than she had imagined. He had layers like an onion that would have to be peeled away to really know him. She replaced the pendant on the table. Somehow it didn't feel quite the same, and her initial excitement was now dulled by his thoughtful explanation. He picked it up and placed it in her hand.

"Please...if you like it?"

"Oh no...I couldn't possibly accept it. It's," and she almost said "worth so much," but caught herself in time to say "so beautiful. What's the green stone?"

"Jade. Beautiful isn't it? These stones," he pointed to a rusty coffee can, "are all that's left from what my father found near Rock River, about ten miles west of here in another canyon. I don't know where he found them. He never told anyone, and then someone killed him."

"I'll treasure it always, Mike. Thank you." She gave his hand a squeeze.

The day passed quickly and soon the sun had fled, and the high-altitude night air carried a chill. In mid-November night temperatures sometimes hover near freezing in northern Mexico. It felt so good to be out of the mine that she had difficulty sustaining anger. Her reluctance to become intimate was also dissipating. They sat huddled beneath the stars; her head against his chest, watching the flames dance joyfully. The fire mesmerized them, and they sat silently, each reconstructing the day within their own perspective.

She should hate him, but didn't, she realized. Mike was very likable, but his world was totally foreign. He reminded her of a television character out of *Wagon Train* or *Rawhide*.

Ruth nestled against him, feeling content. The smell of a man and her head on his chest heightened her awareness of him. The fire glowed warm and romantic and she relaxed. It would soon be bedtime, and the cheerful pop and crack of the fire lulled her into complacency and provided a soothing balm to her spiritual wounds. What would surely follow no longer distressed her and she allowed herself to remember a night not too long ago.

The eyes of the jaguar glowed huge and yellow near the fire, but Ruth paid it no mind. The cat would appear suddenly, then depart for who knew where. Mike showed it little attention, and they seemed to communicate without speaking.

She shifted her weight and looked into the night sky. The Milky Way twinkled like diamond rhinestones on velvet cloth, and the magic of two nights ago crept back into her soul. "I'm ready for bed, Mike," she said unexpectedly. "Where do we sleep?"

He stiffened, surprised, and replied, "I sleep next to the jewelry room on the first level."

"Do you need to prepare it for us?"

He hesitated, and then said, "I'm sure I do. Wait here and I'll call you." He disengaged and walked to the cliff dwellings, disappearing into the darkness of the overhang.

Ruth stood and stretched, watching him pad away and scurry up the ladder. He moved like the jaguar: smooth but with hidden strength. She felt unexpectedly complacent, and the recent horror of the mine seemed distant. She circled to the other side of the fire to better hear the soft murmur of the hot spring. The campfire illuminated steam tendrils rising into the sky, and she felt drawn to the water. After swimming three or four times a day the last two weeks, she remembered that she had missed her swim today. Dipping a foot to test the water and its warmth caused her to shiver with delight. Acting on impulse, she quickly stripped naked and sat on its smooth edge momentarily before sliding into the warm, percolating water. It felt delicious against her skin, and she dog paddled from side to side, swimming lazily in the water. Moments later she heard a familiar sound—the rustle of clothing—and turned to see Mike, naked also, standing in silhouette. His eyes glittered hungrily with reflected firelight, and he stood tall and well-defined. She could see that he was erect and ready. She felt herself flush and looked away momentarily before turning to meet his eyes.

"Mike...?"

"Yes, Ruth."

"I may not be able to stay with you very long."

He remained silent for what seemed an eternity, then said. "Yes...though it makes me sad. We are very different, but it's probably best. But I still want to make love to you."

"Yes...I can see that." She stared at his erection. "Can you swim as well as you run?" she asked in a husky voice.

"Yes...I love to swim."

"Good, because I'm not sleepy anymore."

He dove into the water and surfaced in front of her. Hungry for affection and thankful for her life, she reached for him. His face was flushed with desire and he pulled her to him, crushing her breasts against his broad chest. Their legs churned rhythmically to keep them afloat. They embraced, and their hands explored each other's bodies as their legs moved sensuously in the warm liquid.

The water felt like fluid satin caressing their skin, and she felt his tumescence against her belly when he sought her lips. She struggled at first, then capitulated, his strong arms and hungry mouth stoking her passion like a bellows inciting furnace coals. Feeling wanton, she succumbed to a ravenous sexual hunger and wrapped her legs tightly around his waist. He groaned with passion and they moved to poolside where a smooth stone lip extended from the edge just below the water.

Trembling with repressed desire, he spread her legs and she braced herself on the ledge as waves from the pool lifted and buoyed her breasts like tiny ocean swells. Her head was thrust back with closed eyes, awaiting the intimate stroke that would consummate their love. He mounted her slowly and tenderly, pushing into her with a groan of delight. He hesitated, then closed the gap and held her tightly. His body shivered with passion. Their eyes met and they began the primal movement of sexual union. They moved languorously, wanting it to last forever, pausing only to kiss and give small love bites before beginning again.

Ripples of pleasure surged from their groins and caused them to groan and then stiffen. They would stop, then start again, trying to make it last. Soon the pleasure became too much and she felt her explosion coming, so she squeezed tightly with her legs and urged him on. He moved his hips against her in a circular motion until, suddenly, he stiffened and arched into her, crying something she didn't understand. She quickly followed, going limp in his arms with ripples of euphoria blossoming into rapture.

Fluorescent moonbeams lit the canyon like dim flickering lamps, and the jaguar sat watching like a voyeur from a nearby cliff. With the moon bathing them in streams of silver luminescence, they talked and played and, inevitably, joined their bodies again, and then one final time before finally leaving the pool.

Bored with the foolish antics of humans, the jaguar tucked her head beneath a paw and closed her eyes. The cat slept fitfully, her dreams disturbed by unknown enemies. After the two humans had gone to sleep, she slunk down the mountainside and lay close to the fire. She watched the flames dance until they grew tired and the coals glowed in a tired, withering death. Soon her eyes grew heavy and her chest moved slow and rhythmic as a chilly stillness crept into the canyon.

Fr. Martin Bites a Snake

The Land Cruiser rocked and swayed when Luis drove into a rushing creek of white water. Normally a dry bed of rock and gravel, the frenzied stream boiled and broke against large rocks and shallow cataracts. Yesterday's storm had swept through the Copper Canyon area, leaving every creek and river a torrent of activity. Luis, David and Fr. Martin had searched until they found a safe place to cross this wide but shallow creek. After walking up and down the bank and speculating on its depth at midstream, they had decided to enter at this spot.

The fifty-kilometer drive had begun well enough. The first twenty had been a slow journey southwest over a series of dirt and gravel roads before arriving in a broad valley with round weathered mountains. They had driven through one ramshackle Indian town after another, each like the last: chink log cabins and outbuildings with piles of multicolored corncobs drying in the sun on corrugated metal rooftops. The strong odor of livestock and open sewage wafted through the windows, and Fr. Martin talked nonstop about every town and who he knew in each.

The dirt road ended when they arrived at the foothills, then deteriorated into little more than a series of rocky paths and sheep trails. Travel slowed to a near crawl as the terrain became rugged and Fr. Martin directed them away from the beaten track and deeper into the foothills of the Sierra Madres.

It was tough going, and the sun moved steadily away as if avoiding them, finally perching behind the huge, threatening spine of the sierras and pausing, taunting them with its disappearing light before dropping behind the distant cordillera for the night.

Luis changed the Jeep to four-wheel drive and everyone held their breath when the front end of the Jeep dipped into the water. "How far?" queried a disgruntled Luis. "What happened to the roads?" He craned his neck through

138

the driver's window to watch the car's tires as he crossed the stream. "One of these times we won't be so lucky and this car's going to get stuck in the middle of the river."

"Soon, captain, soon. Your patience will be rewarded. If not for the rain, we would already be there." Fr. Martin held on to the back of Luis' seat. "The paths are still clear enough, and I could find my way in the dark. Have faith."

Luis mumbled something.

"What?" asked Fr. Martin.

Luis waved him off, then looked at the professor who was absorbed deep in thought. *Probably thinking about those darn ruins*, thought Luis. "Hey, *gringo*. Where do we sleep tonight…in that tent?"

"I don't know…sure, why not?" agreed David. "It's probably cleaner than some of these cabins I've seen."

"How much farther, padre?" Luis looked into his rearview mirror to find the priest. "The sun's going down and I don't want to be eaten by a grizzly." He goosed the Toyota as they reached the opposite bank, climbing up and over to dry land. Soon they followed the trail again.

"Don't joke, captain. My brother assures me that grizzly bears still roam the Lost Canyons."

"Yeah? Well I've got a .30 caliber bullet for one if it gets to sniffing around." Luis took a quick peek into the mirror to see if the priest was baiting him.

"See that path?" Fr. Martin pointed toward a copse of pines. "Go that way. On the other side is the village where my father was born."

"How far?"

"Five minutes…no more." Fr. Martin perched on the edge of his seat. "Watch for sheep."

"Sheep?" said Luis.

"These people all raise sheep. They live in the lowlands year around. The other Indians call them Los Ranchos because of their dedication to raising livestock."

"Your father was a rancher?" asked the professor.

"No. My father lived like an itinerant mystic. He worked as a healer, but ended up a misfit who supported himself by making a little jewelry once in a while."

"I thought you said he was a shaman."

Fr. Martin frowned, then replied. "He was…I mean, he did what little he could to get by. He was a poor excuse for a parent."

"How did he die?"

"Someone killed him over there…Rock Canyon, I believe." He pointed northwest. "Mike found him, or his remains. Father had arranged to meet a trader to sell some jewelry, but never returned home."

Luis had the headlights on, even though only one worked, and he cautiously navigated a well-worn path through the trees. Suddenly the forest ended. They crested a hill and drove down into a grassy valley dotted with small cabins, herds of grazing sheep and a well-used network of paths. The moon shone like polished ivory and the first evening stars began to appear.

Luis stopped the Toyota and they all stared; Fr. Martin at the small community below and Luis and the professor at the forbidding mountains to the north and west. Even in the declining light of evening, the *cordillera* appeared harsh and majestic.

"Jesus," breathed Luis, intimidated by the thought of what lay beyond. "We're going into that?"

"Early tomorrow morning," replied Fr. Martin. "We can set up camp over there," he pointed to the far side, near the mountains, "then I need to talk to a few people. You're welcome to come along if you wish."

They skirted north of town and pitched camp. Their tent, a blue polyester bubble, supported itself with thin, connecting fiberglass rods. They decided to erect it very near to where Fr. Martin had indicated they would leave tomorrow on foot. By the time the Toyota was unloaded of the remaining supplies, darkness had fallen. They piled into the empty Land Cruiser and descended into the sloping valley, drove a few kilometers, and finally arrived at the village where they would leave the car and buy a burro to carry their supplies.

The town, if it could be called such, was nothing more than a collection of chink log cabins on a meandering stretch of road. A few of the larger, more prosperous-looking buildings lay off the main thoroughfare, away from the poorer homes. The town had no pattern and there didn't appear to be any stores. Isolated and homogeneous, the few people they encountered stared with curiosity at the sight of the one-eyed Toyota and its cargo of three men.

"Any of these cars run?" asked Luis, eyeing the cadavers of old pickup trucks in varying states of having been stripped for parts.

"Maybe a few," replied Fr. Martin. "The really big ranchers can sometimes afford an old truck." The priest waved at someone who didn't recognize him, then said, "Around the curve, captain. See the house with the light in the window?"

Luis parked the Toyota in front of a rundown cedar plank house with rusted corrugated steel roofing. The yard was barren of grass and strewn with bits of trash and wood chips. Several men with weathered faces smoked cigarettes and stood in groups talking in low voices.

"Something's going on," said Fr. Martin. He craned his neck out the window to look around. "I think someone's sick," he added.

Two men approached the Toyota and Fr. Martin called out to them. They waved and called out his name and seemed happy to see him. Father Martin accepted a cigarette, although he didn't light it, and listened while one of them talked rapidly and pointed toward the cabin. The other stood and listened, then went to the cabin door, knocked once and entered.

Within moments a short Indian woman stormed from the house. Three braids of hair hung from her head, and she wore wool clothing against the chilly night air. Several fetishes hung from her neck and a rope belt at her waist. Her face a mask of stone, she walked straight to Fr. Martin.

"We don't need any Jesus magic tonight! Leave before a spirit steals this poor girl's soul."

The priest's eyes narrowed with disapproval. "I want to see her myself, *señora*. I can only hope that I arrived before you poison the child with one of your filthy potions. If it is Pine Needle Girl, she is probably just experiencing the monthly discomfort of a woman and the cramps will pass without your help."

The old woman sputtered with rage. "What do you know about what's between a woman's legs? You…who…who…have yet to find your own sexual organs! Leave us before an evil spirit steals all our souls."

They began to argue in Tarahumara, and Luis and the professor looked about sheepishly before wandering back to the car. A man and woman, probably the owners of the small *rancho*, hurried outside to intervene in the shouting match. The woman pulled the old shamaness away from an angry Fr. Martin and directed her back into the house. The woman reappeared again to hug Fr. Martin and they talked quietly, stealing furtive glances at the house. Finally, the priest shook hands with both and grudgingly returned to the Toyota, waving to a few people he recognized as he approached the car.

"Evil bitch," he said, getting into the Land Cruiser. "She's probably killed more people than the measles."

"Look, padre…we didn't come here to fight a whole town of Indians. Do you think you could keep a lower profile? That old woman looks like she eats grizzly for breakfast. Let's get that donkey and get back to the camp. What do you think, David?"

"Sounds good," agreed the professor. "I'm tired, and a donkey will take some tending to anyway."

"Sure...sure," grumbled the priest. "Turn left. Go about a quarter of a mile...see that big house? That's the one."

This *rancho* had an even larger group of people milling about. As before, Fr. Martin shook hands and greeted everyone before introducing Luis and the professor. Moments later someone ushered them through the front door. Candles burned throughout the house and a woman, apparently the house matron, gave Fr. Martin a tearful embrace while her husband shooed the hangers-on outside.

A smoke-stained picture of the Virgin of Guadalupe hung prominently above the stone fireplace and served as the centerpiece of the large room. The Virgin stood with her hands at her sides, palms outward, a halo above her head and her heart exposed and illuminated in golden light. The room contained coarse pine furniture and tools. It served as a kitchen, living room, bedroom or storage for anything that needed to be somewhere other than outside.

This is where Fr. Martin had expected to purchase a donkey and store the Land Cruiser, but a rattlesnake in the corral feed trough had bitten the couple's daughter one hour earlier while she was tending the livestock. Candles flickered at the head of her bed. Except for her frightened eyes, she lay perfectly still on a mattress stuffed with cornhusks.

Father Martin examined the child's leg, then announced it was time for prayer. He would ask Jesus to heal the child and he would lead the prayer himself.

Luis groaned. "Let's go outside, *gringo*. I can't stand to watch this charade."

But David, always the anthropologist and a life-long hater of snakes, decided to stay and witness what followed. "Go ahead, Luis. I want to see this."

"You've got to be *loco* to stay here with...."

"Be quiet," hissed the professor. "I've got a feeling you're going to remember this. He's up to something."

Fr. Martin called for everyone outside to come in. While Luis and the professor observed from afar, everyone circled the child's bed and joined hands. Fr. Martin led them in prayer. Shadows flickered and danced wildly when the candles sputtered, casting dim light about the room like phantoms trapped in a cave. Fr. Martin prayed with passion, beginning slowly and speaking in a hushed tone. Soon he was pleading. Tears streaked his cheeks as he begged and cajoled the Holy Spirit to descend on the child and save her soul from the evil spirit of the snake. Many in the prayer ring looked frightened and wide-eyed while others resolutely held their eyes tightly clenched as Fr. Martin's oratory led them to an emotional peak.

"Jesus...." whispered Luis, but the professor nudged him to be quiet.

"Bring the snake to her," ordered the priest. His eyes burned like coals and his hands shook.

Snake? thought Luis and David at the same time, alarmed. Their eyes met.

The professor stole glances at the floor and look about uneasily.

Luis bent to whisper in David's ear. "I don't want to see this...let's go."

But the professor stood riveted. "Be still and watch," he urged. "You can tell your kids about it some day. I'm not leaving until it's over." He continued to look around furtively as goose bumps rose on the nape of his neck.

An old man had left the prayer circle and returned with a snake. He held it firmly behind the head with one hand and by the tail with his other. The snake appeared mature—about three feet long—and the professor's knees wobbled and he held his breath.

"Jesus...." muttered Luis again, looking to locate the front door.

The old man released the snake's tail. It hung limply for a dangerous moment, then began to writhe and jerk. It opened its mouth, exposing two curved, menacing fangs, and Luis felt the professor jerk beside him. The candlelight glittered on the fangs, but the old man squeezed tighter and it closed its mouth. The professor expelled his breath. The old man grasped the front of the snake's head, pinching its lower jaw and snout tightly together, and offered it to the small girl. But she turned her head and whimpered.

"What the...." Luis stammered, appalled.

Fr. Martin touched the man's arm to volunteer his services, and the old man turned to offer Fr. Martin the snake. The priest said another short prayer, then took the child's hand in his. Everyone in the room held their breath as Fr. Martin bent and bit the snake's head while it jerked convulsively.

"Incredible...." breathed the professor.

Luis could have sworn the priest's eyes rolled back into his head. "Told you he's *loco*," Luis repeated, shaking his head in disgust.

The old man took the snake back outside to be placed in a pit. If the child died, the snake would be released because its evil spirit had won. If the child lived, the snake would be eaten, its evil spirit neutralized and cast out.

"He's good," said David, motioning for Luis to follow him outside.

"He's got balls is what he's got…or he's *loco*." Luis shook his head.

"No…he knew it would work."

"What do you mean?"

"He looked at the girl's leg and it wasn't swollen. The child isn't in shock, either. The snake didn't inject any poison. Sometimes snakes don't inject poison into an animal that's much larger than them. He could tell the girl hadn't been poisoned."

Luis' face lit with understanding and he nodded agreement. "You're right," he agreed, reluctantly, "he's good. But the wrong snake got bit. Good God, *gringo*, he's a priest! How can he do that?"

"Luis, the Catholic Church has never had problems incorporating the beliefs of primitive people. They just turn their heads. I can give you a hundred examples in Africa, New Guinea…even here in Mexico. How many Christmas parades in small Mexican towns have you attended that celebrate the tradition of Christ being born in their own town?"

"None."

David ignored his answer. "Well I've witnessed several, and I can give you more examples in South America where…."

"Don't bother," Luis cut him off, "I'll take your word for it. Uh oh…here comes the snake charmer." Luis turned to watch the bearded, sandaled priest approach.

"Gentlemen, I hope I didn't alarm you with the short ritual. Sometimes one must sacrifice convention for the expedient in order to demonstrate faith and the power of the Holy Spirit when working with the unsophisticated."

"Save it for the Indians, padre. It's about what I expect from you now."

"Luis!" the professor interrupted. He shot the *federale* a "back off" stare, then stepped forward to greet the priest. "Very interesting, Fr. Martin. I'd like to discuss it more with you later. It was an intriguing…no…a breathtaking experience," he corrected himself.

"What about the donkey?" Luis affected a bored expression.

"We've been given a donkey by this man," the priest pointed at the house, "and I'll bring it along with me later when I return to camp. I've a few more minutes here, then I plan to go by the rancho we stopped at earlier to see the Garrazas and their daughter if that satanic bitch is gone, that is," he added. "Don't wait up, gentlemen. The car will be safe here. Can you find your way back by yourselves?"

Sure," said Luis, taking it as a challenge.

"Uh…I guess so," said David, hesitant, looking at the night sky and thinking of snakes and scorpions and other heat-seeking critters waiting to find his bedroll. "When do we leave?"

"Bright and early. Get a good night's sleep, Professor Wolf. Tomorrow will be a very difficult day for you."

"What about you?" Luis' statement stood like an accusation.

"Captain, God has blessed me. I need little sleep, and I have much to do tonight."

"More snakes to bite?"

"Please, captain. I know you don't like me, but don't let it affect your good sense. You shouldn't make fun of things you don't understand."

"Yeah, Luis," agreed the professor. Then to the priest he said, "Thanks, padre, and thanks to the man who lent us the donkey." He offered his hand to the priest, who shook it, but Luis declined and turned to walk the dirt road toward camp.

"Come on, *gringo*. I'll hold your hand if you want."

"An irritating man, your friend the captain," said Fr. Martin, glaring at Luis' backside.

"Aw…he's not so bad. Luis has a rough edge that takes some getting used to."

"He's got some big surprises waiting for him in the mountains." The priest shot Luis an angry look. "He may not last the day."

"What does that mean?" asked David. It sounded like a threat.

"Nothing. Tell your friend to watch for bears. It would be a shame if one crawled into bed with him tonight."

The Garden of Gethsemane

The sun blazed. It radiated a steady stream of heat and hung like a blazing chandelier in the blue sky, watching the progress of the three adventurers and their donkey while they negotiated up, over and through a seemingly endless array of rock formations and canyons. The scenery was a spectacular collection of wind-eroded arches, mushrooms, spires, and other curious shapes that seemed familiar yet had no readily identifiable form.

"Didn't know it could be so hot this high up," complained Luis, already in a bad mood. His face and neck shone red with sunburn and his khaki shirt clung with sweat. He had slept poorly waiting for Fr. Martin, who didn't arrive until late morning after celebrating Mass with the Indians, and then the priest and David had talked philosophy all morning while climbing the trail. With no book learning or formal education, Luis felt excluded and a little miffed at the professor, who readily discussed Spinoza, Kant, and St. Thomas Aquinas in between frequent gasps of air.

The trio had agreed on a method: thirty-minute hikes followed by fifteen-minute rests until noon, then thirty minutes for lunch followed by the same pattern in the afternoon. At fifty-two, David thought himself to be in remarkably good shape, but after a hard trek uphill beneath a relentless sun he was ready to quit for the day when they stopped for lunch in the shade of a mountain. Luis fared a little better, but struggled also. Fr. Martin, a Tarahuamara Indian who had spent his whole life at high altitudes, showed no sign of fatigue.

Luis pulled David aside when the priest went to relieve himself. "Quit encouraging him with that philosophical blather, *gringo*. That guy's head is too big as it is. I can't think for all the noise coming out of you two."

"He's a brilliant man, Luis, and he knows...."

"He's *loco* and you know it," interrupted Luis. "Remember that snake stuff last night?"

"Aw, Luis. You're so suspicious sometimes."

"Look, David. This may just be an archaeological expedition to you, but I'm looking for a kidnapper." He poked a large finger in the professor's chest. "Don't forget it. If you want to help," he shot a furtive glance in the priest's direction, "get that guy talking about politics or his brother. Maybe he'll slip up and tell us something."

"Why don't you ask yourself?"

"Because he's a liar and hates my guts, that's why. I'm warning you, *gringo*, don't get too close to this guy."

David frowned and wiped his forehead, too tired to argue more. He plopped heavily onto the ground and leaned back against a towering rock wall that sheltered them from the sun. Shade was at a premium this high above the tree line. A narrow wisp of stream glittered far below. Soon they would be moving through this narrow, rocky pass and descend into the valley before crossing the stream and moving eastward, up and over another mountain wall and down into another valley. The donkey wasn't much to look at, but had plodded along without complaint. It stood stoically and fully loaded while they munched on corn tortillas and black beans.

Fr. Martin returned and reached for the bag of tortillas.

"Where did all the shade go?" Luis asked idly. "Must be the worst part of the day to be climbing a mountain."

"We're above the tree line. The air's thinner up here," volunteered the priest.

"I noticed," said the professor. "I hope I won't hold you two up later when I have my stroke."

"We'll be sure to put lots of heavy stones on your grave so the animals can't dig you out," offered Fr. Martin, cheerfully. "Actually, you appear to be in quite good condition."

"I try. Say, padre…I've been meaning to ask. Do these jade stones come from the same place as the cliff dwellings? Is there a mine near the ruins?"

Fr. Martin seemed troubled by the question and so he rephrased it. "Are the stones mined at the ruins? No, the green stones come from farther east…probably along the Rock River somewhere. Mike might know. Why?"

"Well, that makes sense, I guess," the professor sighed. "I took some core samples from a stream at the mouth of the Aguila Canyon and they contained trace particles of jade. I don't remember seeing anything called Rock River on the map."

"It isn't on any map. If I remember correctly, three small rivers empty into the Aguila Canyon in the area in which you refer," said the priest. "The easternmost river flows from Rock Canyon, but only in the rainy season. Usually it's a dry gulch."

This reminded Fr. Martin of something, and he pursed his lips as if deep in thought, then said, "Tell me, professor. Are you familiar with the Archaeological Antiquities Act?"

"Yes…I have to be. Unfortunately the laws are not as strict or wide in scope as they need to be."

"How so?"

"Enforcement is lax and problems of definition abound in the law. In most cases it's difficult to prove that an artifact has been looted from a specific site. Forgeries are everywhere and sold openly, and most customs officials are not trained to distinguish what's real and what's a commercial fraud."

"What about the archaeological sites themselves?" asked the priest. "What sort of protection do they have?"

"We're doing better there. The Act established a committee of academics from several universities to review requests for site protection and make recommendations regarding the designation of 'National Treasure' for an archaeological site."

"Do you know anyone on this committee?"

"I'm on the committee."

"Really!" Fr. Martin clapped his hands. "How convenient."

"In what way, padre?"

"Professor, I'm sure that you'll want to have these ruins designated a National Treasure."

Luis couldn't keep quiet. He had to say something. "What's in it for you, padre? How can that help you?"

Fr. Martin, loath to talk with Luis, frowned and looked away. He thought to ignore him, but said, "Development."

"Development?" Luis didn't understand.

"Building the Aguila Reservoir will dam up several major rivers, causing irreparable damage to the Lost Canyon area. It will also result in the wholesale development of property, which will eventually affect the ruins. The Indians will be removed and their land sold from under them. Whole villages will be destroyed and the families dispersed. It will be the end of the Raramuri."

"What about all the jobs and the…."

"Jobs and land development equate to the destruction of Indians, captain.

148

But I don't really expect you to understand," he condescended. "Even if you won't listen to me, maybe you'll listen to your friend here."

"Pompous asshole," muttered Luis. He shot the priest a gangrenous look. "So that's why your brother kidnapped the diplomat, huh? And all by himself. Seems like a lot for one guy, especially if he's a harmless little religious ascetic living off the land. Think he had any help?"

The conversation was beginning to heat up and David paid close attention. Fr. Martin, looking uncomfortable, shifted his weight to the other leg and reached for his rosary. "What does that mean?" He looked away, evasively, but he had caught Luis' inference.

"Most kidnappings, especially those motivated by politics instead of money, are the result of a plot by two or more people. What we need to discover is the other person or persons that helped plan and execute this. Frankly, padre, I don't believe for a second that your brother did this all by himself. There's got to be at least one other person involved." Luis stared him straight in the eye. "And he's probably around close by," he added.

"Perhaps so," Fr. Martin, looked away again, "but you would know more about that sort of thing than me. I'm just a country priest." He suddenly stood to go, already having revealed more than he intended and having said more than he should.

Good God, he's lying! thought the dazed professor, who had watched the whole thing. *But which part? Who is he trying to protect? Surely he's not involved; he's a priest.*

David looked to Luis, who had an "I told you so" smirk on his face. The professor raised his eyebrows and nodded slightly to acknowledge that he had seen the same thing. Though unclear what he had witnessed, Fr. Martin's discomfort was very visible.

"I think my back's locked up, we better get moving," said David.

"Yes, professor," the priest agreed absently, a troubled expression on his face. "Today is the hardest day and we have far to go. Tomorrow we follow the river deep into the canyons and we'll make better time." Fr. Martin had a distant look in his eye. He took the donkey's halter rope and led the animal down the winding path into the valley. Luis and the professor followed.

The philosophy discussion had ended and the two men resolutely trailed after the robust priest, breathing heavily and concentrating on their next step. As the day waned and the sun crested the western mountain wall, Luis and David marched numbly and exhausted, struggling to keep up. With the donkey in tow, Fr. Martin had gone ahead, oblivious to the others and now substantially distant from them. He showed no sign of slowing.

"Bastard's trying to punish us," growled Luis between pants. "Hope he breaks a leg."

"No...he's thinking about what you said. He's changed somehow. Did you see the look on his face when...."

"David, he's *loco*! Can't you see that? Smart people can be just as crazy as everyone else. This priest is a dangerous man. I'm not going to let him out of my sight and you shouldn't either. He's using you for something...something to do with archaeology and saving the ruins."

They struggled along, slipping and stumbling, their feet blistered and heavy backpacks rubbing them raw. But neither was willing to quit. That would allow the priest the satisfaction of gloating, and so they followed obediently, each silently reviewing his own situation.

The professor reconsidered Luis' assessment of Fr. Martin. David had been caught up in a fantasy regarding the ruins and had ignored the problem of Fr. Martin and his story. What really bothered David is that the priest seemed as anxious to give up his brother to the *policia* as he was to give the ruins to the professor. Why, all of a sudden, had Fr. Martin decided to give up his brother, reveal a family secret, and who knows what more could be expected? Why did the priest act so uncomfortable when answering questions about the jade mine? Had he lied about the mine? If so, why? What was his real motivation—the Aguila Reservoir? Or, as Luis had stated so simply, was Fr. Martin crazy and motivated by something obvious only to himself?

Imagining that blisters were rising on the nape of his neck, David groaned and shifted his uncomfortable backpack to adjust its carriage. The trek had become unbearable, so he faded out of reality, imagining he had returned to Mexico City and that he and Alexandra were visiting the floating gardens of Xochimilco. The scent of flowers on a cool breeze held him mesmerized and he began to fantasize, plodding along, placing one foot after the other.

Fr. Martin's mood had changed from joy and exhilaration to depression and despair. How had it happened? he asked himself. He knew the answer, though, and remembered when it had occurred—after the fight with Mike. The encounter had left him angry and bitter and with a sense of loss. It was an old paradigm; high expectations with low realizations, leading to depression. The *federale* had been the catalyst for this spiritual crisis, he decided—always suspicious, always coming at him with a snide remark or an accusing, open-ended statement. He felt like he was being pursued by one of Satan's couriers of guilt and temptation. Luis had tricked him into talking, and Fr. Martin had fallen face-first into his simple little trap.

His inner voice, The Beacon of Wisdom that guided him unerringly, fell suddenly mute and dark. Fr. Martin felt frightened, aware that something was terribly wrong in his life. The Light and Voice had always pointed the way for him, but now he reacted blindly, based on his decision to betray Mike and the location of the ruins in order to save God's Plan. God had revealed His design to Fr. Martin, hadn't He? What had once been firm and vivid was now illusory and ephemeral. When celebrating morning mass, he had been shocked to discover that the familiar sense of awe and reverence he always experienced was absent when the wine and bread became the Body and Blood of Christ. Why? he asked again. Hadn't he always followed the Inner Voice of God? Now the Voice had gone strangely quiet. The priest felt that his soul had fallen into a cold void with no boundaries and no place to anchor, a spiritual free fall. He jerked the donkey's halter rope and gripped his rosary with his free hand and began to pray feverishly, stepping in rhythm as he climbed the winding mountainside. But his prayers became distracted by images of Mike moving in and out of his consciousness, breaking his concentration and feeding a growing torment.

Fr. Martin quickly realized his deficiency. He was no longer in a state of grace. He had sinned, and guilt rode him like a burden of stone on a swaybacked mule. Fear joined with guilt and grew like a malignancy. His breathing came quicker and he wanted to run.

But why guilt? Why? Then images of Mike presented themselves as proof of his shame. He saw himself and Mike as their conspiracy unfolded: planning the bombings at the chemical factory, destroying roads and equipment and kidnapping the female. Mike was always the reticent, reluctant follower of the older, wiser brother, and now Mike's image appeared to the priest as a silent accuser who had abandoned a flawed calling. The superstitious, unlearned brother now held the higher moral ground.

But I did as You wished! he screamed silently at his God. *I followed the path You laid for me. I sacrificed everything for You! Tell me, please*, he begged. *Send me a sign. Guide me, Lord Jesus. Remove this stain of guilt. Tell me what I have done and what I must do to seek Your forgiveness. Do not take Your Light from my life!* But his inner shadows darkened with the evening gloom and he wept quietly as he walked.

Fr. Martin led the donkey onward, never looking back to see how his struggling companions fared. The sun slid behind the western canyon wall and evening shadows grew long and ominous. His mood continued to fail when no resolution presented itself, and a shadow coated his mind like chimney soot. He slipped into a numb panic.

The donkey began to jerk its head in protest, and once stopped entirely before Fr. Martin became aware that the day was done and his companions far behind. He cast about for a likely spot to spend the night, then began to set up. Working silently and making good progress, he had a fire going when Luis and the professor stumbled into camp.

David slumped with fatigue and had a glazed look in his eyes as he trudged into camp, but Luis was near choleric and sullen. The *federale* layed his rifle against a boulder and threw his backpack onto the ground while glaring at Fr. Martin. Luis wanted to lash out at the priest and put him in his place, but he held his tongue upon seeing the priest's tear-streaked face. *Good God! What now?* the *federale* wondered. A grown man crying openly like it was nothing. This guy really was crazy.

The priest would not respond to attempts at conversation and acted as though his companions didn't exist. Luis and the professor exchanged curious glances while they ate cold beans and tortillas again. Their camp lay high above the canyon floor on the mountain's east side. They stared into the fire, unseeing and listless from extreme exertion. Only the crack and pop of the flames disturbed the pacific evening, and the night air grew chilly as the full moon spewed cold fluorescent rays into the valley. Fr. Martin, now muttering to himself, stood abruptly and walked uphill into the gloom, disappearing from sight.

The professor yawned and stretched. The fire mesmerized him and he wanted to go to sleep. Luis, however, remained wide-awake. When Fr. Martin didn't return, the *federale*, always suspicious, went in search of him. He returned shortly and whispered urgently, "Come on. You've got to see this."

"Can't make it, Luis...too tired. Go away." David eyed the tent.

"Come on...just for a minute."

The professor groaned and tried to stand and straighten his back. "You go ahead. I...."

Luis hissed again and gestured urgently.

When the tired archaeologist had finally straightened himself, Luis held a finger to his lips and motioned for David to follow. He led them uphill and around behind a splatter of boulders. He pointed upward. The professor followed his finger until he saw the shadowy profile of the priest in the moonlight above on a rocky crag. Fr. Martin on his knees, hands folded in prayer, his head tilted upward into the heavens. Tears streamed from his eyes and his face was as a mask of torment.

"Good, God," whispered David, but Luis shushed him. They watched silently as the priest prayed and wept, sometimes cajoling, sometimes begging his God for forgiveness. Occasionally a snatch of words or anguished syllable broke the stillness. But David grew tired of watching and felt embarrassed to be spying on the priest in such a private moment. The scene seemed eerily reminiscent of Christ's passion in the Garden of Gethsemene before his crucifixion. The professor shivered.

"Let's go. We don't belong here."

"Go ahead. See you in a bit. I've got some thinking to do." Luis stared churlishly at the priest. He turned again to the professor. "Told you he's *loco*."

David waved him off and stumbled down the mountain to his tent and sleeping bag. *One thing about these guys*, he thought. *You never lack for entertainment.* He lay in his bag, finally comfortable, nearly asleep, his eyelids like lead. *What a pair*, he thought. *One of them crying and praying and the other spying and scheming.* Then a wonderful silence cloaked him and he became oblivious to the deep insistent ache of his body. He went limp, his mind blank and he breathed shallow and slowly.

The earthquake struck at dawn. The donkey, sensing the impending disaster, had begun braying and jerking at its tether. Moments later the tremors hit, starting with a slow jiggle, moving through the earth in jolts. And then a loud whine pierced the air as the mountains groaned and shifted. Wave after wave swept the ground like towels rippling and snapping in the wind. Frightened and groggy, Luis and David were thrown against each other inside the tent. Frantic and confused, they struggled to exit the tent opening, but kept slipping and falling. The roar and crash of falling rock filled the air as pieces of the mountain dislodged, sending errant missiles and huge boulders sliding and rolling to the distant valley floor, causing landslides up and down the canyon. The ground shook for a full thirty seconds, but it seemed an eternity to the terror-stricken men in the tent.

David couldn't breathe and his legs wouldn't hold him. He fell twice, called to Luis for help, then finally made it to his hands and knees. He lunged through the opening, leaving Luis inside the collapsed tent, struggling like an insect in a web of silken honey.

Then it stopped and the professor could breathe again. His heart felt thick and pounded slowly and painfully. Stumbling, he went to help a shouting, furious Luis from his polyester trap.

"Luis! Luis! It's an earthquake."

"*Hijo de chingada*! *Cabron*! Get me out of here!" yelled the *federale*. "David…where's the door to this…."

"Here…here…hold still, you big ape." The professor grabbed a piece of the tent wall, found the entry, and helped Luis shed the collapsed polyester confinement.

"Jesus!" exclaimed Luis, panting, his eyes wild. "You okay?"

"No…yes…guess so," gasped David. "That was like Mexico City in '85."

"Yeah, I remember." Luis plopped to the ground, his legs weak from fear and his breath coming in short gasps. He took several deep breaths to calm himself, then surveyed the canyon from where he sat. Below them, a film of yellow dust floated like a thin cloud over the canyon.

"Where's that crazy priest?"

"Oh, Lord," said the professor, jumping to his feet. "When did you last see him?"

Luis pointed above. "Stayed until I almost fell asleep. He was there when I left."

They left at once and headed up the mountain to the rocky overhang where they'd last seen him. A rockslide blocked the path, and they had to circle around to approach the line of boulders from where they had hidden to spy on Fr. Martin. But the big rocks were gone. The terrain had changed; the jutting balcony had collapsed and broken free and slid down into the valley.

"Fr. Martin!" called David. "Fr. Martin! Are you okay?" They searched frantically all along the mountainside.

"You didn't hear him return to the camp?"

"He was there when I left," repeated Luis, pointing to the missing ledge. "Let's go down and look."

"*Chingada*! You don't think he was in the slide, do you? He wouldn't have prayed all night, would he? Nobody can pray that long." David talked nonstop as they carefully picked their way down to a large mass of debris and rocks.

"Look!" Luis gasped, holding up a broken rosary. "He was in it!" His eyes followed the trail of devastation until they rested on a pile of rock below. Quickly they slipped and slid down the gravel-strewn mountain until arriving at the canyon bottom. A bloody, twisted leg with a torn sandal protruded from the slide.

"Oh, God...." choked the professor, squatting, then looking about frantically. He began to dig, throwing and casting aside the rocks.

"No, over here," directed Luis, "he's over here. Careful, David. If he's not already dead, we'll kill him trying to save him."

Hastily but carefully they moved rocks and debris until the priest's broken body lay exposed. His limbs were horribly twisted and blood seeped from an unknown wound.

"He's dead," said Luis.

"No...look, his eyes are moving!" Indeed they were. Blood-red and frightened, they darted chaotically, looking first at David, then to Luis.

"Can you talk, padre?"

Large tears had pooled in the priest's eyes, and he whispered, "How bad?"

"Bad," replied Luis, "real bad." He looked away.

The priest's eyes moved to David. "Tell him to leave," he whispered.

"Huh?"

"Tell him...to leave," he gasped. "No time...argue...please?"

Luis couldn't stand to watch anyway. He had seen much mayhem in his life, but this was hideous: twisted arms and legs, protruding bones and the priest's face a mass of purple and red. He was a dead man. The *federale* walked away, overwhelmed, and fell to his knees and retched.

"Hear my confession," the priest struggled to whisper.

"I'm not a priest...I can't give absolution...Father, you've got to hold on," pleaded David.

But the priest stared beyond him at the rising sun. "Beautiful...." he croaked, and a crooked smile came and went. Flecks of blood appeared on his lips and his rasping breath came shallow.

"My fault...did it all...Mike innocent."

"What?" The professor bent to hear, holding an ear close to the priest's mangled face.

Fr. Martin hesitated, gathered his strength and said, "I did it all...Mike's innocent...bombs, kidnapping, everything."

"You did it?" The professor asked, incredulous.

"...Mike innocent," the priest repeated. "Protect him from...captain. Luis...not...understand," he gasped, and pain twisted his face into a rope of agony. Luis returned and stood grimly watching.

The priest closed his eyes momentarily when a tidal wave of pain drenched him. They fluttered open again, and he stared at David. "Tell him...tell him...love him...my brother...."

"How?" asked the professor. "Where are the ruins?"

The priest said nothing, then closed his eyes.

"Where?" pleaded the professor. "How far?"

The eyes opened again and Luis knelt. "Follow river...north...all day. Go east side of falls...." he coughed, then moaned pitifully, his saliva thick with blood and bubbling into froth on his lips. He whispered. "Cross mountains to...side."

"Which side?" interrupted Luis.

"East." Blood began oozing from his right ear. "Follow new stream to hot springs...warm water...west of stream...hidden beneath a wall of rubble."

"But where...how will we know if it's hidden, padre?"

"Beautiful...." said the priest again, feeling the aura of death coalescing around him. He never spoke again, and he watched the progress of the orange globe rising above the eastern canyon wall. And then he died, his eyes wide open, staring in death at God's eternal promise of renewal as it slowly crested the canyon wall and bathed him in a grisly, revealing light.

"Let's bury him, David." Luis had a ghastly expression on his face. "He's dead."

"What are we going to do, Luis?" The professor acted as if he hadn't heard.

"We're going to bury him, then we're going looking for that waterfall."

"And that's all?"

"That's enough...you okay, David?" The *federale* watched his friend anxiously.

The professor stood and looked around. He spotted the polyester tent on the ridge above, but the donkey had disappeared. Their adventure had turned into a disaster. He looked at Luis, and then at the priest. "Yes, you're right, I guess." He looked north into Cactus Canyon and considered its sheer walls and forbidding terrain. "Well, let's start piling them on."

"Piling what on?"

"The rocks...got to keep the carrion eaters from his body."

Luis shivered. "Sweet Jesus," he said, walking to the nearest pile of stone. He took a deep breath and said, "Ready?"

"Sure, guess so." The professor reached to catch the stone Luis tossed, followed by forty or fifty more piled on top of Fr. Martin in the shape of a cross.

Luis looked approvingly at the grave, and then turned to go. "You can say a few words if you wish, David. I'll break camp."

"And that's it, huh? That's all there is?" The professor stood stricken with sadness.

"That's all there is for him, *gringo*. We're still alive. Say a few words and let's get out of here."

Disaster

Upstream at the ruins before the disaster, a red-orange haze had presaged the dawn and forced the night shadows to flee, revealing harsh lines that gave shape and definition to the canyon and ruins. The warmth of dawn had fallen on an intimate tangle of arms and legs; Ruth and Mike, naked and comfortably entwined as only lovers can be, enjoyed the sweet exhaustion of carnal exertion. The ground had felt firm and smooth beneath the blankets and the hot spring percolated a constant, soothing whisper.

After a night of passionate love, short naps and more lovemaking, Ruth had discovered that, at least for now, she couldn't fall asleep inside the ruins hidden beneath the cliff. Her cabalistic imprisonment had created a sickening dread and insomnia replete with fleeting, wakeful nightmares. Horrid phantoms and unknown terrors lurked on the periphery of her dreams. It would be some time before she could sleep inside a protective enclosure again.

After the sun had set, Mike had led the way up into the ruins with a torch. Upon seeing two hammocks in the sleeping room and imagining a stygian darkness of hell when the torch died out, she had asked if they could please sleep outside, under the stars. With only a star-studded dome for a ceiling, the warmth of the coals and the hot springs would coax her toward tranquility and sleep. Her phobia had probably saved their lives.

It began with a pitiful, low moan from the jaguar, which turned into a threatening, low-throated growl of protest. Mike's eyes flew open but he remained still, reluctant to disengage himself from the welcoming thighs and warm, soft breasts of his companion. Both were semi-awake and listening when the first tremors rippled through the ground.

"Uunh...." said Ruth responding slowly, disengaging from Mike. "What's going...."

But Mike moved quickly from under the covers and had just gained his feet when the first jolt rocketed through the canyon and knocked him to the ground. Ruth cried out and floundered helplessly on the ground as waves of energy equal to several hydrogen bombs surged from the earthquake's epicenter and spread throughout the northern Sierra Madres. The roar was deafening, like a hellbound locomotive, its throttle locked on full as the earth cried out.

Crack! Like a cannon shot, the limestone cliff-face above the ruins fractured. At the far end of the canyon, a huge chunk of limestone overhanging the ancient city collapsed in a hail of boulders and inundated nearly half the cliff dwellings. Visibly fractured, the remainder of the overhang seemed held in place by no discernible force. It appeared ready to collapse at any moment, threatening to fall and destroy the remaining half of the ruins.

The earthquake lasted only thirty seconds, but seemed an eternity to the naked lovers when being tossed about and struck by flying debris.

The earthquake ceased as suddenly as it began. They lay gasping with hearts thundering. A cloud of dust and grit rolled from the foot of the landslide, and a thin cloud of dust rose halfway up the canyon walls and hovered above them like a ceiling of dirty glass.

Naked and stunned, Ruth stood while Mike gasped for air. He reacted slowly, as if just waking, but gained his feet and stumbled toward the shattered ruins at canyon's end. His face was stricken with disbelief as he walked to the far end of the canyon where the landslide had destroyed and buried the ruins. Halfway there, the western wall shifted inward and a muted roar leaked from within as the gold mine's ceiling and walls collapsed. A billowing dust cloud belched from the one remaining entry, as Mike stood mute and watching, his personal universe changed in one fell moment.

Still naked, he walked the north face of the canyon to inspect the damage. Half the ancient town had vanished beneath a blanket of limestone and shale rubble. The remaining overhang appeared cracked and ready to fall at any moment. He stared helplessly, hands hanging impotently. The ancient city had stood virtually untouched for a thousand years, but now was half buried with the remainder threatened with the same. With the collapse of the gold mine, the entire topography of the narrow canyon had altered. As he watched, spring water from within the mine gushed from a jagged slash in the mountain and ran in a steady stream toward one of the tombs partially buried in the rockslide.

Ruth, meanwhile, located their clothes, discarded for last night's lovemaking, and quickly dressed. She felt guilty, like an errant child caught in a forbidden act. Finished dressing, she scooped up Mike's pants and carried them to him. Naked, his face long with anguish and his broad shoulders sagging, he accepted them wordlessly, slowly put them on and cinched the drawstring at the waist.

"Mike, the spring quit moving." Ruth saw that the stream had ceased to flow and its surface lay placid.

Alarmed, he trotted to verify her claim. Quiet and serene, the waters were inching downward into the reservoir, exposing the worn walls of its rocky container. A look of utter sadness and defeat gripped him. He dropped to his knees and silently sobbed like a man who believes he has lost everything.

Ruth, overwrought and confused by the quake, nonetheless recognized how much the canyon with its hot springs and ruined city had meant to him. Now it lay in ruins: a Garden of Eden destroyed by nature's wrath. She bit her lip and thought of what to say. The quick terror of the quake had left her weak but with only a few scratches and bruises. She would heal, unlike Mike who had been dealt a mortal wound to his spirit. She walked and stood close to him, looking down into the spring, feeling out of place. Words could not restore the pristine beauty of the canyon and the aged city. Helpless to give solace or mend the hurt that infected his soul, she just stood quietly and available to offer support.

Mike sat by the pool and stared with numb indifference. Bright sunlight flickered like diamonds on the pool's serene surface and Ruth could see the glint of pooled tears in his eyes. He maintained a stoic silence as the water sank even lower. Soon the water hid from the sun and became a dark cavity of unknown depth, its walls worn smooth from thousands of years of upwelling geothermal water. For eons it had flowed down the gentle canyon slope through a waterworn trough and trickled beneath a wall of debris and rock before finding its way into the stream outside the box canyon.

"I've got to leave a while," he said, looking up at Ruth.

"What…where are you going? What will you do, Mike?"

He shrugged. "Think about things. Maybe I'll go see my brother…who knows?" He stood, gave her a bleak smile, then turned and walked toward what remained of the ruins. He stopped in the shadow of the overhang and looked up to study the spider web of fractures. Much of it was eclipsed in shade and he couldn't tell how badly it had been damaged.

"You probably should stay out here where it's safe. I'm going to move my belongings. It will take a day or two to get organized, then we can leave."

Leave? she thought. The unspoken had been voiced. Impulsively, she blurted, "What about me, Mike? I'm sorry about…about this, but I want to go home." She felt terrible saying it, afraid that he would see it as desertion when he needed her most.

He looked toward the rubble, and then again at her. "Yes." He hesitated, considering her loss from his life also. "I'll take you to Batopilas and you can contact the *policia.*" Then a look of apprehension crossed his face and he gave her a furtive look.

"Mike…I won't tell anyone…I promise," she reassured him. "I would never tell anyone about you or this place. I'll make up something."

He considered her statement, then said, "Do what you want. It doesn't matter anymore…nothing matters." He turned and disappeared into the shade of the cliff.

Oh, Lord, she thought, *I'm going home, it's really going to happen!* She roiled with conflicting emotions: elated yet guilty, hopeful but apprehensive. But it wasn't over, she reminded herself. Batopilas was days away and anything could happen. She turned again to look at the empty pool, then in the direction Mike had disappeared. Suddenly the ground shuddered as a mild aftershock rippled through the mountains.

"Mike!" she screamed, fear jerking at her gut. She spread her legs to brace for another tremor, but none came. She remembered where he had gone and ran toward the ruins, worried that he might be killed if the cliff collapsed.

"Mike…Mike!" she called, running to where a ladder leaned against the dwelling walls. She had a foot on the bottom rung when he appeared.

"Don't come up! It's too dangerous." His eyes were wide and flashed a warning.

"Get out…you'll be killed," she pleaded.

"I'm not leaving without my things. Go away." He turned his back to her.

"I want to help."

"No, it's too…."

"Please…it'll go faster." She crossed her arms stubbornly. "I'm not moving until you let me help."

He groaned, but then said, "Okay…just a few things. Get off the ladder and I'll toss them down to you." He left and reappeared with arms full. Standing at the edge, he threw baskets and packages of goods to her while she scurried back and forth with them out into the canyon. They worked feverishly, pausing only for another frightening aftershock, then finished up.

A large assortment of goods, jewelry, tools and household items lay piled near the spring. Mike stood debating where to store them. After more sorting and repackaging, he decided to use a room in one of two entrances near the east end of the ruins where the overhang had not collapsed. Four openings into the mountain, two on each side of the ruins, were visible from the hot spring and she assumed the gaping holes were simply entrances into another mine. When she asked, he shrugged and changed the subject to eating.

They prepared a quick meal of tortillas and beans and ate in silence. The food seemed dry and tasteless and neither had much appetite. Ruth inquired where the jaguar had gone, but Mike ignored her. She then tried to offer condolences about the earthquake, but to no avail. Stoic and laconic, he avoided her eyes and grunted terse replies. Occasionally he grasped a gold jaguar pendant at his neck and stared far away. Finally he stood and walked to the west end of the canyon again to see the damage.

He climbed up and down the rockslide looking for a place to begin. The decision made, he began tossing rocks aside, intent on clearing the rubble from the selected area. He soon tired and decided to reenter the mineshaft from the central room in which Ruth had been imprisoned. From there he would have access to the other tunnels. But upon investigating, he found it collapsed and full of rubble. Disappointed, he returned to the rockslide and began to carry stone away.

Mike worked slowly and methodically for nearly three hours as she watched. The jaguar returned from wherever it had gone, and lay watching in the shade. Occasionally she yawned and exposed ivory teeth, or licked her fur clean of dust. When Mike showed no sign of completing his task, the jaguar laid her black head on the ground and slept a restless sleep.

Ruth attempted to have Mike stop and rest by bringing him a gourd of drinking water. He would drink, say "thanks," then return to his mysterious undertaking. He seemed worried and intent on an important task, but refused to discuss it with her. He worked tirelessly, his lithe body sleek with sweat and his muscles rippling with exertion. But like the jaguar, Ruth grew tired of watching, and as the afternoon began to dwindle, she drifted away to explore the canyon on her own.

Just as Mike had tried earlier, she went to the mine entrance and shaft leading to the central room, but the thought of what lay inside caused her to shiver and she abandoned the idea. Instead she walked unheeding along the narrow canyon, examining it in detail for the first time. Birds chirped a late afternoon conversation and the sun had dropped behind the western peaks.

Short shadows grew long as she inspected every hidden nook and sought out every stand of mesquite and every grove of hemlock before finding herself at the gravelwalled entrance at the east end of the canyon.

The barrier rose nearly twenty feet and extended almost thirty in length. Narrower here, the canyon walls appeared sheer and towering on either side of the canyon. Tall hemlocks stood vigilant on each side. A sudden impulse seized her. Freedom lay on the other side. She glanced furtively for Mike, and, not seeing him, scurried over the wall, slipping and sliding as she climbed. Reaching the top, she looked back into the box canyon, then slid down the embankment. Her heart beat a rapid solo and she felt guilty, but exhilarated to be out of the four-walled canyon. A persistent sense of daring pushed her to keep going, and so she looked around for a place worthy of exploration.

Where the spring's well-worn water path met the gravel wall, it spread into a fan-shaped trickle and seeped downhill in tiny strings before dropping three feet into a narrow, rocky stream that meandered through towering forests of madrone and hemlock. The water trail was still moist, but only its path remained now that the spring had died. Soon there would be no trace, and the last clue to finding the canyon and its ruins would disappear. Ruth walked along the stream's bank. Despite the earthquake and half-day spent moving Mike's belongings, she felt lightheaded and unburdened, knowing she had narrowly escaped a close encounter with disaster.

She looked down into the clear water and experienced a small surge of joy upon seeing the enormous number of colorful rocks in the streambed. She knelt and reached into the water, but jerked back in surprise. The water felt warm. High in the mountains the water should have been icy cold. Why would the water be warm? She stood and walked alongside it, pondering the question. The stream, she realized, had damp banks, yet flowed only a trickle. Then suddenly she understood. Whatever had caused the hot spring in the canyon to die had also killed others in the area. The stream's water had diminished because hot springs fed it, and all must have stopped flowing. This caused a sense of foreboding. What had happened? What had caused the hot springs to die?

"Ruth."

She jumped with fright. "Mike!" she gasped, stumbling as she whirled to face him. "You scared me to death."

"Why did you leave? I've been looking...."

He saw the stream, or what remained, and jumped from the gravel wall and ran to the bank. He looked upstream, and then walked its edge, stopping twice to inspect areas where water no longer seeped into it. If not for the runoff from the violent thunderstorm two nights ago, the stream would be nearly empty.

"What's going on?" She sensed his fear and shivered, hugging herself tightly. "Why did the springs dry up?"

His shoulders sagged. "The mountain is sick and dying. An evil spirit has stolen its soul. We must leave soon."

Ehhh? Ruth thought. *The mountain is sick?* But she saw that he was sincere, and choked back a sarcastic retort. *He really is an Indian,* she reminded herself. *He believes that nonsense.* She knew it probably had something to do with geology, but as to what she didn't have a clue. She had taken a class in physical geology twenty years ago, but could recall nothing about hot springs and only little regarding earthquakes. She remembered Love Waves, one of three types of earthquake waves that traveled through the earth's crust. A cute name, it had been easy to memorize for the test. But Mike's reaction of dread and fear fueled her own anxiety and she felt a sudden urgency to leave—now.

"Mike…why don't we just leave? I'm scared."

"Tomorrow," he said. "I'm moving things tonight. We'll leave tomorrow."

"What things? We can move your belongings into the cave right now if…."

"No. This is different…and they're not caves, they're tombs."

"Tombs? You mean like dead people?"

"Great leaders of the Jaguar people, the ancients who built this city. Their graves are holy and must be protected. When the mine collapsed, water poured into the tombs."

His mood changed without warning. "Come back inside," he ordered sternly, turning and walking to the gravel-walled entrance, climbing up and over without waiting to see if she followed.

"*Sieg heil*, Herr Himmler," she growled, petulantly. Her patience had grown thin with this place and she angrily followed and climbed the wall. Her hands, arms and knees were all bruised and scratched and she had long since bitten her nails to the quick when a prisoner in the mine. She scrambled down into the shaded canyon and brushed dust from her clothes and arms while inspecting herself for damage. Mike strode toward the west end of the canyon to the rockslide. Feeling lonely and useless, she again sat by the empty spring and stared down into its black, bottomless depths. A loathsome melancholy depressed her and she sat listlessly, dejected and thinking, *Got to get out of this place. Got to get out of here.*

A reddish-brown female grizzly bear, Ursus horribilis mexicanos, slowly waddled upstream with her three-hundred-pound cub in tow. Like all grizzlies she had poor eyesight and hearing, but earlier she felt certain that she had detected the rancid odor of a human animal. It must have been a trick. The scent had fled and it had been futile to follow the winding uphill stream.

She moved ponderously from a summer of feeding. The instinctive seasonal urge toward lethargy and the need to hibernate tugged at her constantly now. If not for the playful antics of the cub, she would already be in her cave. The earthquake had driven her into the forest, bellowing in frenzy and calling for the cub, but when nothing more occurred she had spent the day foraging in the brush. The aftershocks had stopped and the stink of humans had disappeared, so she wandered about aimlessly, hoping that her nose would lead her to a meal.

The cub raced past her and the sow reluctantly followed, unknowingly passing the entrance to the box canyon as she walked downstream. Irritated and tired of following her offspring, she changed course and disappeared into the shady gloom of the forest. She stood on her hind legs, extending almost eight meters, and grunted a warning to the cub. Feeling drowsy, she lay down beneath a rocky crag, wallowed in the pine needles and dirt to arrange her bed, then placed her head on a broad forearm and waited for the cub's return.

Although the night air felt chilly, the tomb maintained a constant ambient temperature. Mike loaded gold artifacts into twine baskets and threw them over his back to transport to the other end of the ruins. He had opened and rearranged another tomb to make room for the new arrivals: three Jaguar kings and their burial furnishings. This tomb had been partially destroyed and the landslide had covered its entrance. He had spent the whole day and most of the evening laboring to uncover the entrance and clear a passage into the burial chamber. Fortunately, the tomb had been placed to the side of the cliff dwellings and therefore spared the bulk of falling rocks.

Fatigue was a constant companion now, and a growing uneasiness gave him gooseflesh and shivers. Moving the bodies and belongings of the Jaguar Kings was not an enviable task. The souls of the dead hovered near. He could sense them, and each piece of gold carried to the other tomb increased his anxiety and sense of doom. Mike was unsure why he felt compelled to undertake this, but knew it was of no benefit to anyone if the godkings lay entombed so that the living had no knowledge of their existence—past or present. The grave serves as a visible symbol of eternity in the afterlife, not death. It represented their culture and belief system. The tomb promised continuity between past and present, and the souls of the dead would become angry if they remained entombed and ignored.

Midnight had come and gone. He had declined making love with Ruth, but had done everything he could to soften the impact of his rejection, holding her tightly until she had fallen into a restless sleep. The seriousness of his task took precedence over his own desires and the wistful wants of the white woman. Mike could think of nothing but the Jaguar Kings and their huge store of gold statues, shields, weapons, and jewelry. Respectfully moving three mummified bodies without damaging them had been the major task, but upon successfully placing them in the east tomb, he had decided to move everything—gold, furniture, statues and pottery—in order to be done with it. The water damage from the spring was significant and another earthquake might collapse and seal the tomb forever.

Completing this task before returning Ruth to her people would give him peace of mind. It had been a mistake to bring her to the sacred ruins, and he wondered if their ancestors' spirits had expressed their anger through the earthquake. He should never have listened to his brother. Despite his intelligence, Martin had failed to learn many important things; even though their father had done everything possible to instill a sense of awe and understanding of the earth's forces in his oldest son. But the Jesuits at the mission had had their way with him, teaching him the word tricks of philosophy and novelty of science. Martin was proof that a keen mind had little value if intuition was muted by intellect and arrogance. Returning Ruth would give him more time to accommodate the changes taking place. This way he could plan for himself and the ruins. His future lay inextricably entwined with the ancient city: they were each part of the same spiritual clay.

Two more loads remained and then he could seal the tomb and rest. It was nearly 2:00 a.m. when he finished, bone tired but mind simmering with activity. He had accomplished plenty, but much still remained. He would return Ruth to Batopilas, a three-day venture at best, and talk with Martin. Although he felt justified in abandoning Martin's plan, he felt guilty for striking him. He loved Martin, his only relative, and couldn't imagine not having him available as a source of solace and quiet empathy. Unfortunately their last several meetings had been rancorous and weighed heavily on his mind.

Upon returning to the bedrolls near the fire, he found Ruth awake and staring into the flickering coals. She had awakened and waited patiently until he finished. The black cavity of the hot spring loomed close by, a reminder of the early morning earthquake. He sat next to her and aimlessly tossed pebbles into the yawning blackness. A slight breeze blew cool against his bare skin, and he groaned audibly as he unlaced his sandals and fell back onto his bedroll.

"I couldn't sleep." Ruth inched closer to him. "I watched what you did."

He looked at her curiously and said, "You watched, but you don't understand what or why I did it."

"Tell me...teach me," she said, reaching for him. The blanket fell away, exposing her breasts, two perfect ovals with large brown nipples.

"I'm dirty...I've been working," he warned.

"You smell like a man." She reached for the drawstring on his pants, but he caught her hand.

"Why are you doing this?"

"I told you...I can't sleep and you smell like a man."

"That's all?"

"Yes...that's all." She met his gaze straight on.

He encircled her with his arms and laid her back onto the bedroll. Silver moonlight sparkled in her eyes and illuminated the pearl white of her breasts. He looked into her eyes and cupped a breast, then gently traced a circle around its nipple until it contracted and grew small and hard. He lowered his mouth to the other and began to suckle it.

She shivered and groaned and her legs parted reflexively. He reached for her furry nexus and gently cupped and caressed the pouting lips. She sighed and reached again for the drawstring on his pants. He shed them quickly and knelt between her legs, his erection fiercely unbonneted and swollen with desire. He hesitated, tickling her inner thighs with his fingertips, delaying the love stroke until one of them was nearly delirious with passion.

"You will never forget me," he said, lowering himself to enter her.

"Yes...and I think I never will know you."

He plunged into her like a diver parting the water, unable to control himself, lost in an unbridled passion.

She locked her legs around his waist and stared glassy eyed into the star-spangled sky, concentrating on ripples of pleasure that became waves of bliss. He moved against her rhythmically, coaxing her toward the rapture that would cause her soul to temporarily flee the body. Suddenly she went rigid and climaxed, jerking and trembling uncontrollably before going limp. Her big toes curled upward.

Mike moved urgently, seeking his own release from the swollen, rising excitement in his loins. Then he arched into her and his hips pounded a staccato until his own cataclysm seized and held him enthralled.

He rolled aside, spent and utterly exhausted. It had been a physical release, pure and simple—no word of endearment, no love pats or bites, no love at all. He had used her and she had used him. When he turned to look at her, she stared wide-eyed into the sky.

"You okay?"

"Yes." She rolled away, discouraging conversation. "I think I can sleep now."

A Fateful Day

The professor sniffed, then twitched. The hiss and crash of cascading water created a steady, relaxing sound and produced an airborne mist that floated on a light breeze. He sniffed again to make sure. Yes—the aroma of freshly brewed coffee riding a wispy morning draft to his nose. It titillated his consciousness, and he was unsure if he was dreaming until the bittersweet fragrance became stronger and he awoke. Luis had brought the beverage in his pack, and it smelled rich and dark. David salivated with anticipation and attempted to rise from the ground, but couldn't. Every joint in his body had locked up. He felt more stiff and sore than he could ever remember.

After two nightmarish days of climbing up and over mountains, then down into endless winding valleys with thick forests, they had followed the stream as Fr. Martin instructed when he lay dying beneath the avalanche. The waterfall, which had very little water cascading at its apex, stood sheer and impenetrable. A deep pool of clear water lay at its base and David, exhausted from three days travel over paths unfit for mules, had stripped and dove into the pool—much to the chagrin of Luis who, of course, was a city boy. He yelped his disapproval and reached for his rifle, muttering of snakes. The water revived him and David did the breaststroke and taunted the *federale* to join him.

Upon arriving yesterday, they had searched for a path Fr. Martin had assured existed, but both sides were daunting, and the cliff escarpment on the west offered no hope of scaling without professional equipment. The eastern wall appeared slightly better, though still intimidating. It was climbable, but rose nearly 400 meters: a rugged, gruesome-looking cliff face that sent shivers up the spine and weakness to the knees. Both felt a sense of dread, and the professor sat on his bedroll and frowned while Luis tossed stones and psyched himself up.

Their situation did not invite envy. Fr. Martin, their guide, was dead. Only twenty percent of their supplies could be transported because of the missing donkey. In their exhausted condition it would require a Herculean effort to successfully negotiate the cliff.

"Need some help?"

"I can make it," said David, still trying to rise. "If I can just sit up...."

"Here." Luis offered a hand. "Don't be so proud. It took me half an hour to get out of my bedroll. You'll feel better once you're moving around."

"Thanks." The professor accepted a hand and held tightly as Luis yanked him to his feet. The academic groaned, straightened himself and attempted to stretch.

"Good Lord...don't think I've ever been this sore before." David tested every joint for tender muscles and ligaments. He had so many aches that he couldn't lift an arm or leg without a body part protesting.

"I need to check into a hospital."

"You'll live." Luis poured him a cup of coffee. "Better get tough, *gringo*. We're going up that cliff this morning." Luis' face held an expression of grim determination, as if he had been studying the wall all morning.

The professor accepted the proffered cup, then followed Luis' eyes up the jagged, layered wall of limestone and chert. He shivered. "Maybe we ought to go back."

"What? And not find those cliff dwellings you're salivating over?" Luis teased, knowing that David would not turn back.

The professor smiled wanly and stretched again, but didn't argue. Luis was right. There was no turning back. They had come too far to quit. David didn't know if he could find his way home anyway, and the return trip would be just as treacherous. His body, however, still protested, and when he looked at the eastern escarpment for a possible trail along its face, his stomach did somersaults. Yet the only path lay up and over the cliff. Luis and David: two men on the same trip but obsessed with different missions.

Since yesterday's earthquake and Fr. Martin's death, a full realization of the seriousness of the endeavor had come home to roost. It had been foolish to leave Batopilas without telling anyone their plans. Neither wife knew their whereabouts and David had convinced Luis not to inform his superiors of their plan. In retrospect he recognized it as the type of foolishness one would expect of the young and inexperienced, not two middle-aged professionals.

He thought again of the ruins as Fr. Martin had described them and a stoic resolution fixed his face. Time to get moving. In archaeology, luck awaited no one. The relentless aspirant became the achiever of academic acclaim. David gathered his things to pack and break camp. Something would happen today—he felt it. A strong sense of intuition gripped him and a sickening foreboding caused his adrenaline to surge. He turned to see Luis, who was gazing back into Cactus Canyon. With rifle held in both hands, Luis scowled and craned his neck, then climbed a nearby boulder to look further back into the valley.

"What is it?" asked David.

"Nothing...thought I saw something." Luis jumped down and walked past the professor to appraise the eastern cliff wall. He laid the rifle on the ground, sighed audibly and frowned.

"It's probably just the donkey."

"Yeah...probably. Some Indian will sell him or eat him." Luis looked toward his friend. "If I could catch him, I'd shoot him." He retrieved the rifle again and threatened the phantom in the valley, then joined the professor in striking camp. Luis doused the campfire with the remaining coffee and finished his pack. He checked the slide action on his .45 automatic, slid in a clip of shells and firmly holstered it. He reached for his rifle.

"Let's do it," said Luis. "This is a red letter day. If we make it over this wall without getting killed, we'll find that Jaguar Feroz character and the diplomat."

And the ruins, thought David. The ruins were why he had come. Why did this discovery have to be complicated by politics and murder? But his intuition remained firm and his sense of foreboding intensified. He shivered, looked at Luis and said, "I'm ready when you are, captain. Lead the way."

Ruth awoke before dawn. She had slept fitfully, spending the night recalling all that had occurred the last two weeks. It was an incredible tale, she decided, and swore to write it all down if and when she made it out alive. *If*, she reminded herself, the conditional word. Mike had promised to begin taking her back today, a three- or four-day trip. Unable to sleep for the excitement, she had risen early to prepare. She found, however, that little could be accomplished without him, and so she aimlessly walked the perimeter of the box canyon, thinking of what might happen when they reached Batopilas. In the early morning light she saw the hazy outline of the tomb in which he had placed the bodies last night. Next to it lay the one in which he had stored his belongings. Curiously, he had not allowed her inside, preferring instead to take things from her hand at the entrance and carry them himself. She hadn't cared. Entering another cave was the last thing she wanted to do.

The big cat had left sometime during the night, but she saw that it had returned. It lay on the first floor of the cliff dwelling watching her every step. Racing tingles still sped up and down her spine when she saw the beast, but two days of its coming and going had inured her to any real feeling of threat.

She forced herself to look away and walked toward the avalanche at the west end of the canyon where her prison had once been. Skirting the foot of the debris, she walked toward the tomb entrance Mike had spent the afternoon and evening uncovering. It was now only a black oval hole, but seemed threatening, and a sudden fright visited her. She looked above at the fragmented overhang, seeing fine web-like cracks in the limestone. She began a slow retreat, sensing the imminent danger of falling rock.

Strong hands gripped her from behind and she cried out. "Mike!"

"Ruth. What are you doing?"

"Jesus, Mike! You scared me to death." She went limp. He released her.

"I didn't mean to scare you. It's dangerous over here. You should stay at the other end."

"Yeah…sure." She brushed hair from her eyes. "Well, are we still on for today?"

"Are we still on for what? What do you mean?" He seemed genuinely confused.

"Are we still leaving?" she asked, patiently. You're not going back on your word, are you?" A fear that he would renege flashed through her mind, but she didn't dwell on it. She knew him well enough now to know that he kept promises.

"Yes…about noon. I have a few things to finish here, then we'll travel as far as the waterfall this evening."

"The waterfall?" She didn't remember any waterfall on the journey from the train. "Are we taking the same route as last time?"

He eyed her curiously, then said, "No. Our path will be longer, but safer." He motioned with his head. "Come on. Let's eat and make ready." He turned and walked away, expecting her to follow.

Yes, let's eat, she thought, feeling a familiar hollow in her stomach. Since being kidnapped, she couldn't remember not feeling hungry, and the fare Mike provided did little to satisfy her craving for rich, fatty foods. She looked at the length of twine that served as a belt for her pants. Her waist had shrunk six to eight inches in two weeks, and skin hung loosely from the backs of her arms. She appraised her thinness and decided she liked the new look—a lot. The plumpness of middle age had disappeared and she felt strong and supple from endless hours of swimming in the mine.

A sure-fire way to get rich with an exercise/diet plan, she chuckled quietly, following his steps to the front of the canyon, excited at the prospect of returning to civilization. She felt alive and exuberant, nearly giddy with anticipation.

"Why are you laughing?" he asked.

"Oh…nothing. Just a private joke." She took his arm and coaxed him forward. He allowed himself to be escorted, and very quickly they rekindled the comfortable intimacy that had served them so well.

They shared a sparse meal of crumbling tortillas and a knobby, onion-flavored white root. Their meal completed, they began to pack for the journey to Batopilas. Mike's mood had shifted perceptively. His depression had changed to a reluctant acceptance of events and he, too, seemed anxious to depart.

Ruth felt a stirring of passion watching him move and listening to him talk. She recalled the intensity of his passion during last night's lovemaking and the coldness of her response afterward. It had been the low point of their relationship, and she thought to say or do something in a gesture of reconciliation, but then decided it would only embarrass them both.

When they were packed and ready, he stood next to her and together they surveyed the ruins one last time. His arm fell naturally to her waist and she laid her head on his shoulder. It was a somber moment, and Ruth again reflected on the incredible events that had brought her here.

"It's really over, isn't it, Mike? For both of us, I mean."

"Nothing is really ever over, Ruth. What we see or do is with us forever. Even when the soul leaves the body it carries the sum total of our knowledge with it. For you things are changing, but for me it's all the same. Even though the earthquake destroyed my home and you are leaving, I will not change. But your life, I think, will never be the same again." He bent to retrieve the webbed bags of goods and slung them across his shoulder. "But that can be good…and in your case, it probably is. Come on," he said, extending a hand, "let's get you home."

Luis lay exhausted on the ground after scaling the cliff wall. The professor lagged twenty feet behind, beginning to fail badly. His strength was waning and he gasped for air. His grip trembled when he searched for a handhold on the mountain and his legs burned and shook. One error in judgment and he would plummet to his death.

He had been a half hour on the wall, an incredible effort for a fifty-two-year-old man, and felt as if he might expire at any moment. His heart beat a staccato and his arms tingled through the ache. Scratches and bruises covered his arms and knees but he ignored them, intent on the prize above: the top of the cliff. He glanced below and a sickening vertigo caused him to swoon. He leaned into the mountain and held tightly, looked above and began to climb. His left foot found purchase and he shifted his weight to see if it would hold. It did, so he pulled himself up, then repeated the action, his effort focused only on the mountain and his body. He couldn't go down. If he didn't reach the top, he was a dead man.

"Come on, David. You can do it," encouraged Luis, looking over the edge. "Come on."

"Shut up, Luis," growled the professor.

"Huh?"

"Shut up. Don't talk to me…I'm concentrating."

"Just trying to help…."

"Shut up and go away." The professor took another step and pulled again, paused to make sure that his hold was secure, then took another step.

Luis bit his lip, unable to watch the slow, painful progress of the archaeologist. Midway through his own climb up the wall he, too, had finally realized the foolhardiness of this middle-aged adventure, and the thought of losing his friend drove him from the edge.

"Luis…give me a hand," came a gasp from below.

The *federale* rushed to cliff's edge and lay down, extending an arm to the white-faced academic. His large fist engulfed the professor's. He squeezed tightly and pulled with all his strength, slowly dragging his friend over the crest of the cliff. One final tug and David looped a leg over the top and pulled himself over.

They both lay panting, considering the enormity of their accomplishment.

"I'll never go anywhere with you again," gasped the professor.

"Oh yeah? You're the one who said you would come with or without me."

"I said that?"

"Yes."

"I must have been crazy," panted David.

"Yes."

"Yes, what?"

"Yes, you're crazy…but so am I for listening to you."

They rested an hour in a copse of shady madrone pine. The professor ached and his legs trembled, but he felt surprisingly good considering what he had just put his body through.

Luis, ten years younger and stronger, recovered quickly, anxious to be off. He looked about, wary, searching the shadows. They had entered the land of The Fierce Jaguar and must pay very close attention. Neither knew the distance to the hot springs or cliff dwellings. Furthermore, Luis didn't have a plan if they did find the Fierce Jaguar at the ruins, a sobering realization requiring serious thought. Everyone had relied on Fr. Martin to resolve the issue by guiding them to the ruins and convincing his brother to release the diplomat. Now they must accomplish both without his help.

They agreed to follow the stream and hope to find the hot springs. Luis would go first and David would follow. The creek wound through heavy forests of hemlock and pine within a peculiar valley of high walls and sheer palisades. Lush foliage, trees and an abundance of wildlife made it seem a miniature Garden of Eden: eerie and strangely incongruent with the surrounding mountainsides that had only juniper and cactus in rocky soils void of water.

Luis took off his gun belt and handed it to the professor.

"Here…you might need this."

"Luis, I haven't shot a gun in years."

"Yeah…but at least you've shot one." He stood to go, but David sat looking at the pistol, turning it over in his hand, a shocked expression on his face.

"I told you this was dangerous work, *gringo*."

"But I'm an archaeologist, not a cop," pleaded David.

"Today, you're not. If I don't get this Jaguar Feroz guy, then you don't get your ruins, do you?"

The professor reluctantly belted on the gun. "I guess I hadn't really thought about it that way."

"Think about it, David? You better not be thinking of anything else until it's over. Understand?"

"Yes…I understand." David withdrew the pistol, jacked a shell into the chamber and reholstered it. He sighed. "Let's go, *macho*."

The Attack

Barely visible patches of pale blue sky leaked through the forest canopy. David traipsed slowly through the trees fifty feet behind Luis, but on the other side of the meandering streambed, heading slightly up into a mountain forest. Thin, cool air swelled his lungs, and sections of the forest canopy limited visibility to ten or twenty feet. The climb up the wall had left him bruised and fatigued, but he resolutely placed one foot in front of the other and tried to pay attention. Luis insisted that they maintain this pattern of stalking the priest's brother: one on each side of the stream with the professor fifty feet behind, as more territory would be covered in this manner. A skilled woodsman, the Indian had an intimate knowledge of the wild canyon country. He lived here and they were trespassing. They must find him before he found them.

David frequently lost sight of Luis, and the oppressive shade and gloom of the forest fueled his earlier premonition. Danger seemed to lurk in every darkness and shape, only to be exposed as a rock, limb or natural object. His fear of being surprised and unprepared grew with each moment and he sometimes left the forest to look for Luis and assure himself that all was well. They had agreed to meet at the stream every ten minutes in order not to separate, and so far their meetings had been uneventful. They had discovered no springs or cliff dwellings—indeed, nothing but birds and scurrying rodents. Luis' nose had led them to the spoor of a large animal, but both agreed it wasn't human.

The more David thought of the gun and the jaguar man, the more certain he was that he had crossed a line and stepped out of his element. His hand touched the checkered wood handles of the .45 and it felt strangely disparate, as if it didn't belong on him. Its steely hardness reminded him that he should be carrying his wood-handled rock hammer instead of allowing it to dangle from his backpack. *A gun-toting archaeologist*, he thought, and a shiver wracked his body. He picked up his pace, spooked by the darkness and his mission, when a distinctive *snap!* disturbed the heavy quiet of the forest. He stood rigid and tried to identify the direction from which the sound had come. His adrenaline surged and he could hear his own heartbeat, but nothing more. A minute of waiting only produced the sound of his breathing.

Unable to stand the suspense, he bolted for the stream, trying to restrain himself from calling out to Luis, whom he felt sure had continued to walk upstream while David stood scared and unmoving in the trees. Upon arriving he glanced at his wristwatch, then upstream to make sure Luis hadn't witnessed his embarrassing retreat from the forest phantoms. *Ah...* chingada, he cursed silently, standing streamside, feeling abashed. *Get a grip, David*, he chastised. Christ...he'd almost jumped out of his skin. He looked at his watch, then upstream for Luis. A rendezvous was scheduled in three minutes. He was contemplating a slow jog to catch up when he noticed the bare, eroded ground of what had once been a narrow channel of water flowing from the forest. He had nearly passed by, but years of field archaeology had honed his ability to notice the trivial and unimportant, especially those related to rock and dirt. His eyes followed the path into the forest, and he saw that it had once carried a substantial flow of water, but was now dry. Forgetting his fright, he stooped to test the center of the eroded channel: a mixture of silt and fine sand. When he poked his thumb two inches into the soil he found damp earth.

He rolled it between his fingers. Why would water be so close to the surface? Was it the result of the storm three days previous, or just a well-worn path for runoff? Somehow he didn't think so. At this altitude water would evaporate quickly, and mountain soils were notoriously porous and dry. But then again, this ecosystem was like no other he'd seen. A lifetime of considering similar cause and effect dilemmas took over and he followed the water trail up into the forest. Twenty yards into the trees the incline became steeper and the water trail branched out. He pursued the wider source trail and arrived at a rocky limestone bowl with a dark hole approximately one meter in diameter.

He stared quizzically, his lips pursed, and then like so many times in the past, he understood. It was a spring, or used to be. He examined the area more closely and a flood of thoughts begged for attention. Fr. Martin had said to look for hot springs flowing from beneath a wall of rubble in the area of the ruins, but this one wasn't flowing, although it must have recently. The wet core of the path remained as proof.

Could it be Fr. Martin's spring? Springs flowed most of the time, didn't they? But then why had it stopped? He tried to recall his geology, and finally decided that they didn't always flow. They were dependent on rainfall, ground water level and such things. This probably wasn't the area to which the priest had directed them.

Disappointed, he glanced at the time and jerked with alarm. He had missed the assigned meeting and Luis had gained nearly ten minutes on him. David would be left behind! He bolted for the stream, his backpack swaying in rhythm as he stepped off the distance. *Damn it anyhow*, he berated himself. If they became separated, Luis would really be upset. The professor was becoming a liability. He jogged to the stream, and the effort left him breathing heavily. *Chingada*! He couldn't remember when he hadn't been tired. He walked briskly, ignoring the forest and his assignment as he tried to locate the federale as quickly as possible.

As he moved upstream, a persistent sense of having missed something important tugged at him. What was it? he wondered, irritated, and glanced at his wristwatch. They were scheduled for another meeting in five minutes. Would Luis wait, or come looking for him?

The stream turned ninety degrees, became narrower, and the water flow decreased visibly. The forest wall extended to the bend in the river and blocked his sight. He stood on a rock and leaped to the west side. Gaining his balance, he stopped to adjust his backpack and get his breath. The rustle of brush and a grunt startled him. He turned toward the sound and gasped!

Thirty yards ahead, a bear cub had wandered from forest's edge. Farther upstream, Luis was kneeling in the midst of shallow cataracts to fill his canteen. A huge grizzly sow had spotted the *federale* between herself and cub and she tore from the underbrush to protect her child. Luis was unaware of the bear's charge, but when he stood he spotted the cub and David at the same moment. The professor stood motionless, almost catatonic, before finally screaming an alarm.

Luis turned to look behind and saw the bear. The grizzly stopped short, awkwardly raised herself on hind legs to a full height of eight meters and began walking toward Luis, bellowing in anger. Luis' gun lay on the stream bank. He turned to flee but the bear pursued him with lightning speed. A sweeping claw caught him on the back and lifted him airborne, depositing him in the middle of the creek. The water began to turn crimson, and the sow bellowed in rage while Luis cried out and jerked spasmodically. He crawled, tried to stand and fell.

David finally reacted. Drawing the .45, he shouted and waved his arms wildly, running toward his friend. The bear sow had waddled forward to finish Luis off; David's charge startled her. She barked an instruction to her cub and the two bolted for the cover of the forest.

Luis again attempted to sit up, but fell into the water face first, mortally wounded. The professor holstered his gun and hauled his friend to the bank where he could see his wounds. Luis had a vacant expression and his eyes were glazed, but he didn't complain about pain. Blood steadily oozed from his back. David turned him to his stomach to strip off the *federale's* shirt. This elicited a groan and yelp, and Luis fought to gain his feet. The professor cursed angrily and physically restrained the bigger man. When Luis finally lay still but groaning on his stomach, David stooped to look.

He nearly gagged. Beginning at the spine and shoulder, the flesh had been torn and hung like a bloody rag. His scapula, the bone of his shoulder blade, shone white and pink. Blood flowed profusely, staining scarlet the gravel bank and streaking the water. The professor had never seen such a terrible wound in his life and had no idea how to stop the bleeding. He felt completely helpless as Luis' life slowly trickled onto the soil. With a grim expression he dropped and opened his backpack, searching for something to stop the bleeding. Luis jerked and called out something unintelligible, and David turned to see what disturbed him. A pair of sandaled feet stood next to his friend, and David looked up into the face of a Fr. Martin look-a-like— except it couldn't be. The priest was dead! The jaguar man, Mike, had discovered them. Next to his side stood a white woman with a look of horror etched on her face. She bit her fist and stared at the gaping wound on Luis' back. One tear streaked a grimy path to her chin, but she quickly wiped it away and took a deep breath.

"He'll die if you don't get some mud on it," said the Indian.

"Huh," said the stunned professor, expecting a bloodthirsty murderer.

"I said he'll die if you don't put some medicine on the wound."

David collected himself, tried to hide his surprise, and added, "I don't know how to do that. Do you think you can save him?"

"No," said the Indian." He looked at David for the first time. "Martin sent you, did he?"

The professor hesitated. "Yes…I guess you could say that…your brother sent us." He looked toward the woman, whom he assumed to be the kidnapped diplomat, but she stood, wide-eyed and mute by the bear's carnage.

He pleaded with the Indian. "Help us out and I'll tell you all about your brother, okay? This man is my best friend."

"It's him...that jaguar...."

"Hush, Luis." The *federale* had tried to stand again, but the professor pushed him down. David looked imploringly at the Indian, then back to Luis.

"He's the *policia*, isn't he?" said Mike.

"He's a man, like you and me, and he's going to die if you don't help him."

"He'll die anyway...if not today, soon."

"Please," pleaded David. "Your brother said you're a medicine man."

The woman approached Mike and, much to David's surprise, took his hand and muttered something.

"You're sure," he asked the woman. "He may not die for three or four days."

When she nodded her acquiescence, Mike turned to the professor and said, "Help me pick him up." He stooped to help the wounded Luis to his feet.

"Where to?" asked David, then saw the woman already leading the way. With Luis' good arm strung over his shoulder, the Indian followed the woman across the stream to a very large pile of rubble. She crouched, then began to scramble over the hill.

"I'll need some help," he said to the professor.

"Where are we going?" David asked, dismayed. "He'll die if we don't do something quick." He moved to his friend's other side and helped lift him. They half-walked, half-carried Luis, staggering over the entrance into the box canyon.

When they reached the other side, the professor's eyes grew wide in astonishment. The ruins! Finally. He had found the cliff dwellings, and the excitement of the moment nearly caused him to lapse into an academic mindset. But a groan from Luis returned him to reality. They lay him down near an empty spring and Mike walked and entered what appeared to be a cave entrance before returning with a basket of cloth, herbs and plastic bottles.

"Start a fire," he said to no one, beginning to work on Luis' back. The woman moved first and David followed, feeling useless. His mind raced. Everything had happened quickly and he'd had no time to adjust. He tried to make conversation.

"Are you Ruth Johnson, the American diplomat?"

"Yes." She gave him a weak smile, bending to pick up firewood and hand it to him. "And you are…?" She laid two more small pieces in his arms.

"Uh, David Wolf," he stammered. I'm…"

"You're not a Mexican…are you a cop?"

"Oh no," he gestured toward Luis, "my friend is the cop. He's a Captain of the Federal *Policia* from Chihuahua. I'm an archaeologist."

"An archaeologist?" She stopped and looked at him, nonplussed. "They sent an archaeologist to look for me?"

"Well…no, actually, you see…."

"Hurry up over there," called Mike, "you can talk later."

They quickly finished gathering wood and returned to build a fire and boil water. Mike stanched the bleeding and spent much time cleaning Luis' massive injury. The *federale* faded in and out of consciousness, groaning and shivering, and cried out when Mike washed the wound with an astringent of hot water and packed it in a poultice of smelly herbs. He then prepared tea from Belladonna leaves and insisted that Luis drink. Mike explained that Belladonna, a powerful narcotic, would substantially ease Luis' pain. His ministrations complete, they moved the *federale* into the shade of the overhang.

It had been only an hour since the bear's attack, but Mike said he could do no more. Now they would wait for Luis to live or die. If he made it through the night, they would give him more tea for the pain. The bear had broken Luis' shoulder blade and the terrible wound would surely fester and become infected, and then gangrene would set in if fever and blood loss didn't kill him first. His wound was such that if he didn't receive treatment within twenty-four hours, the infection might advance too quickly to contain.

"He's tougher than he looks," said David, swallowing a lump in his throat. "He saved my life once." He became maudlin with emotion. His fatigue, events of the last two days, the earthquake, Fr. Martin's death and the bear's attack on Luis now overwhelmed him. He slumped to the ground. They might as well be in a foreign country on the other side of the world. Although a return trip was possible in one hour by helicopter, it would take at least three or four long days to reach Batopilas on foot, and David realized that his friend probably wouldn't last more than a day or two before succumbing to the inevitable infection. He knew that Mike had done all he could. And now the professor wanted to cry out at the futility and injustice of life, but felt too tired, and so he stood and walked to Luis. He peered closely at Luis' wound and saw that it could easily cause death. A large lump grew in his throat and he sat next to his friend, resigned to the inevitable.

Ruth pulled Mike aside and engaged him in a hushed, heated conversation. She gestured emphatically as she talked, but Mike frowned and shook his head in disagreement. He started to argue with her, then abruptly walked away and stood above the *federale*. Ruth glared at his back and looked as if she wanted to push him over a cliff, but she would not be so easily put off.

"Tell him, Mike," she demanded, hands on hips. "Tell this archaeologist and his friend that you refuse to help them. You told me you'd never hurt anyone in your life."

"It's okay," said David, trying to calm her. "What else can he do? It would take three to five days to get him to a hospital. It just isn't possible."

"But Mike can...."

"You're an archaeologist?" Mike said with sudden interest.

"Uh...yes. I'm a teacher at the National University in Mexico City."

Ruth stepped between them. "He can help you," she said to Mike. "If you save his friend, he'll help you. I know he will. Won't you?" She turned to the professor for confirmation.

David didn't understand why she pressed so insistently. The Indian had already done more for Luis than he could have. Why was she badgering him for a miracle? Everyone was stressed, but he supposed that she had suffered more than anyone. He tried to be patient with her.

"...er...ah...Ruth, I appreciate your concern for Luis, but it would take the intervention of God to save him now. I think Mike has...."

"No! No! No!" she huffed emphatically. "You don't understand. Mike can run to Batopilas in six or seven hours. Can't you, Mike?" Her eyes dared him to dispute it. "You could direct a helicopter back to pick all of us up."

David felt suddenly dizzy, and realized that he was holding his breath. *Carramba!* Was it was true? Mike was a Tarahumara and many of them were incredible runners. He looked at the lean, muscled frame of the jaguar man. The guy had shoulders and legs like a stallion. His long muscles bulged like the weave of thick rope and rippled in cords when he moved. He looked like entrant in an Iron Man contest: but six or seven hours of running over mountains? Was it really possible? No one could run up and down mountains for seven hours, could they?

"You've done it before, haven't you, Mike?"

The Indian looked at his sandals, embarrassed. "He's probably going to die," he repeated, but the conviction of his earlier pronouncement was lacking. "Anyway...they'll throw me in jail when I get there."

"No they won't," interjected David. "They don't even know we left

Batopilas or where we went. Honest. I could send a letter with you. Why…" he stuttered, seeking the right words, "…why you'd be a hero, Mike. Your brother made it clear that none of this is your fault. He told us that you had nothing to do with the bombings. He said that…"

"My brother came with you? Where is he? Why isn't he with you now?"

The professor looked at his boots, over to Ruth, then into the black pools of Mike's eyes. "He was killed in yesterday morning's earthquake. He died in a landslide. We buried him in the valley below the falls."

The Indian's shoulders sagged and he turned to walk toward the eastern wall of the canyon and the avalanche that had buried half the cliff dwellings.

Ruth and the professor watched his retreating figure.

"Oh, God," she said, looking miserable. "Now he probably won't do it." She sat heavily on one of the large stones near the spring and looked mournfully at the professor, then at Luis, who moaned and tried to shift his weight. "I don't know about you, but I can't remember the last time something good happened." She appeared on the verge of tears, but the look was quickly replaced with a hard expression. She glanced away, wanting to be left alone. "I don't think I'll ever get out of this place," she muttered.

David thought to comfort her, but didn't know what to say. "It'll be okay," had a superficial ring considering the misery she must have experienced the last two weeks. Maybe she just needed to be left alone. She must have found her own way of coping with adversity. He looked at Luis instead and recalled his robust features and gregarious mannerisms. He could visualize Luis' large hands moving as he talked and the many curious positions of his mustache, depending on his moods or facial expression, and the white teeth behind the wide joking smile. The memory saddened him and he felt mildly nauseous.

Deciding he couldn't comfort the woman, he strode off to find Mike, his eyes feasting on the ruins as he walked the canyon's perimeter. David joined him near the base of the rockslide. The Indian no longer shed tears, but an eternal sadness hung on him.

"Tell me," said Mike, "how can you save this place from thieves and developers? Ruth already knows about it. Now you know the location, and the earthquake has destroyed most of it." He turned to face the professor. "How can you save it?"

David thought quickly. He would have to be convincing, but honest, and he would have to tell the Indian something he really wanted to hear.

"First of all I know people…influential people. That isn't a brag, it's a fact."

"Go on," said Mike.

"I can ensure that the ruins aren't looted and that any graves in the vicinity are not defiled. I can arrange to have this landslide removed." The professor pointed to the obvious damage. "And…I might be able to arrange for you to be its caretaker." He hesitated, wracking his brain for something that might influence the priest's brother, but could think of nothing more. Finally he threw up his arms. "What do you want? Ask. If I can do it, I will."

"The Aguila Dam."

"What about it?"

"Can you stop it?"

He saw the serious expression on Mike's face, and felt tempted to lie, but sighed miserably and said, "No. Your brother asked me the same thing, but I told him that I could only protect the cliff dwellings by having them declared a National Treasure."

"A National Treasure?" The phrase rolled slowly off Mike's tongue as if he savored a delicious food. "What is a National Treasure?"

"An archaeological site protected by law. Money is budgeted to develop it and to…."

"Develop?" Mike seemed agitated at the word's connotation.

The professor grimaced. He must be more careful. "Repair…clean…restore, you know, beautify it." David emphasized the last word.

"Beautify," Mike repeated, "and repair?"

"Yes. I can see that the earthquake caused this damage. We can have it removed and the mortar work repaired. Then we can maintain it in good condition forever."

"Forever?"

"Yes. If it's a National Treasure, the Antiquities Council is required by law to maintain it."

The professor became hopeful. He had run out of promises and sensed that the Indian was reconsidering, perhaps on the verge of relenting and running to Batopilas. Mike could call Chihuahua for help and return with a helicopter for Luis. David shifted his weight to the other foot, looked about uncomfortably, and tried to remain patient while the Indian brooded. When the jaguar man walked away without answering, the professor was tempted to go to his knees and beg.

Mike skirted the landslide and stared into the empty tomb. He voiced a *shk…shk…shk* sound and a set of glowing, yellow eyes appeared. Then a large black jaguar walked from the darkness within.

David gasped and his anal sphincter nearly relaxed. First the bear and now a jaguar. A jolt of adrenaline fueled his fight or flight response and he turned to yell a warning to Ruth, but stopped when he saw the cat nuzzle the Indian. Together they rounded the base of the slide and approached the trembling professor.

"Where is Martin buried?"

David stood paralyzed, his eyes darting from cat to Mike and back to the cat. He saw that it had very large canines exposed beneath lips curled in a perpetual snarl. He had seen jaguars from a distance in the southern jungles, but never this close.

"She won't hurt you," Mike stated matter-of-factly, sensing his distress. "She's my friend."

"A day's walk from the falls...at the base of the eastern wall. You'll see the landslide," David croaked. "His grave is shaped like a cross."

Mike gave him a wan smile and walked to join Ruth by Luis. The cat followed and sniffed the air and growled when they drew close to Luis. The professor wanted to join them, but couldn't bring himself to approach the jaguar. He pretended to investigate the ruins and walked halfway down the slope, stopping short, but close enough to see what transpired. He did notice, however, that Ruth was unaffected by the cat, and when Mike spoke to her, she seemed to perk up. Suddenly she jumped to her feet and threw her arms around his neck. Mike hesitated, then returned her embrace, and the next thing the professor knew they began a slow, passionate kiss.

Hey! he thought, *these two aren't exactly strangers.* This thought led to another and he quickly discerned the nature of their relationship. *They're lovers,* he told himself. *He kidnapped her and now they're lovers. Go figure. What the hell's been going on up here?*

David was still trying to find the nerve to approach when Mike disengaged from the woman and began to stretch. The Indian shooed the sniffing, curious cat from Luis, then kissed the woman once more. She nuzzled his chest and they murmured endearments.

"How about that letter?" Mike called to the professor, stretching again. "Come on down. The cat won't hurt you."

David tingled with trepidation, but decided he would just try to ignore the jaguar. Besides, if the woman could do it, he could also.

"Sure," he replied with a confidence he didn't feel, inhaled deeply and said. "Let me get my backpack." He walked to the spring and retrieved his field notebook. He avoided looking at the cat and scribbled a message and two phone numbers for Mike to call upon reaching Batopilas.

"The first number is my wife, Alexandra. Call it first. Believe me. If she can't get a helicopter here in time, no one can. She has more connections than El Presidente. The second number is the American Embassy in Chihuahua. Call it last. Do not—I repeat, do not—call anyone in the Army or the Federal *Policia*. They'll fight over who has jurisdiction and some of them are powerful and crooked enough to plunder this place. Any questions?" He handed the letter to Mike.

"I hope they don't put me in jail," said Mike, his face creased in worry. He walked to Luis one last time, stopped to feel his forehead for fever, then searched for a pulse at the jugular. "Be sure and give him more tea when he wakes up." Then he waved a casual goodbye to the professor, lowered his head to receive a peck on the cheek from Ruth and walked toward the gravel-walled entrance. The cat followed, and together they climbed up and over.

Just like that, thought the elated professor. *No argument, no conversation and maybe he'll save us all. Can he really run that far, that fast?* He looked at his wristwatch. It said 3:34 p.m. and the sun was moving behind the western mountains and thick forests. Long shadows stretched thin and crooked, and the western end of the canyon was already cloaked in shade. He must begin his investigation of the cliff dwellings at once.

Ruth stared at the gravel wall, her face void of emotion. She sat on one of the large stones and absently toyed with a lock of hair.

Curiouser and curiouser, thought David, *but this isn't Wonderland*. He wanted to get her story and see what she knew about the cliff dwellings, but Luis groaned and shuddered in his sleep and David went to him.

"I'll watch him if you want to look around," she offered.

"Tell me what you know first," he asked, looking first at Luis then to the cliff dwellings. "We've got at least ten hours. Start at the beginning."

A Surprise Visitor

Late afternoon shadows stretched long and the creek bed outside the canyon now moved at a mere trickle. Mike glanced at the stream, then back at the rubble wall guarding the entrance. Hurt and despair hovered on the periphery of his mind like circling birds of prey. His home and playground of thirty years was threatened. Only the staid forest on either side of the stream appeared untouched by recent events.

Why Tata god and his wife had allowed evil spirits to desecrate and destroy the city of the jaguar people eluded him. What had he done wrong? Had his reluctant and ill-advised alliance with Martin resulted in this disaster, or did something subtler and not readily discernible lie at the root of the problem? How had he angered the spirits and why had he drawn their attention? Unlike his father, he had always felt particularly deficient in divining the intent of the supernatural or understanding the spiritual cause-and-effect of their sometimes-capricious behavior. Supernatural forces had caused this host of misfortunes—of this he had no doubt. His uncertainty lay in not knowing how to restore the spiritual harmony of his personal universe.

Perhaps Ruth had caused the calamity? Her soulful eyes and willing body had distracted him from his daily rituals and observances. By obsessing on her, his last year's abstention from passion had resulted in a reawakening of his body and a burgeoning carnal spirit that he had not thought possible. His thirst could not be sated, and after tasting the nectar of her love he dreaded her absence from his life. But it must happen. They were too different. Their spiritual and secular orientations stood in opposition.

With the death of his brother, Mike was now the last of his family. Although his mother might be alive somewhere, her ways had always been alien to him. Even though she had a strong passion for life, her commitment to children and husband had been noticeably absent early on, as if she had intuited that she would always be an outsider and that her children would remain with their father and live out their lives as primitives in the sierras.

Martin. His brother's name and image coursed through Mike's mind like the long roll and echo that precedes thunder in a stormy sky. Always a brilliant malcontent, the presence of his soul lingered angry and far from his body. Mike sensed him and felt cowed and somewhat fearful that his brother's spirit had come here.

He must go to Martin, he decided. It would be best to take the shorter route through Rock Canyon, but he felt the pull of Martin's grave and the need to calm and propitiate his brother's soul so that it would do no evil. Mike felt homesick already, here, standing outside the entry into the canyon, but bit his lip and stretched yet again in preparation for the long run. The archaeologist seemed to be a good man. Like most white people, he didn't seem to be very smart, but would do his best to protect Ruth in Mike's absence.

He continued to stretch the long muscles of his legs before beginning the grueling run to the white man's town. Beside him the jaguar issued a low-throated growl and stood tense, focused on something in the forest. She snarled and crept low in the brush and went into stalking behavior. Mike shushed and coaxed the jaguar back to his side. Now was no time to hunt, and if the bear was hiding the bush he didn't want the cat to antagonize her. The grizzly would soon return to her winter lair and bother them no more.

He took a deep breath and began slowly, allowing his body to warm up while his heart rate rose gradually. He felt strong and moved with grace and confidence as he followed the winding stream toward the falls, striding effortlessly while the cat galloped at his side. Arriving at the falls just as the sun slipped behind the western range, he negotiated the cliff face in only a few minutes. He had ascended and descended the wall regularly since he was eight years old and knew every niche and foothold on its face.

In the gray dusk of evening his legs flashed rhythmically as he trailed the streambed south into Cactus Canyon toward his brother's grave. Martin's spirit would lead him, and Mike would sing The Gift of Death Song for his brother and say goodbye before continuing on to Batopilas. A feeling of sureness and rightness regarding his mission pushed aside the doubt and distraction of the last two weeks. Upon arriving at Martin's grave he cried without shame, sang and left a few food items for Diablo on a large boulder so that he would not capture Martin's soul and use it to torture the living. Then Mike sung a song from their childhood and ended with an invocation to his brother to bother him no more.

His mind at peace, he ran toward Batopilas again. He felt energized, and as his sandals crunched the earth as a familiar meditative rhythm settled within and allowed him to run tirelessly. His spirit soared and his soul rose from his body and went ahead to guide the way. The jaguar ran at his heels, a feral animal chasing a wraith. As his long legs stretched to eat the land, he realized that he ran not to save the *federale*, but to save himself. His home and way of life were imperiled.

Omar sat in the pine forest across from the rubble-filled entrance to the canyon. He had waited patiently, regaining his strength and forming a plan. The need for haste had come and gone. The goal that had eluded him for thirty years lay on the other side of that burgeoning hill of gravel.

It was here all time, he chided himself. He remembered once, twenty-five years ago, when he had explored this very area, walked these forests and agonized over his inability to find the ruins and share in the knowledge of gold and jade that the old shaman would not divulge. Omar had sent the leathery old heathen to hell where he belonged, and then waited patiently these many years, knowing that the shaman's offspring would one day lead him to the secret.

He began to wax philosophical regarding his long wait and the purgatory of living and working in a heathenish Christian country. Allah had shown His infinite wisdom in waiting so long to reward Omar's tenacity. A young man would not appreciate the wealth nor recognize the honor of being chosen to discover this place. But appreciation is proportionate to the difficulty of acquisition and Omar planned to satisfy his every desire and nurture his lingering proclivities of hedonism while indulging long-suppressed sadistic fantasies. After all, he was all alone and no one would ever know.

It had been child's play for a man of his abilities to track this luckless trio. He had burglarized their cabin and found the professor's core sample reports. Everyone in Batopilas had known they left together, and following their Jeep had proven much easier than tracking a man. Unfortunately it had been many years since he had hiked and climbed the sierras and the torturous pace of that devil priest had nearly returned him to the comfort of his Batopilas home. But the earthquake and the priest's death had galvanized him to succeed. He felt certain that Fr. Martin had told the archaeologist and *federale* the location of the ruins. Why else would they have continued onward?

The cliff face at the waterfall had nearly bested him, but he had years of experience climbing difficult mountains. They had nearly lost Omar at the falls, and he had run to keep up, finally overtaking them here, outside the ruins just as the bear attacked the *federale* right in front of his eyes. Thanks be to Allah for small favors. It saved Omar from having to kill the infidel later.

Now the filthy Indian and his snooping jaguar had left. To where he didn't know and it didn't matter, because Omar would take what he wanted and go. Only a female and hapless academic lay between him and his destiny. He smiled broadly, baring his diamond-studded teeth, enjoying his situation immensely. First he would bend them to his will, then make them carry the treasure to bury at a location known only to him. Then he would kill the professor and the woman.

No…wait, he thought. *First, I'll enjoy the woman and I'll…*he paused, feeling inspired. A sadistic fantasy had captured his imagination. A hundred different games could be played with her, and Omar knew for sure that she would beg to die before he would oblige her. A convulsive shiver wracked him and he felt himself becoming erect.

Not yet child, he massaged his groin, *I'll feed you later*.

The professor listened keenly to her story, a straightforward narrative that from beginning to end lasted only ten minutes. He let his own imagination fill in the gaps. She was a strong woman, this American diplomat, and he wondered how he would have fared had he been abducted and thrown into a dark damp mine for two weeks. The thought made him shudder.

The news of a gold mine next to the ruins perked his interest, but he supposed it was little to be excited about when captive inside. The gold mine would explain how these people had supported themselves. No doubt they had traded gold for food and other needed items. But with whom and for what had they traded? Much needed to be studied and he had little time. He would have to enter the cliff dwellings themselves to study this culture further.

Her ominous report of the dead hot springs struck a familiar chord. He recalled Alexandra's vague message from Dr. Atunez regarding seismic activity. He felt a burning in his stomach and a tingle of fear. He should have paid attention. He wasn't a geologist, but knew that hot springs and geysers were created by magma heating the granite bedrock, or by tremendous pressures from the earth's core causing intrusions of magma from the mantle into the crust. Hydrothermal energy could be wonderful or threatening. It appeared that the numerous earth tremors of last month and the colossal earthquake yesterday morning had not resulted from shifting tectonic plates. The magma below was under pressure and had shifted upward. The area would continue to have earthquakes until the magma ceased moving. He might be sitting on Mexico's next volcano.

The talk of tombs and treasure lifted him to his feet and to the grave entrances. Night would fall within the hour and it was imperative to investigate as much as possible now. With luck a helicopter would arrive within ten hours to rescue them. Although he had not been inside, a quick perusal of the cliff dwellings told him that they were not Anasazi in origin. They were unique, this previously unknown civilization of stone masons, miners and jewelers.

He lit a torch and set it near a tomb entrance, and moved stones aside to enter. This was poor archaeological method, but Ruth's narrative had made it clear that the tomb had been entered just recently. According to her, Mike had emptied the contents of another tomb at the west end and transported everything to this one. The impending darkness and the possibility of a shortened stay had created the urgency, and so he would endeavor to see what lay inside the tomb without moving or changing anything.

"I don't think Mike wanted anyone to go into the tombs," Ruth objected.

"I can't protect what I don't know exists," he replied, continuing to move stone aside. "Keep your eye on Luis, okay?" Within minutes he leaned against the wall, gasping for air. Ten minutes later he called for Ruth. "Can you help me with this last one?"

Together they pushed it aside to expose a dark passage.

"Did Mike move that by himself?"

"I'm sure he did."

"Strong guy." David looked about, then gave a "here goes nothing" look. He stooped and entered the tomb. The passageway was wider than the entry suggested, and he walked carefully, peering into the darkness while his torch cast lurid shadows onto the walls and ceiling. He came to a large room. The ceiling, rough cut and slanting downward at the rear, rose six meters at its highest. The rock and gravel floor stretched nearly forty meters in each direction.

Biggest tomb I've ever seen, thought the professor, lifting the torch and walking to the middle of the room. He slowly turned in a circle, pausing only when something caught his eye. His excitement, palpable when entering the passageway, now boiled. The remains of an ancient culture lay scattered everywhere. The grounds outside had been scoured clean years ago, probably by Mike's father, and placed inside this large room. Pottery, baskets, metates for grinding corn, blankets and items of unknown usage lay stacked against the north wall: all-in-all a treasure trove of material culture that an archaeologist needs to identify, classify and research. It all sat in this room waiting to be studied. He didn't even have to dig it up. And who knew what lay above, untouched in the rooms of the cliff dwellings? Perhaps much of it just the way it had been left the last day the city's occupancy?

Stacked into boxes near the western wall lay a collection of modern implements: plastic milk cartons, tools, a chain, a wood chest with a large old-fashioned lock and two shovels—probably Mike's belongings. More boxes were placed on either side of the passageway, and a closer inspection revealed cooking implements and more tools.

A glint of reflected light from polished metal drew him to the east wall. He took two steps forward, then stopped. A cold chill raced along his spine and an involuntary shiver shook him. Two skeletons, one on the floor, the other in a chair, lay as they had died. When he moved the torch closer, he saw that both were chained to the wall. They had been captives.

This wasn't a tomb, he thought. A jail maybe, or a storage room at best. The bodies and treasure of which Ruth spoke must be in the other tomb. David knelt to examine the shiny chains. He tried to lift one to gauge its weight, but grunted with effort, surprised at its heaviness. He could barely lift it. Upon closer scrutiny, he dropped it, too stunned to speak. Gold! A thick gold chain! *Incredible*, he thought.

He moved the torch from side to side, slowly appraising the artifacts. Near the wall sat a three-legged table with a pile of what looked to be clothing next to a pottery vase with a lid. He walked to search further and had nearly arrived when a flicker of light from beneath the table caught his eye. He lowered the torch and saw a helmet. He gasped! The helmet was of the style worn by Spanish Conquistadors—and now he recognized their armor on top of the table.

How had Conquistadors come to be chained to the walls of a dungeon in the Sierra Madres? How had they found this place? How many hundreds of years had they lain waiting to be discovered?

His mouth felt like cotton and his breath came rapidly. An incredible discovery and it could only get better. A steady stream of tingles raced from spine to fingertips. Heady stuff. He stood ingesting his favorite narcotic—discovery—and felt himself becoming intoxicated.

On a whim, he reached for the lid on the vase and leaned over to peer inside. He started to close it, but saw that paper had been shoved inside and that it lined the inner surface of the vase. Temptation tugged. Should he or shouldn't he? It certainly wasn't appropriate, and the paper might crumble into a thousand pieces when he tried to extract it. *Just this one thing*, he told himself. The lid might have sealed the vase and perhaps no moisture had penetrated within. If it started to crumble or tear, he would leave it be. David had noticed a torch holder near the room entry, so he carried the vase with him and mounted the torch in its holder.

The mouth of the jar stretched wide enough to easily take his fingers. Slowly and carefully he extracted the paper, or papers, as they turned out to be: two of them. They were dry and crisp and had yellowed with age, but held firmly considering their age. The lid had protected them these many years and he had no doubt that whomever had left them knew it would be quite sometime before their discovery.

He placed them under the flickering torch light, careful not to singe, yet near enough to read. His heart beat duly and he felt lightheaded. With trembling hands he read the archaic Spanish.

I DO BELIEVE I AM THE LAST ALIVE, AND I SHALL SURELY STARVE. EVERYONE IS DEAD FROM THE SMALLPOX. DIEGO'S INDIAN GUIDE CARRIED THE POX AND TOGETHER THEY DIED FIRST. AND NOW THE FILTHY INDIANS FALL LIKE FLIES IN OCTOBER.

WE FOUND IT! THE FIRST OF THE SEVEN CITIES OF CIBOLA! BUT VELASQUEZ IS DEAD AND I WILL DIE SOON UNLESS I FIND THE COURAGE TO CUT OFF MY LEG AND FREE MYSELF FROM THIS ACCURSED CHAIN. A GOLD CHAIN, BY GOD! YAY, I AM BITTER. MY FAMILY WILL NEVER KNOW THAT I AM THE GREATEST OF THEM ALL! THERE IS MORE GOLD IN THIS MOUNTAIN THAN THE KING AND QUEEN OF SPAIN, GOD BLESS THEM, HAVE IN SEVILLE. AND THE ROOM NEXT TO THIS ONE HAS MORE GOLD THAN A FLEET OF GALLEONS CAN CARRY.

IF YOU READ THIS, REMEMBER ME! I AM SIMON GONZALEZ DE LA MADRID OF NEW GALICIA, SENT BY THE MOST ILLUSTRIOUS LORD, DON ANTONIO DE MENDOZA, THE VICEROY OF MEXICO CITY, TO EXPLORE AMONG THE HEATHENS AND BRING PROFIT AND HONOR TO THE CROWN. REMEMBER MY FAMILY! VELASQUEZ AND I MUST NOT DIE IN VAIN AND WITHOUT OUR FAMILIES ENJOYING THE PENSION OF DISCOVERY PROMISED BY HIS EMMINENCE

THE VICEROY.

SIMON GONZALEZ DE LA MADRID
JUNIO 16, 1537

Amazing! Almost unbelievable. A Conquistador in search of the legendary Seven Cities of Cibola: the cities of gold. An Indian guide with small pox had led them here, and a small, but whole civilization had been wiped out. Astonishing, but sad. Yet another example of an old theme in the history of the New World: European diseases, guns and steel decimating and destroying the high civilizations of Middle America while Conquistadors relentlessly sought gold, subjects and souls.

He read the paragraphs again to commit them to memory, then returned the papers to the vase and replaced it on the table beside the armor. He retrieved the torch and walked to the eastern wall where he found more gold implements: bowls, figurines, a small shield with a jaguar design, a spear and several knives—all within view of the Spaniards, but out of reach. It must have driven them crazy. As Cortez had told the Aztec god/king, Moctezuma, "Spaniards suffer from a disease that only gold can cure." Being bound until their death with gold chains couldn't have made their lingering deaths easier.

Nearly spent, the torch flickered, so he decided to go outside and get another. The discovery had rejuvenated him. He could explore all night. The last three days be damned! He quickly navigated the narrow passage, deep in thought, oblivious to everything going on about him. He was entrenched in an academic wallow and felt that he must share his discovery with someone before he burst.

"Ruth!" he exclaimed, exiting the mountain passage, "you'll never guess what I...."

But instead of the diplomat, a large man stood waiting with Luis' rifle pointed at the professor's stomach. When the light from the professor's torch shone on the intruder's face, it smiled broadly, revealing diamond studded teeth. The torch sputtered in David's hand, and a nauseous, sinking feeling nearly put him to his knees.

"Yes, *gringo*," smiled the jeweler. "Tell me all about it. I'm anxious to hear."

*

194

Stunned! Upon being surprised, Ruth had stood petrified while visions of a horrible death raced through her mind. Who was this reptile with diamonds in his teeth? She had never seen anything like him before. His eyes shone black and empty and he had thick, hard muscles. His wide, cruel smile revealed gemstones set into his teeth, and he had the manner of a cold, brutal man. When he placed the cold tip of the gun barrel to her forehead and dared her to cry out, she stood perfectly still. When he raked her body with his eyes and made coarse statements filled with sexual misogyny, she felt more afraid than she could ever remember.

She wanted to cry out and run. But where would she go? If she stayed, something terrible would happen, yet if she ran, he would shoot her like a dog. He had finally found her: the man all women fear in nightmares. True, he had come for the gold, but he would not leave before torturing her and killing David. He couldn't chance having them reveal his secret to anyone. She had seen some of what Mike had transported from the tomb and its worth couldn't be calculated: probably millions. This creep must have followed the professor and the federale, then waited until Mike left for Batopilas.

Ruth had survived a living hell the last two weeks, but she was still determined not to succumb to a whining helplessness and become a passive victim. Damnit! She had been so close to leaving and believed that she had already survived the worst that one could experience, but here stood: a grinning, sadistic killer with diamond-studded teeth. "What do you want?" she asked boldly, trying to mask her fear.

He lowered the gun barrel and slapped her so hard that her ears rang. He stood over her, hand poised to strike again.

"Shut up, American bitch. If I want something from you, I'll step on you." He showed her his teeth. "Don't do or say anything until I tell you, and you'll live longer. Understand?" He jammed the gun into her solar plexus and she grunted and fell to her knees as rivers of pain flowed from her middle.

"Where is the other American...the archaeologist?"

She couldn't breathe to answer and he raised the gun to strike again.

"Ruth," came a muffled voice from within the tomb, you'll never guess what I...."

Omar swung the rifle barrel to the hole in the mountain and stepped forward to meet David as he exited the tunnel. The professor stopped, struck dumb. Looking first at Ruth on her knees, then at the gun pointed at his stomach, a look of recognition swept his face.

"Yes, *gringo*," smiled Omar. "Tell me all about it. I'm anxious to hear."

The professor stood impotently with his torch sputtering. It barely cast light to see ten meters, but he quickly appraised the situation. Ruth cowering on the ground and the rifle barrel at his stomach told him all he needed to know.

"You lied," accused David.

"No. I purposely misinformed you. I've searched thirty years for this place and now I must kill you to protect its secret."

"Take some gold and go," pleaded the professor. "There are many pieces inside this room. Take it. I'll never tell anyone."

"Gold?" said Omar. "Yes…I'll take a few pieces of gold, but I came for the jadeite. It's the jade that's priceless. It's the finest quality jade I've ever seen. It's worth ten…no, a hundred times the gold."

"Then you're going to be disappointed. If there's any jade here, I haven't seen it."

The diamonds disappeared and the gun barrel jabbed the professor's stomach. "What do you mean?"

"The jade deposits are miles from here…somewhere in Rock Canyon."

"There's no jadeite? You lie!" Omar swung and cracked the rifle butt against David's head, dropping him like a stone. Omar straddled him, daring him to rise, but the professor lay unconscious.

"Where's the *federale*?" he shrieked angrily at Ruth. "Where is he?" The torch sputtered benignly on the ground.

"Dead," she croaked, cowering in the darkness, taking a step backward. "A bear attacked him and he died. Mike, the Indian, has run for help." Omar glanced at the cliff dwellings, then the tomb entrances. The Indian had gone for help, but it would be least a day or two before he returned. He stood torn with indecision. It would take days to comb the whole city for treasure and darkness would drastically impede the search. But he would not be denied. He would grab what was easily available and bury it, then return later to retrieve it. The jade would have to wait. The archaeologist probably told the truth, and Omar had little time.

The diamonds reappeared. "Start there," he motioned with the gun.

"Where?"

"There…the other tomb."

"It's covered with stone. I can't…." Then she stopped. His facial expression would have stopped a charging bull. She looked at David, shot a furtive glance to where Luis lay and acquiesced. "Sure, mister…anything you say. Take it easy."

She entered the adjacent tomb entrance and began carrying stone while Omar kicked and cursed the professor into consciousness. Groggy, his face swollen, David painfully gained his feet and also began removing stone from the unopened tomb.

Omar urged them to move faster, threatening and cajoling until, finally, all three joined to move a large boulder from the tomb entrance.

"Stand aside," growled the jeweler, holding up a torch. The light revealed the outline of a jaguar head above the entry. David jerked with recognition. This, he realized, really was a tomb. He knew it. Turning to Ruth, he said "Did Mike open…?"

"Shut up!" screeched Omar. "Don't talk." He tossed a rope to the ground at David's feet. "Tie up the whore and come with me."

David and Omar held torches as they entered the passage. The professor went first, his mind a torment of conflict. Even though it was imperative that they escape or kill this diamond-toothed horror of a man before he killed them, David couldn't shake his sense of excitement when entering the tomb. He became passive and willingly took the lead into the tomb.

"Move it, infidel," ordered the jeweler, shoving the professor away and stepping inside. They held their torches high and then gasped in unison.

"My God," muttered David. Gold lay everywhere.

"Praise Allah," said Omar, his diamonds flashing in the wavering torchlight. "You have a long night ahead of you, American pig."

"How so?"

"You're going to carry all this to a different place and bury it for me."

"You can't be serious," said David, moving his torch to the other hand and surveying the room. It wasn't possible to have this much gold in one room. It just wasn't possible. Everything shone red-orange and bronze, reflecting light like a flaming, gilded hell. Shields, swords, figurines, ingots, incense burners, statues of deities and dead kings lay in piles. The treasure trove of the jaguar people! The inventory of goods with which they had traded for food and the wealth of their time: turquoise, green obsidian from the Valley of Mexico and cacao beans from the southern Maya—all worthless by today's standards.

"Grab those small statues," pointed Omar, reaching for two heavy ingots to carry in his left arm. "We're running out of time."

Mike Goes to Jail

Mike rested on a boulder west of the Batopilas Bridge, looking into the sleepy town nestled comfortably beneath the eastern canyon escarpment. It was a sparkling clear night and moonlight reflected from the crashing, hissing cataracts of the Batopilas river while he relaxed and listened to the soothing sounds of moving water. He was torn with indecision. Now that he had arrived, where would he find a telephone? The *farmacia* had long since closed, the *policia* might arrest him and the old priest at the church might not let him in. He would sit and think awhile.

He began to hum a song, but then stopped, alert and listening. Intuition warned that someone was watching. He waited patiently for the person to identify themself, but then rose to leave when they didn't. Then a tall Indian youth walked onto the path in front of the bridge and Mike relaxed. He recognized the youth's profile—Ribi, Omar's son and a friend from the old days at the mission school. He had stood in the shadows and watched him arrive. Ribi was a half-breed like himself, and they had both suffered the taunts and rejection of peers when attending the mission school.

"You have run far, jaguar man; I smell your sweat," Ribi stated in Tarahumara. "It's a good night for the long run."

Mike walked to his old acquaintance. "Yes…but tonight I run to help a friend. I need to make a call. Do you know anyone who has a telephone?"

Ribi shrugged. "I'm on my way to the cantina to see a girl. Maybe you can use their telephone."

"Do they allow Indians in the cantina now?"

"No," answered Ribi. "The cantina is closed, but Lasa waits for me near her window at night. Come and walk with me." He motioned with his arm. "Maybe she can help. It's been a long time since we talked, jaguar man. I hear stories of you, but you have let the priest and my father come between us."

"Omar killed my father," accused Mike.

"Yes…I believe he did." Ribi hung his head in shame. "I've been worried. My father left town three days ago and I think he followed your brother and the policia into the Lost Canyons."

A spasm of fear caused Mike to shudder. "Omar followed Martin and the *federale* into the mountains?"

"Yes. That's what my father's house girl said."

"Ribi, I need your help." Mike joined him at the bridge and they crossed the river together. "Let's go see your Lasa and I'll tell you what has happened. I have a plan."

They walked the Camino Real south into town. Only a few lights shone from within any of the homes as most of the town had long since bedded down. They crossed the cobblestone streets to the zocalo, tried to avoid the eyes of those lurking in the shadows and skirted around the empty market. A few patrons from El Perdido Otra Vez weaved their way home. Some staggered drunkenly and the corner across from the cantina had a group of four inebriates singing a mournful love song.

Mike and Ribi rounded the corner and walked the alley to the rear of the cantina. Ribi knocked lightly on a wood-hinged window, waited, then tapped again when no one answered. Thinking it a waste of time, they had turned to leave when the window flew open and a small, pock-faced prostitute stood with a candle in her hand and a finger to her lips.

"Lasa…." Ribi began.

"Shhh." She waved for them to be quiet, looked behind her to see that no one listened, then turned to see whom her lover had brought along. Her eyes grew wide when she saw Mike, and a look of wonder spread across her face.

"El Jaguar Feroz," she muttered, surprised. "Why did you bring…."

But Ribi, aided by Mike, was already climbing up the side of the building and had a leg through the window of her bedroom. Mike followed, moving quickly and furtively through the window into the whore's small living area. Sparsely furnished, the room had a few unframed photographs and magazine pictures pinned to the walls. In the corner, a much-used bed sat slumping and rumpled in the corner, and the girl's few clothes hung from a rope attached between two walls.

While Mike told his story the diminutive prostitute poured each a glass of *ponche* made from fermented sugar cane. The story became longer and the drinking cups were refilled. Finally Mike recounted his departure from Ruth, the subsequent bear attack and the meeting with Luis and the professor—the reason he had run all night to a telephone. He showed them the paper with the professor's telephone numbers and they passed it among themselves before laying the paper on a table by the prostitute's bed.

"I always wondered about that place," said Ribi, brushing hair from his eyes and adjusting a red headband. "I think now I know exactly where it is. It's good that your family kept the secret for so many years or the white men would have destroyed it." He left unspoken the fact that Omar had killed Mike's father trying to obtain its secret.

Lasa grew still, then her head jerked, and she placed a finger to her lips and ran to the door. Loud voices, a crash and more shouting erupted from within the cantina. She motioned frantically for them to exit through the window, but Ribi reached for her instead.

As the young couple embraced to say good-bye, someone pounded loudly on the cedar plank door. Mike and Ribi bolted for the window as the door burst open and three armed men rushed into the room and seized them.

A grinning Colonel Cedras entered with a pistol in one hand, the cantina's madam grasped in the other.

"So...you do keep customers after hours, do you, Flora?" He leered at the madam, then at Lasa. "Can't control your little *putas*, eh?"

Colonel Cedras smiled happily. Things were finally looking up. The escape of the Chihuahua *federale*, the archaeologist and Fr. Martin into the mountains had left him short tempered and petulant. The unexpected departure of Omar had confirmed his suspicions of a plot and had left him positively livid with anger. The jeweler, his old smuggling buddy, had planned to cut him out of this one. But when Cedras learned that Mike and Ribi had arrived in town, the Colonel came running. When he finished extracting information from them, it would be Omar on the outside looking in at the real players.

Although he and the jeweler had once shared a mutually satisfying business arrangement, Cedras couldn't stand the diamond-toothed bastard. Besides, he wasn't a Christian and the Colonel had purposely ignored his foreign sexual perversions and complaints of citizens in the community for too long. It was time to send the freak back to Afghanistan or put a bullet in his head.

Motioning with the gun, he pointed at Mike and Ribi. "Lock up these two. I'll be down later to question them. He released the madam's arm and she began to protest her innocence while readjusting her nightgown.

"Colonel, I can explain...." began the madam, beginning to dissemble.

"Yes," he interrupted, holstering his gun, "and you'll get your chance, but first I think you owe me something, don't you, Flora?"

The madam smiled, understanding him immediately. "Of course I do," she agreed pleasantly, happy to see that it was business as usual. She turned to glare at Lasa. "Accommodate the Colonel in any way he desires…."

"No," said Colonel Cedras. "Not her, you."

"Absolutely not," objected the horrified madam. "This little slut caused the problem, she can fix it. Besides, I'm retired, I don't do…."

"Get out," the Colonel drew his gun again and motioned Lasa toward the door. "I don't have sex with Indians; I want the good stuff. Shut the door behind you." He turned the gun on the madam and gestured to her nightclothes. "Take them off, Flora. I've been waiting a long time for this."

Lasa looked quickly at the grim-faced matron, then at the leering, gun-wielding Colonel. At twenty-five and already a veteran whore, she had acquired knowledge far beyond her years. And any fool knew that the person holding a gun was the real boss, especially if he had a badge. She unobtrusively picked up the note Mike had left and pulled the bedroom door closed behind her.

Darkness shrouded the cantina and the contrasting odors of cigarettes, sour beer and sweet brandy pervaded the room. The wood floor creaked in protest and only a small candle from the madam's open bedroom cast dim light into the cantina's interior. Lasa hesitated, looked at the instructions and phone numbers on the paper, then decided. She had a feeling the *federale* would take his time and enjoy her boss at his leisure. She ran to the madam's room and sat at her desk. Lasa squinted at the note as darting shadows danced wickedly from the candlelight onto the smoke-stained walls. She thought of her Ribi and El Jaguar Feroz and how Indians were treated in jail. She took a deep breath and dialed the first set of numbers on the paper.

"Bueno…." came the sleepy, irritated reply. "Who is it?"

"Is Alexandra Wolf there?"

"Alexandra? Who's calling? Does she know you?"

"This is an emergency, *señora*, it's about her husband, Luis."

"Luis? Luis Alvarado is my husband. Who is this?" asked Angela.

"Please…I…you don't understand, there's so much…."

"Who is it, dear?" Alexandra's calm voice floated into the parlor. "Is everything okay?" She tied the sash of her nightgown and rubbed her eyes.

"It's someone calling for you about Luis." Angela started to hang up. "It's some nut."

"No, wait," said Alexandra, taking the telephone. "I'll talk to them. It might be important. The boys haven't called for three days, you know."

She carried the phone to the kitchen table. "Yes," she said, "this is Alexandra Wolf. You have information regarding my husband?" She listened politely, frowned and her eyes grew wide with alarm.

"Who is this?" she demanded.

"My name is Lasa, I...."

"Where are you calling from, Lasa?"

A short pause, then she heard, "Batopilas."

"Batopilas? How do you know my husband?"

Alexandra's face shifted from frowning perplexity to unwelcome surprise, then turned pink.

"What? You work where?"

"What's going on, Alexandra?" interrupted Angela. "What's happened to Luis?"

But Alexandra waved her off and reached for a pencil. "Go ahead, I believe you. This is too crazy not to be true." She wrote rapidly while Angela looked over her shoulder. Alexandra asked questions and scribbled information, shaking her head with dismay at the answers. Finally she thought she had it all: names, places, times, and events. Luis lay dying in a remote archaeological ruin while David tended the female diplomat kidnapped two weeks earlier.

Alexandra, disappointed and upset, tapped the pencil against her teeth. David and Luis had been hanging out in cantinas and her husband had lied to her by omitting his real intentions. She swore a silent oath. When she got him back the closest he would get to an archaeological site would be excavating the rose beds in their backyard.

Angela, tearful, collapsed into a chair. Luis attacked by a grizzly and dying in an unknown, remote location? She began to sob and then a cry escaped her mouth. Her neck slumped with the pain of a woman who believes that she is a widow.

"Stop it," commanded Alexandra, walking to Angela's side and hugging her. "It isn't over yet, *corazon*. We don't know that he's dead. There's still a chance. Now quit crying, I need your help. Let's talk this through." Alexandra paced the floor, occasionally looking at the information she had scribbled on the pad.

David's right, she thought, *we can't let the policia or army become involved. Luis will die while they argue and fight among themselves for the spoils at the ruins.* She walked to the telephone and dialed the number the puta had given her, but then thought better of it and cradled the phone.

No, she decided, it wouldn't work without the big guns. This time she dialed an unlisted number in Mexico City. She had decided to take a big chance, even though failure was a very real possibility. It was time to lean on her late husband's old friend, the Atomic Ant. If El Presidente couldn't help, nothing else would. The number clicked, connected and began to ring. Her heart skipped a beat in anticipation as she gripped the telephone in her small hand. It had been two years since she had last talked to Carlos and he had been very disapproving of her remarrying. No one answered and she started to hang up when someone muttered, "Bueno...who is this?" The tired voice was familiar. "What do you want? How did you get this number?"

"Carlos?" she asked, hoping against the inevitable.

"Who is this?" The voice was angry. "It's 3:00 in the morning!"

"Carlos...it's Alexandra Wolf, I'm calling about an emergency. David is...."

"Alexandra...is that you? What's happening? Where is David now? I told you not to involve yourself with an archaeologist. They're immature rock hounds and drinkers. I warned you...."

"Carlos...I know where the diplomat is."

"Huh?" He didn't understand. "Alexandra, why don't you call tomorrow when...."

"Carlos, wake up! The kidnapped American diplomat...I know where she is."

She thought he had hung up. Finally he said, "How could you possibly know? What are you saying, Alexandra?"

"Listen...I need your help," she pleaded.

He groaned. "No! Absolutely not!" he fumed. "Call tomorrow when I've had some sleep...and you get some too."

"Then I'll call the American Embassy in Chihuahua and El Paso to tell them where the American diplomat is."

"What! Are you insane? Those bastards have been beating me to death for weeks."

She let him shake off the sleep and think a moment, then said, "You've got to help, Carlos. Two phone calls will do it...please?"

He groaned and cursed. "What do you want, woman? If you so much as breathe a word about this I'll..."

"Hush and listen," she chastised, in control again. "There's this man in Batopilas, a Colonel Cedras who is holding two Indians who know how to...."

Ten minutes of explaining left her mouth dry and her palms wet. The Atomic Ant hadn't said a word and she fidgeted restlessly, afraid that he might turn her down.

"You'd be a hero," she added, trying to forestall a negative answer.

"Alexandra, you don't know squat about politics. Let me think." He sounded disgusted, and a long silence ensued.

Angela gripped the phone and steeled herself for an answer. She could imagine what he must be thinking and silently reviewed his dilemma. The Americans had been roasting him for his inability to find the diplomat or kidnappers. He needed closure on the affair and maybe her idea would work. Carlos could give the United States a chance to fall on its face and mess up. He could put the ball in their court and turn his head. If they were successful, he could take credit. If not, he could condemn their action and profess no prior knowledge.

"Okay," he said, finally. "Give me the number of the Embassy in Chihuahua."

"But the *policia* in Batopilas...."

"That's easy. It's big brother to the north I'm worried about."

She gave him the number. "Carlos, the next time someone says you're short, I'm going to kick them in the knee."

He chuckled, then grew quiet. "Alexandra if we pull this off everything will be fine. If it fails, your family will lose everything in PRI, and I mean everything. Understand?"

"I don't care anymore, Carlos. When my husband died, I got out of politics. I hate it. I just want David back, can't you understand that?"

"An archaeologist," he said again, as if the word left a bad taste in his mouth.

"Yes, and he's a hell of a man...and Carlos?"

"What now?"

"Tell them to send a doctor on the helicopter, okay?"

"Yes, Alexandra. Anything else?"

"That's it. We're on our way to the Embassy right now." She hung up, then shuddered.

"Get dressed, Angela. We leave in five minutes."

The Valley of Death

The moon had disappeared with its soft light, hiding the evil deeds being perpetrated in the highland valley and its ancient cliff dwellings. Ruth, weary beyond measure and nagged by fear that chewed at her sanity, had lost all track of time. She and David had worked all night retrieving gold from the tomb and carrying it over the gravel-walled entry. From there they had toted it upstream through the forest into a narrow, hidden ravine. But they would never live to tell their stories. Omar couldn't leave anyone alive who knew of his evil, the location of this incredible treasure or any trace of what had occurred. Every moment increased their peril.

They marched single file in the darkness: David first, bent and stumbling, and then Ruth and finally Omar with his rifle and torch. She could feel his lascivious eyes burrowing into her back, watching her every move. She had rubbed dirt on her face and arms to make herself unattractive and her hair was a tangle of filth. What could the cretin possible see in her? Ideas she didn't want to entertain caused her to shiver and become sick to her stomach. She had resolved to escape, but hadn't yet come up with a plan. Omar didn't allow talking, and she sensed a quiet desperation in the professor. What had happened to David's gun, anyway? Didn't he have a pistol strapped to his waist when she first saw him? Where had he put it? If only....

Was Luis really dead? speculated David. Was she telling the truth in the tomb? If so, he felt deeply saddened at the death of his best friend and the situation had turned nearly hopeless. Each time they returned to the ruins he tried to see Luis, but darkness obscured the *federale* in the black shadow of the overhang. Omar showed no interest in a dead body. He had taken Ruth's statement at face value, anxious to finish hiding the treasure.

Ruth was to be trying to communicate something to him with her eyes, but he found it impossible to decipher every nuance of gesture, and Omar didn't allow conversation. The professor's broken and swollen jaw pained him greatly. Throbbing, unrelenting pain accompanied every step. Once he had stumbled and fallen and Omar had kicked him repeatedly in the ribs, and now every breath was accompanied with a knife thrust. The outlook seemed more desperate each minute. If Mike didn't return soon, chances were that he wouldn't come at all—with or without help.

David now knew true hate for the first time in his life—a black, seething cholera that welled from deep within. He wanted to kill the jeweler and he wanted to do it now. Normally a mild man of discreet passions, the realization had stunned him, but he no longer cared. He watched haplessly as the pig leered at Ruth, and held no illusions regarding the jeweler's intentions. They would both die as soon as he didn't need them anymore, and that time was drawing nigh. One or two more trips would fill the tiny ravine. He couldn't talk out a plan with Ruth, so he must act alone and soon and hope that she followed his lead.

Where had he placed the pistol? he asked himself for the hundredth time. He cursed silently. He didn't even remember taking it off. "The absentminded professor," he muttered bitterly, his lips scabbed and thick from being struck by the rifle stock. They had left Luis' rifle lying beside the stream and the pistol lay who knows where?

And what of Mike? he wondered. Would he really try to bring help? The odds were not good. Except for the woman, of whom the jaguar man seemed to be very fond, Mike certainly had nothing tangible to gain. Except, remembered the professor, David had promised to help protect the ruins. But did Mike really trust him? Or would he be content with saving his own neck and be quit of the miserable white wretches who had profaned his home? If El Jaguar Feroz didn't return very soon, they were all dead.

Luis' hand tightened around the wood grips of the .45 automatic and it felt good. The feel of the pistol gave him comfort. But the rattlesnake warned him again and he froze, afraid that the snakes (he believed there were two) would sink their fangs into him. Perhaps they were attracted to his warm body on this cool night, or maybe the Indian had purposely put him here to die. He didn't know and it didn't matter now. If only he could clear the cotton from his mind.

Whatever the Indian had given him to drink had begun to wear off, and pain grew by the moment. He tried to lay unmoving, but cold chills and fever wracked his body. Shivering might incite the snakes. Where had everyone gone? He thought he had heard a familiar voice earlier, but could barely recall anything after the bear had attacked. He must have gone into shock.

The professor had left Luis the pistol, but he couldn't see in the dark and he lay on his stomach unable to move. His back and shoulder felt as though they had been ripped from his body. Where had the rattlesnakes come from? Where were David and that Indian? How could he escape the snakes? A flood of questions surged through his mind as he slowly gained his bearings. He knew he couldn't lay here forever. He must make a move soon. He had just gathered the nerve to ignore the rattlesnakes and lurch to his feet when he felt the one on his left slither and crawl over his back again. He began to sweat steel splinters, and he wanted to whimper, but held his breath, gripped the gun and prayed to the Virgin of Guadalupe for her intercession.

Hail Mary, Full of grace

The Lord is with thee

Blessed art thou among women....

The United States Invades Mexico

The moon had slipped behind the western wall of the Batopilas Canyon and only a few stars battled to stay up. Colonel Cedras walked slowly—slightly tipsy but happy—feeling that he had made a major conquest tonight. Not money or drugs, mind you: he had had his way with Flora, the madam of El Perdido Otra Vez. He had taken what he wanted like a man, and that's the way it's supposed to be. A man took what he could when he could get it. You held on to what you have or someone else would take it: one of life's immutable laws. Although she had acted pissy and ready for him to leave, he knew she would never forget him. The bitch could count herself fortunate that he didn't shut her down. Flora might be the only woman in Mexico who owned a whorehouse. Prostitution was a man's business. Only a man could control women. Didn't she know that?

The Colonel whistled a tune as he walked the five blocks to the police station. He had more luck than most guys, he decided. He had access to sex without bothering his wife, money from his numerous smuggling enterprises, status in the community and a family he could show off. What more could a man need? Other than money, that is. You could never have enough money.

Colonel Cedras looked at his watch. 4:34 a.m., nearly time for *huevos rancheros* and a plate of sliced avocados. But first he must go to the jail and interrogate those two filthy Indians. The prospect soured his mood and reminded him of Omar and that damn *federale* from Chihuahua. Where had they made off to? As he turned the corner, he became aware of a rapid whump, whump, whump sound. He searched the sky, but saw nothing. What the hell was making that noise? It sounded like a helicopter or something. What would a helicopter be doing in Batopilas? Where was the sound coming from? He picked up his pace and took long steps toward the clamor, which drew him ever closer to the police station. Upon rounding the corner at Calle Morelos, he stopped dead.

Two helicopters sat at the station: one on the roof heliport, the other on the front lawn. Both birds had U.S. flags emblazoned on their tails. Soldiers in camouflage dress, holding automatic rifles stood near them, looking wary and ready for action. He rubbed his eyes. Two U.S. helicopters? In Batopilas? Was Mexico being invaded? He shouldn't have drunk so much brandy.

Colonel Cedras puffed out his chest and walked to confront the invaders. Who the hell did they think they were, anyway? He hoped that they were lost, because he would make them wish they had never seen him before.

"There he is," shouted someone over the din. "It's the Colonel."

Cedras lowered his head and circled to the side door of the helicopter. He had never seen one quite like it before. Long and sleek, the tubes on the helicopter's side reminded him of the engines on a Mexicana Airlines jet. It looked fast and had guns, cannons that looked like they could blow up a tank. Suddenly he didn't feel so confident.

"Cedras," came a voice from behind. When the colonel turned and saw who called his name, he nearly messed his pants. Jose Antonio Gonzalez Corso, the Inspector General of the *Policia* Federal from Chihuahua stood in front of him. Cedras feared the Inspector General more than any man alive. He immediately began to fawn and dissemble before him.

"Cedras," continued the Inspector General, obviously irritated at being up at this hour, "I'm taking the two Indians with me. I want you to know that I'm very unhappy that you detained them for no reason, arrested them for no cause and that you are out whoring around like the reprobate that you are."

"Yes, sir…I understand, Sr. Gonzalez. I was just about to release them myself and…."

"Don't lie to me, Cedras. I'm fed up with your shenanigans down here. If I ever get called out here again for an emergency, I'll cut off your *cojones* and send them to your wife in a jar. Understand?" He turned to walk back into the station.

"Of course, Excellency. Take them. Take anything you wish. I'm not sure why you're here, but…."

The Inspector General whirled around. "I'm not here, Cedras…and neither are these people." He pointed to the American soldiers and the helicopters. "If you so much as breathe a word of this, I'll personally destroy your career and see that you are relieved without pension. Do you understand this also?"

"Of course, Inspector General, I have never seen you or these men before in my life. You can trust me, Excellency."

"I doubt it," sneered the Inspector General. The tall, broad-shouldered patrician turned on his heels and marched into the station while Colonel Cedras stood humiliated, feeling out of place.

"What are you looking at?" he hissed at a sniggering underling. "Get inside and see if you can help out." He looked to the roof heliport and saw that the helicopter had a red cross on its side. The open door revealed several passengers—two of whom appeared to be women. What in the world? Civilian females in an army helicopter?

Mike and Ribi trudged wearily from the jail and were placed in separate birds. The soldiers boarded the helicopter and the Inspector General appeared. He spoke briefly with someone the colonel didn't recognize, then entered the helicopter on the roof. The other man, obviously an American, ran down the stairs two at a time and jogged to the helicopter near Cedras. He ignored the Colonel, shouted orders to the pilot and shut the door. The engines roared and the blades whipped furiously, driving the Colonel away from the helicopter and toward the station. The big bird on the roof lifted first, hovered momentarily, then shot away at an incredible speed when its jet engines fired. The helicopter near him raced after the first. They headed west, moving toward the Lost Canyons, and in two minutes had shrunk to black dots in the early morning sky.

The Huntsman and the Prey

The starry blaze wavered and lost its brilliance as a white band of luminescence in the east strained to lift the shroud of darkness. The Sun god had awakened and the light of day would expose the sins of night.

"Last load," said Omar, gesturing toward the tomb with his rifle. "You Americans work slower than anyone I've ever seen. Into the tunnel, bitch." He motioned with the gun. Ruth hesitated, looking to the professor for some kind of sign, but he was gazing toward the overhang where Luis lay.

Omar shoved her toward the tomb and raised a fist to strike her.

"No!" shouted David, stepping toward the jeweler. "Leave her alone or I'll...."

"You'll what, American swine? Hurt me?" Omar turned the gun on the professor. "Giving up, *gringo*? Want to end it all right now?" He brought the rifle to his shoulder and his finger lay heavy on the trigger.

"No...I...just don't touch her. Please don't hurt....."

"Shut up!" roared Omar. "Get into the tomb! Go!" he commanded, pointing the gun at Ruth, then again at David.

Ruth obeyed, ducking her head to enter the darkness. David followed her lead and Omar fell in behind with a torch and rifle, walking closely on the professor's heels. When David stepped into the burial room behind Ruth, Omar struck him behind the ear with the rifle butt, knocking him senseless. He fell limp and unmoving.

Ruth screamed and rushed Omar. He cradled the rifle in his arm, stepped aside and put a quick fist into her stomach. She fell gasping to her knees. He stood and grinned, poised to strike again, but changed his mind. He liked her, he decided. No sniveling, whining weakling, this American. She had fire in her belly and she wanted to fight. So be it, he thought. A plan began to form in his twisted mind. He would find a way for her to fight and play. The

211

jeweler took a length of sisal rope and made a noose, then he slipped it over her neck. She would choke if she struggled or tried to run. Holding the other end of the rope in his hand, he herded her, stumbling and complaining, through the passageway and into the canyon.

She fell to her knees, trembling from anger, her pulse accelerated by an infusion of adrenaline. She felt as if she would explode. She grabbed at the line and whirled to face the sadistic killer. He responded by yanking the rope, choking her, and then tightened the noose more while she struggled, slowly applying pressure until she fell and nearly passed out. Then he relented and eased up so that she could breathe, then stood over her while she gasped and pulled at the rope around her neck. He loved it. This would be more fun than he anticipated.

"Get up, slut," he commanded. "Help me roll this rock in front of the hole."

"What?" she gasped, pulling at the noose. "We can't, you crazy bastard! He'll die. You can't bury him alive in that tomb."

Omar pointed his rifle and fired a shot between her legs. She screamed. He fired near her head, and then took aim at her chest.

"Okay!" she screamed, okay!" She climbed to her feet. "Asshole," she said, her teeth clenched with anger.

"Ahh," said Omar, smiling approval at her outburst. "You will get your chance, American whore. As soon as you finish restacking this stone, you and I will play a little game. I will allow you escape, then I'll find you—and I will find you, whore." He reached and rubbed his groin suggestively. "When I do the games will be over." He flashed his diamonds, grinning broadly and raking her body with his eyes.

"And then," he continued, his smile growing even larger, "I will do terrible things to you…things that will cause you much pain." He searched her face for a sign of weakness, but she stood her ground.

"You're a perverted, sick animal."

"I feel quite well, thank you, and I'm very excited at the prospect of our game." He motioned with the rifle. "Help me with this big one, then get to work stacking stone, whore. I'm anxious to get started."

Ruth stood with fists clenched. She wanted to scratch out his eyes. A game? He wanted to hunt and torture her like an animal. How had he lived so long without someone killing him? Rage fueled her resolve. The last two weeks had been a complete immersion in a psychological hell—yet she had survived. Her spirit had been reforged and tempered. She had become hardened emotionally and her mind was nearly oblivious to suffering. Her past and future were all contingent on the next instant: every moment to be experienced as an excruciating, poignant experience.

She pushed everything from her mind but her hatred and Omar's diamond-studded teeth. She would gain strength and focus from her animosity, and the image of his smile would put wings on her feet. Ruth would flee the repugnant beast like a possessed woman.

She jerked the rope and went to stand by the boulder. "Let's do it. I'm ready when you are."

Omar's diamonds flashed appreciation, accepting her challenge. He directed her to the other side of the boulder, then lay down his gun. They struggled mightily, slipping on the rocks and gravel before finally rolling the boulder in front of the tomb entrance. They both leaned against the stone, panting with fatigue.

He isn't in that good of shape, she realized, appraising her captor. He must be close to fifty. If she got loose, he'd never catch her.

"Okay, *puta*. Start stacking stone." He jerked the rope again and she faked a stumble, falling toward his feet. She held a large rock in her hand and as she pretended to fall, she shifted and brought the rock down with all her force and weight on the instep of his foot.

Too late, he saw it coming. The bone snapped and his jaw dropped as pain rocketed through his body. He screamed and dropped the rope, falling to the ground to clutch his foot. Ruth butted him in the face with her head, smashing his mouth and teeth bloody, rolling him over backward. She tore the rope from her neck. Omar reached for her, but the pain stopped him. She moved for the rifle, but he lurched and grabbed it instead.

She bolted for the canyon entrance. He bawled a warning and aimed the rifle. As she crested the gravel wall, he squeezed off a shot. The bullet struck low, hitting her in the thigh, pitching her forward and down the other side of the gravel wall. He raised the rifle again, but the excruciating pain in his foot prevented him from firing again.

"Bitch!" he screamed. "Whore! I'll flay the skin from your body!" But the pain commanded his attention. He tried unsuccessfully to stand, but couldn't. He hobbled painfully, reduced to hopping on one leg. The game had begun, he realized, and they had both drawn blood. What she didn't know, however, is that she couldn't escape. This area—the forest, the creek, the jutting peaks—was a geographic anomaly. With the exception of the narrow, barely passable fissure between the mountains leading to Rock Canyon, the only way in and out lay in negotiating the steep cliff face near the waterfall, which he felt sure she couldn't descend. She would never find the secret passage to Rock Canyon. He had discovered it only by accident twenty years ago. This area comprised a high-altitude box canyon. If Ruth didn't bleed to death first, she would ultimately arrive at the falls. He would take her there.

Omar began casting about for wood to build a brace. He couldn't stand on the foot, but a tightly strapped brace that extended a few inches below the boot would support his weight. It would be slow going, but he had time. He only hoped to find her before she bled to death. He still had plans for her after the game and a dead body wouldn't be nearly as much fun.

"IN THE PRESENCE OF MINE ENEMIES"

Ruth thought a sledgehammer had struck her leg. Waves of pain issued from her thigh and she could barely see for the tears in her eyes. Fear drove her to try and stand. The beast stood just on the other side and might be coming at this very moment. She didn't know if the blow had hurt enough to slow him, but she must get away as quickly as possible. She shifted her weight onto the injured leg and groaned with pain. Blood dripped from her hand when she removed it from the wound. She ripped her pant leg and bent to look at the damage. Nausea caused her to swoon and she almost vomited. Bloody, fleshy tissue surrounded a hole the size of a golf ball. The bullet had not entered directly; it had hit the side of her thigh and ripped a segment of skin and muscle from the leg. Her stomach waffled, then the nausea returned.

She hobbled toward the stream, glancing furtively over her shoulder, moving alongside the streambed. Blood oozed steadily from the wound, but the leg didn't hurt anymore if she walked than when she didn't. The blood scared her, but not as much as Omar. Holding her bloody thigh with her hand, she blundered along the dry streambed, leaving a clearly marked trail for him to follow. She remembered Mike's statement that they would return by way of the waterfall and that it was safer. David and the *federale* had come this way. Gritting her teeth, she pushed herself to go faster, ignoring the pain, moving with a jerking, skipping motion as she put distance between herself and the insane Omar. She glanced backward again, then hurried onward. Suddenly, two gunshots cracked loudly from behind and she lurched, pitching forward onto the gravel.

Oh, God, she prayed…*Oh, God…Oh, God.*

*

Omar had hopped on one leg to beneath the overhang of the ruins. He remembered seeing a stack of firewood earlier and he needed to build a brace. He would kill that bitch slowly, he swore, very slowly. As he jumped and jerked toward the wall, the warning rattle of a Timber Rattlesnake stopped him. He looked around. There, by the rock! No. Two of them, next to the dead *federale*. They lay coiled, rattles shaking, tongues flicking. He steadied himself, pointed the rifle and then blew their heads off one at a time. Threaten him, would they? He smiled with satisfaction. It felt good to kill something, even if only a snake.

Just as he had hoped Omar found a stack of dried wood in various thickness and shapes. He culled out two, broke one to match the length of the other and strapped them to his leg with sisal rope. The foot throbbed painfully and had begun to swell. The sticks must be tied tightly to support his weight, but when finished the brace nearly cut off his blood. He would to stop periodically to readjust the splint, but must go before the American whore got too far ahead.

He found a stout limb to serve as a crutch and tested it. It would do. Grabbing his rifle, he hobbled toward the wall and creek beyond. It worked surprisingly well, he thought, congratulating himself on his ingenuity. Though hurt, he wasn't bleeding. If he walked at a steady pace, he would find her. The prospect of the hunt thrilled him, and his adrenaline surged with anticipation. The gun felt good in his hand and Omar imagined himself to be a young man again. He struggled up and over the gravel wall and began his pursuit of Ruth.

Luis had fainted. Overwhelmed with pain and the consuming terror of rattlesnakes, he had lost consciousness. The rifle shots had roused him.

Where am I? he wondered. A wave of chills rippled through his frame, and he groaned and tried to move, but he didn't have any upper body strength. He moved his legs, and this caused him to groan again. His lips were swollen and parched and a burning fever pushed him to the edge of delirium. More chills wracked him and he cried out. The cotton around his brain had thickened and he knew not where he was or why. Tears formed in his eyes, and he began to whisper his wife's name.

"Angela...Angela...help me," he whispered. "Please help me." He lost consciousness again and his body began to jerk when the nightmare returned.

He stiffened and cried out as he battled the rattlesnakes in his dreams. He had killed them and killed them but they just wouldn't die…they just wouldn't die….

Panic seized her. Winded and weak, blood still oozed from the wound. Her leg had turned numb and dragged noticeably when she moved, but she had to go on, had to keep running. If she stopped he might find her. His face pursued her, a grinning sadistic countenance watching and waiting as she staggered down the streambed. She glanced quickly over her shoulder, expecting him to catch her at any moment.

"Move it!" she exhorted herself. "Run! Run for your life!" She imagined him to be reaching for her, nearly touching her back. If she quit or slowed, she would die slowly and horribly at his hands. She continued to flee the grinning image in her mind, driving herself onward, pushing herself to the limits of endurance. If he caught her, she would fight. She would kill him. She would do to him what he planned to do to her. She would….

Omar chuckled. Just as he had predicted, the American slut had taken the obvious route. Blood drops lay easily visible along the streambed and every thirty meters or so he found more. This would be child's play. Hoisting his rifle and setting the crutch firmly into his armpit, he began walking as rapidly as he could. The brace worked surprisingly well. At this rate he would be at the waterfall within an hour. He fantasized. What would her expression be when she saw his bone-handled knife? And the breasts. She had such wonderful breasts. He had watched them sway and jiggle as she carried treasure from the tomb. He had plans for her breasts—oh yes indeed.

Mike stared stoically past the doctor and two women on the opposite side of the helicopter. He had told his story and answered their questions. Now they whispered among themselves. The doctor repeatedly checked his medical supplies and asked questions of the pilot and the American from the Chihuahua embassy.

Nearly twelve hours had passed since leaving the ruins and Mike didn't know what to expect. He sat quiet, sick at heart. Omar had entered the Lost Canyons to track the professor and the *federale* and the jaguar man worried. He knew the Arab to be a relentless adversary and cold-blooded killer. The professor meant well, but he was just a…well, he was just an academic—certainly no match for Omar.

217

The pilot asked another question and Mike stood to give directions. His eyes grew wide with surprise. The helicopter flew faster than he thought possible. He saw that they had flown into Cactus Canyon and were following the dry stream toward the waterfall. Minutes later he saw it in the distance. But as they approached he noticed that no water cascaded from its summit, and he grew sad when they passed over.

"Follow the stream bed above the cliff. It used to be a waterfall before the earthquake," he instructed. "Slow down a bit. We're almost there."

"Thank God," said Alexandra, squeezing Angela's hand. "We'll know in a few minutes, dear. Hold on. I'm here for you."

"What's that?" asked the pilot.

"Where?" said the other American, following the pilot's pointing finger. Near zero visibility hampered their search because a forest of hemlock and pine rimmed the stream's edge.

"Down there...thought I saw something...probably just an animal, though."

Mike inched forward between the two front seats. "What did it look like?" he craned his neck to see.

"Well, it's hard to say. I thought it kind of looked like someone walking out of the trees. How much farther, buddy?"

Someone walking out of the trees? What was going on? What if....

"Look! There's another one," pointed the embassy person. "Hey, he's hurt and he's got a gun. What do you figure that's all about?"

"Go back," ordered Mike, filled with trepidation.

"Back where?" asked the pilot.

"Go back. I want to see who that was. It's really important."

"Sorry, sir. My orders are to fly directly to this archaeological ruin and land. I can't stop. There isn't anywhere to land, anyway. Trees are too thick."

"Then turn and go back to Batopilas, because I won't guide you to the ruins unless you fly back to that spot."

"For God's sake, Larry, have him turn around and fly over again. It'll just take a second," complained Alexandra. The embassy person nodded an affirmative to the pilot, who then radioed their intention to the helicopter behind them. He brought the bird to a stop. Turned it around and began skimming the treetops as he flew to where he had seen the man.

"There," he pointed at a shuffling figure on the ground. "It's a guy. Must be chasing that woman."

"What woman?" Mike became frantic, looking everywhere, unable to see clearly for the trees.

"Well...I thought the first one kind of looked like a woman. Whoever it was had long hair and walked kind of funny...limping maybe."

The bird hovered directly over the stream, and the man on the ground shielded his eyes and looked up into the sky. Mike's blood ran cold and an involuntary shudder shook him. A sparkle and flash jumped from the man's face, diamonds reflecting the early morning sunlight. Omar, chasing Ruth, had paused to stare up at the helicopter. The man who had killed his father was now chasing his lover to do the same.

"Land!" he demanded.

"What the...."

"Land! Now! That man is a killer. He's chasing Ruth."

"Ruth?" said the pilot.

"The kidnapped woman," offered the embassy man, his mouth a grim, thin line. "But I don't see anywhere to land."

The pilot banked the helicopter and headed upstream.

"Where are you going?" demanded Mike.

"Trying to find a place to land," he replied. How far to the ruins?"

Mike calculated quickly. "There," he said, "over above the next bend in the stream."

"Can't land there either, Mac. No room. We'll have to land on top of the stream."

"No, to the left...over that mound of gravel."

"Not a chance," said the pilot. Entry's too narrow. We'd never make it."

"You don't understand," said Mike. "Go higher than the trees on each side, then slowly move over the opening."

"Are you blind? There's mountain there."

"Trust me, I know what's there," pleaded Mike. "The other helicopter can land in the streambed. This one is for hurt people, right?"

"You're crazy..."

"Do as he says, Larry. I believe him. Just try it will you?" Alexandra pleaded from the rear.

"Jeezuz H. Christ," muttered the pilot, slowly lifting the bird to the top of the trees. He took a deep breath and guided the bird up and over the small opening, centering it the best he could.

"Good, Lord," said the embassy man, exhaling and taking another breath. "Who would've thought...."

"There, in the middle," pointed out Mike. "Hurry, please."

"Hold your water, Mac." As the helicopter landed, Mike had the door open. He ducked beneath the whipping blades and trotted toward the overhang. "There...by the wall." He pointed to Luis, then ran for the gravel barrier.

"Hey...you!" called out the embassy man. "We need your...."

But Mike ignored him, scrambled over the wall and skirted the second helicopter. It had landed near the streambed and sat with its door wide open. Soldiers had exited the bird and milled about awaiting orders. Ribi was nowhere in sight.

"Indian, where you going?" called the Inspector General. "Stay and help us...."

Mike had circled around and jogged to the stream. His long muscular legs stretched and flexed in the morning sunlight as he quickly ran from sight, sprinting to find Omar before the killer reached Ruth. His legs flashed and moved in a blur, running faster than he could ever remember having run. He leaped and climbed and stretched, running faster...faster...faster, closing the distance between himself and the killer.

"Oh...God!" she cried, struggling toward the waterfall. Where was the damn thing? What would she do when she got there? Her breathing came in gasps and exhaustion weighed on her like a mountain. She had nothing left to give, her reservoir empty. Weak and dizzy from blood loss, she stumbled and fell, but rose and staggered away from the lewd face that chased her. She would kill him. First she would claw out his eyes, then drive a stake through his heart, then she would smash his hideous teeth, then she would....

Omar, livid with rage, cursed the hovering metal bird and hurled invectives. Helicopters! That filthy Indian had brought the army to rescue his friends. That stinking pig of a half-breed had returned in half the time possible. Filthy infidel! The countdown for Omar's death had begun. He wouldn't talk his way out of this one—not this time—but he swore not to die alone. He would take the American whore with him. It was her fault that he wouldn't escape and she would pay with her life.

The smile fled, but he felt energized and determined. He would kill the cunt. He would send her to hell to await his arrival. The jeweler stopped to tighten the brace, and then hobbled toward the falls. Nearly there, he paused to inspect a fresh blood trail. He could sense her presence and smell her blood. A mushroom of elation surged within! Maybe around the next bend she would be waiting for the game to end. *Too bad I can't see through the forest*, thought Omar. *Too bad, too bad.*

Ruth stumbled, completely spent and near to fainting. She tottered dizzily near the cliff face on waterfall's edge.

What now? What should she do? Turn around and circle behind? But what good was that? Then she collapsed, nearly falling over the edge as she did so. She tried to rise, but couldn't. Again she tried, but fell backward and passed out from blood loss.

Omar rounded the last bend in the stream, his face fixed in a horrible smile. There! She lay by the waterfall where he knew she would be. Praise Allah...he hoped that she still breathed. It was important that she see his face and the knife before he cut her throat.

"Omar!" came a scream from behind.

He whirled about angrily and saw the Indian in his red headband. The jeweler didn't hesitate. Shouldering the rifle, he focused on the Indian's chest and fired. It hit! Omar yelped, ecstatic, and shook the rifle above his head in triumph. The Indian had fallen immediately. Omar had sent him to hell with his father and that filthy Christian brother of his. He limped and skipped toward the fallen Indian, a smile stretching the length of his face. The Indian lay on his side, so Omar braced himself and bent to roll the body over.

Stunned! The jeweler's breath caught in his chest when he recognized Ribi. He fell to his knees and cried out in pain, cradling the boy's head in his arms. Tears ran in curdled streams down his grimy face. Ribi, his son—he had killed his only son! He whirled around to see the woman. She hadn't moved. This was her fault, he reasoned. The American slut had killed his son. He would peel the skin from her body and then kill her before throwing her from the cliff.

He tenderly laid Ribi's head on the ground and rose to go do the deed. Choked with anger, his face shone red. Omar hated women. He had always hated women, and he intended to cut this one like he had always dreamed of doing. He staggered toward cliff's edge, pulled his knife and stood above her. A wide smile exposed diamond-studded teeth.

Ruth felt a shadow and sensed someone's presence. She opened her eyes. The face! She screamed!

Omar grabbed her arm and lifted his knife to plunge it into her.

"Ruth!" came an anguished cry.

"Mike! Mike!" she wailed, struggling with all her remaining strength, fighting the grasp of a sadistic murderer.

Omar whirled to see who called. There stood another Indian—the one he should have killed—but first the woman. First the whore must die. He returned to his task and lifted the knife....

The first lurch surprised him and he dropped his makeshift crutch. The second jolt of the earthquake unbalanced him and he struggled to right himself. Ruth, lying on her back, grabbed his knife arm, planted a foot in his crotch and pulled. Omar glided over her, bellowing in terror as he plummeted a hundred meters to the ground and a well-deserved death.

The earthquake came in jerking waves, rolling and bucking as magma from the earth's core intruded further into the crust. Ruth rolled to her stomach and searched for something to hold onto as the earthquake tried to cast her over the cliff's edge. It lasted twenty seconds, but seemed an eternity.

Then it stopped and she lay spent and sobbing, weeping for no reason and for every reason, just crying.

"Ruth."

She looked into the worried eyes of her kidnapper. "You came back," she mumbled weakly, her eyes closing. "You promised you'd come back," and she passed out.

Four American soldiers appeared from around the bend of the stream. They stopped briefly to inspect Ribi's body, and then trotted to the cliff's edge where Mike was trying to revive Ruth. "Here...I'm a corpsman," said a blond-haired, skinny soldier with long fingers. He nudged a pair of wire-rimmed glasses up the bridge of his nose with a knuckle, and then reached for Ruth's arm and took her pulse. He frowned, then checked the wound on her leg. "Gimme me some room," he ordered, and everyone backed away. The medic filled a syringe and gave her an injection, then he expertly cut off her pant leg and began to doctor her wound.

"Over here," shouted one of the soldiers, pointing to Omar's body below the cliff. "How did that...."

"Call for a helicopter," ordered the medic. "She's lost a lot of blood, but she might make it."

A bearded, thick-necked soldier with black paint smeared on his face radioed his superiors and requested one of the birds.

"Yep, I think she might make it," said the medic again. "Going to have an ugly scar though...."

"Sir," said the soldier with the radio to Mike, "the Inspector General requests that you return immediately. They can't locate one of the expedition members and it is urgent that they leave as soon as possible to transport the injured policeman to a hospital."

The *federale* was still alive? wondered Mike. That left only the archaeologist, and Mike didn't recall seeing him at the ruins or along the stream. Had Omar killed him?

Though reluctant to leave Ruth's side, he knew there was little he could do to help. The Medic would do his best and Mike should return to the ruins. He stood and headed upstream, running alongside the stream, moving quickly, deep in thought.

Why is the mountain still angry? Is the city okay, or was it damaged even more? A simmering urgency implored him to run faster and soon his long, muscular legs flashed like pistons. He rounded a bend in the stream, jumped to the other side to avoid the encroaching forest and continued upstream. Then he stopped, startled. A tiny stream percolated from the forested hillside. He stooped to touch the water. It felt warm. One of the springs flowed again! If this one worked, then perhaps the others did also.

He ran imbued with new energy, experiencing his first glimmer of real hope. While he ran, he saw that several of the hillside springs were oozing hot water into the streambed. As he drew near the ruins, a helicopter roared overhead on its way to the waterfall to evacuate Ruth.

A steady stream trickled from below the gravelwalled entrance to the cliff dwellings. He could hear a loud hiss and whoosh from within, but it didn't sound like the helicopter. When he crested the wall a sound directed his attention to the west end of the cliff dwellings. Everyone milled about aimlessly after the earthquake; the pilot sat in the bird and talked on the radio while the American from the embassy shouted orders.

Mike ignored them and stared in wonder. A geyser had erupted from within the collapsed mine, ejecting steaming water horizontally from a two foot hole in the mountainside. It shot nearly sixty meters into the air before landing in front of the helicopter and flowing toward the wall on which he stood.

Urgent cries greeted his arrival. The woman called Alexandra argued vociferously with the embassy man and she shouted and stamped her foot. Mike saw the *federale* and his wife inside the helicopter. Alexandra turned to Mike when he approached. "Where is he? Where could he be?" she asked frantically, her face lined with worry, her hands twisting a handkerchief into knots.

"Who's missing?"

"My husband, David, the archaeologist. Please help. They're threatening to leave without him."

"Alexandra, that isn't true," interrupted the embassy man, trying to be patient. "That Mexican cop could die any second. We've run out of time. We'll send someone back to look for him."

Where could the archaeologist be? wondered Mike. Was he hiding? Mike looked around, distracted. The ruins appeared okay. He found it difficult to focus with so much happening; Ruth, Omar, the earthquake and hot springs. If he had more time, he could probably find David, but....

There, it caught his attention. Someone had tampered with the eastern tomb. The large boulder lay firmly in place, but all the smaller stones had been removed and scattered. Had Omar robbed the tomb? If so, why had he rolled the stone back in front of the entrance? Mike felt a tingle of dread. The dead could harm the living, and if Omar had robbed their tomb and...and what? he thought. That's just it. He didn't know.

"Let's look there," he pointed, walking toward the west end of the ruins. "I need some help."

They rolled the large boulder aside. Inside lay the professor, his fingernails broken and bloody and the side of his face swollen purple. Alexandra cried out and knelt next to her husband.

"Get another stretcher," ordered Larry, "and tell the doctor we need him here, also."

Alexandra bit her hand and tears pooled in her eyes as she followed the stretcher to the helicopter. The professor had regained consciousness and appeared lucid. He couldn't speak, though, and he gripped his wife's hands and flashed yes/no answers with his eyes.

"That's it," shouted the embassy man, stepping to avoid the geyser stream flowing from the collapsed mine. "Move it...everyone. Watch your step. Next stop is the Ft. Bliss Army Hospital."

"Where's the Indian?" inquired the pilot.

"Eh? Beats me." Larry buckled his seat belt and said, "He was just here." Larry looked around the ruins.

"What do you want me to do?" asked the pilot.

"Leave him. We don't have time to organize a search. He's the Mexicans' problem. If they want to throw him in jail, they can come and find him. I'm outta here."

The huge MedEvac helicopter lifted from the ground, turned 180 degrees and moved between a gap in the forest, then over the gravel wall. It hung suspended, then the engines roared, and within moments it was skimming the treetops along the creek bed, now filled with flowing water.

"Will you look at that," said the astounded pilot, pointing up ahead.

"Look at what?" asked Larry.

"There…it's the Indian, and he's got a dog with him. They're running and splashing in the stream. Want me to buzz him?"

"That's not a dog."

"Huh?"

"It's a big cat…looks like a lion or a jaguar or something."

"Want me to take a shot at him? The *federale* on the other bird said he's a criminal." The pilot lightly touched a button on the stick between his legs.

The embassy man hesitated. "Nah. Leave him be. Our information is that he helped our Ruthie out and tried to save her. Looks happy to me. Let him play with his cat. I hope they don't catch him."

The big bird banked a hard right at the falls, quickly gained altitude, then fired its jets and sped north over the Sierra Madres.

With the sun strong and bright in his face, the tall Indian and his companion stood on the edge of the waterfall. He gave thanks to Tata god and his wife for healing the mountain. Large tears streamed down his cheeks, but he smiled happily. With joy in his heart, he spread his arms and began to sing a song of thanks.

* * *

Printed in the United States
1321200002B/310-330